THE
MESSENGER

REX E. HALE

This book is dedicated to the memory of
Piriha Priscilla Potae
1945 – 2011
A woman who gave so much to those in need.
And when it seemed that she had nothing more to give, she gave us hope.

Also by the same author
The Guardian of Seville (2010)

ACKNOWLEDGEMENTS:

In writing the fictional journal of Francisco de Villanova I have drawn inspiration from several contemporary factual sources:

Cristobal Colón – The Journal of the First Voyage of Cristobal Colón—(1492–1504)

Antonio Pigafetta – Report On the First Voyage Round the World—(1525)

Andres de Urdaneta – Chronicle to His Majesty the King of Spain of the armada sent to the Spice Islands under commander Loaysa in 1525—(1537).

1

GHOSTS FROM THE PAST, BARCELONA,

NOVEMBER 2010

After all that he had been through, was this really how it would end? The thought struck him as he gazed into the mirror that hung on the wall of his study. His dark eyes searched for affirmation in the face that stared back at him. He looked older than the thirty-five years that had so far been his life. Wisps of gray had begun to settle upon the dark hair at his temples, and a scar across his right cheek now marred his once flaw-lessly handsome features. There was regret on the face in the mirror, and uncertainty in the eyes. An uncertainty of mind, of thought, perhaps even of love—no, not of love.

All was testament, he now saw, to the trial that had thus far been his life.

The dream last night had rattled him. And even on this beautiful au-tumn afternoon, he could not throw off the sense of foreboding it had brought with it.

He turned and walked across the room to his desk. On it sat a wooden box, which he had placed there earlier. He felt uneasy as it drew his gaze. Pulling back the chair he sat, his eyes still firmly fixed on the wooden con-tainer. He drew breath, and for a moment played with the idea of leaving the box just as it was—unopened. But that could never be—not now— and he knew that.

He reached out and lifted the lid. The box was filled to the top with old letters. His heart beat quickened as he reached in and took one. He unfold-ed it with trembling hands, for as he did he knew that the doorway to his past was about to be opened. A doorway he had firmly shut many years ago.

Dear Papa,

It has been two years since you left us. I stopped counting the days long ago because we seemed to drift even further apart as the numbers grew bigger. Now I have decided to count only the years. Mama and I are well, but we miss you terribly. As you know, today is my fifteenth birthday. Grandfather says that I look more and more like you every day. I have not told him yet, but I don't want him to say that anymore. I am afraid to hear it. I don't want to end up like you. I lie awake at night wondering why you did this to us. I cannot even remember when Mama last smiled. I have even forgotten what her smile looks like. Why did you do it Papa? Why did you kill yourself—why? Mama and I miss you so much. Please Papa, find a way to come back to us, to tell us how you are.
Your son, Roberto
September 16th 1990

He finished reading; the pain that filled his heart was now etched upon his face. Staring for a moment into the room, his eyes searched—but for what, he did not know. He looked again at the letter in his hands—a letter that he had written to his dead father more than twenty years ago. He felt cold, the dream that came to him last night had disturbed old ghosts— voices from the past were calling to him. That's the only reason he now sat before this open box, a doorway to a past that he had all but left behind.

In the 1980s, Roberto's father, Sebastian, had been a prominent and wealthy banker in Barcelona. His wealth and success had earned him both respect and envy. But in the end, neither money nor position could save him.

Roberto never forgot the day that he discovered his father's body. His brains were splattered across furniture and halfway up the nearest wall. Part of his head had been blown away, and a bloodied revolver lay nearby. Roberto was just thirteen years old and those dreadful images would haunt him for the rest of his life.

Sebastian Torres had been an important man in the city, and when his body was discovered, the police immediately suspected foul play. Their investigation was thorough, but in the end there was only one logical conclusion. With the victim's fingerprints all over the revolver, it was obvious that the fatal shot had been self-inflicted. The verdict of suicide was accepted, and the case was closed.

But a puzzle remained—the whereabouts of Sebastian's distinctive signet ring. He wore it always, and the fact that it was missing when his body was found was a mystery.

But for now mother and son had to face the truth; and for them that was the most difficult of all things to do. For Roberto, a single question would haunt him, and for more than two decades it cried out from within. Why had his father killed himself—a catholic committing the cardinal sin of suicide? It was just too hard to accept.

If it hadn't been for his grandparents, Fernando and Nuria, Roberto and his mother would not have survived the emotional trauma that threatened to drown them both. The elderly pair opened their hearts and their home to the two broken souls who appeared at their door.

Mother and son would eventually move in with them. There they felt safe, sheltered from life's storms which broke beyond the borders of the elderly couple's love. They had time now to start again—it wouldn't be easy, but there was no other choice. In this new environment Roberto began to grow again and soon a bond developed between grandson and *abuelo*—his grandfather. Roberto nicknamed the old man *welo*, and over time the pair became inseparable.

Fernando and Nuria lived in Vallvidrera, a suburb in the Collserola hills northeast of the city. A retired merchant banker, Fernando had inherited from his father, Don Rodrigo Ruiz Hernandez, a large villa set high on a ridge overlooking Barcelona. From there the view was spectacular; out across the city and beyond to the great blue Mediterranean and right to the distant horizon.

Although Fernando's father, Don Rodrigo, had been an important man in his time, it was Fernando's grandfather Guillermo who had been the real patriarch of the family's success. It was he who started the business that was to build the family fortunes for the next three generations. At just twenty-five, Guillermo had discovered an unexploited niche in the money markets of his day. And he was quick to realize that his moment of fortune had arrived.

In those early years, few men would loan money to small time farmers and merchants. The risks of default were simply too high. One bad season or a lost merchant ship could mean not only lost profits, but also the loss of an entire loan, and with it potential ruin.

Guillermo however, saw only the opportunities in this risky market and he seized them. By the time his son Don Rodrigo took control of the business, the solid foundations for success had been laid. The business, at that time based in Sevilla, was well on the way to becoming one of the most successful privately owned banks in all of Andalucía. Then in the early years of the twentieth century Don Rodrigo relocated his family and business to Catalunya and the bustling city of Barcelona.

But now, that was all in the past—more than a hundred years had gone by since the family had moved from Andalucía. And now it was Don Rodrigo's son Fernando who owned the villa.

After Sebastian's death, Fernando became very important to Roberto, a secure anchor even into manhood. He often thought back to the times when he and Fernando would sit together on the balcony of the villa. He felt at peace being next to the old man, both of them bathed in the golden afternoon sunlight. They sometimes sat in silence, gazing out across the blue Mediterranean Sea.

Some days, if the light was right, they could just make out the distant peaks on the island of Mallorca, glistening like tiny diamonds against the horizon almost two hundred kilometers away. As Roberto grew older, he never forgot those balmy afternoons in the company of his grandfather. Even the dark, brooding Pyrenees to the north seemed, in those happy days, to shimmer like golden clouds in the afternoon light. But as the warmth of summer gave way to the chill of winter, so went Roberto's life. Yet again his world would change.

It began in his bedroom early one morning, less than a year after his father's death. As Roberto woke, he was greeted by something that at first confused him; then filled him with fear. There at the foot of his bed stood an apparition—the small ghostly figure of a white dog had appeared out of nowhere. What he remembered most from that first encounter was the phantom's eyes—two little glowing embers smoldering in the darkness. He never forgot them, and nor did he forget the choking fear that seeing them brought, a fear so intense that for a moment, it actually paralyzed him. The shimmering ghost, about the size of a fox, eyed him for a few seconds then simply vanished into thin air.

He lay stunned, struggling to figure out what had just happened, and as his senses returned, he could hear his heart pounding in his ears. He glanced furtively about the bedroom fearing that the apparition may still be present—but it took only a moment to see that it had gone.

Flicking back the covers he leapt from the bed. Three big strides and he was through the open bedroom door and out onto the landing.

Was it a dream? He was unsure; his mind was still reeling from the shock.

Should he tell the adults? He thought carefully for a moment, perhaps they would think he was crazy. Somehow this seemed a certainty.

By the time he reached the bottom of the staircase, his mind was made up—it had been just a dream. For the next few weeks he still felt uneasy each time he entered his bedroom. Although he tried hard to deny it, deep down he was still worried that the vision of the white dog might return. However after many weeks had passed, and the little ghost had not reappeared, Roberto finally decided that he had been right all along. It had been nothing more than a dream. But just when he thought the whole thing was safely behind him, the ghost came back.

It happened when he was playing in the park just down the street from where his grandparents lived. He often went there to feed the pigeons that congregated each afternoon near the large fountain, before they flew off in the evening to roost. The shock at seeing the ghost again was so great, that his mind could not cope. His body trembled so violently, that in the end he collapsed to the ground. Even after the apparition had gone Roberto remained motionless, lying as though he were dead.

Soon a startled passerby discovered him, and she helped him to his feet. But by now he had regained his senses, and managed to persuade her that he was alright. After she left, he slowly made his way home.

What he did not know then, on that afternoon in the park, was that he would see that mysterious little creature many more times in his life. So many times in fact, that he would eventually grow accustomed to its visits. But in those early days, it was an experience that only brought to him fear and mental torment.

The visit that day from the ghostly dog, like all its visits, would remain Roberto's secret. He wanted no one else to share the burden that it brought to him. He knew that his mother had her own struggle coping with the loss of her beloved husband. The last thing he wanted was to add to her troubles. And so at the tender age of fourteen, he accepted that the problem of the phantom dog was his alone. That decision was to mark the beginning of his flight from reality. His imagination became his shield. It protected him and took him to a place where nothing could harm him. There he saw only those fragments of reality that he alone could make sense of, and shunned the rest. Soon his mind had become a fortress, and without realizing it, he had become its only prisoner.

Almost two years after the death of his father, the first glimmer of light appeared. Somehow Roberto began to realize that he had become imprisoned in his own secret world. His grandfather, who had been silently observing the changes in Roberto, still clung to hope.

In the solitude of the world he had created for himself, Roberto finally began to understand its nature. By his own hand he was both jailer and prisoner, two opposing entities trapped in a single confused form. He had become a victim by his own will, led and chained within the prison of his own mind. That moment of realization was the spark that lit the first flames of freedom. But it wasn't easy, for still there remained the secret of his ghostly visitor—a frightening secret that he had vowed would forever be his.

It was his grandfather who first suggested to Roberto that he write down his thoughts—the ones that troubled him the most. Perhaps in his wisdom the old man had seen something in the boy's eyes.

"In the writing you take the imagined and make it physical. Once your thoughts have substance you can grasp them in your hands. Somehow this removes that mystical quality that always seems to surround such things."

Roberto seemed receptive, and the old man sensed it.

"By committing your thoughts to paper you move them from here," he continued, pointing to his head, "and place them there," pointing to the blank sheet of paper sitting beside his grandson. "Of course, once you have banished them to the confines of a sheet of paper, you can do whatever you want with them."

By the time Roberto was seventeen, he wrote every day. No longer satisfied with just capturing his thoughts, he wrote about everything. He continued also to write letters to his dead father, something he had secretly begun just days after the man's suicide. In his young mind he thought that these letters would somehow bring his father back to him.

Writing now consumed him. He would spend days locked up in his room, clutching his pen, lost in thought as his hand composed its way across yet another sheet of paper. He became a recluse. His mother and grandmother were worried.

"What is he doing all alone, locked in his bedroom?"

"That's not healthy for a boy his age. He should be out playing with other boys."

"He's so secretive no one is allowed to see what he writes. He won't even discuss it."

"The boy's turning into a hermit," exclaimed his grandmother. Fernando never replied, instead he just smiled. No one knew it then, but one day Roberto would be among the most popular authors in Europe.

2

FIRST LOVE, BARCELONA

Roberto was twenty-two years old when he met Clara Pallares at the Mojito Club disco on carrer Rosellón. An unusual event, because disco wasn't Roberto's thing—and the glitzy Mojito, of all places, hauled him from his comfort zone.

Carlos Barrón Montella, an old school friend who now lived in Argentina, had briefly returned to Spain on vacation. He hadn't seen Roberto in years, and to celebrate their reunion, he managed to talk him into a night out on the town. Carlos, a chubby fun-loving man, simply adored the disco, and the swanky Mojito was right up his alley.

By ten o'clock the Mojito Club was packed. With loud music and flowing alcohol the dance floor had become a heaving mass of human rhythm—and Carlos was in the middle of it all. Roberto stood at the bar watching—he felt like a fish out of water. It was obvious; he was too reserved for a place like this. By now, his instincts were telling him to leave Carlos to it, and go. But in the end he couldn't, his friend *Carlito* would have been disappointed in him.

Then, across the room he saw her. She was tall, blonde, and beautiful—and to make things more interesting, she had noticed him. Before the night was over they had swapped telephone numbers. The following day after seeing Carlos off at the airport, Roberto called her.

Clara was in her final year at university preparing for a career in law. A romantic distraction seemed a good idea, and just the thing she needed before settling into her chosen profession. But Roberto wanted love, and before he knew it, he had given himself to her completely. The quixotic flame of love for him was to rise quickly and flare brightly.

Those close to him had become concerned; they could see that he was heading for a fall. It was obvious that he had become blinded by her beauty, and like a snow-blind explorer, they feared that he would lose his way.

His grandfather though, understood everything. He knew that for too long Roberto had shut himself off from life. He had become a spectator. Perhaps that's why he loved to write. Looking but never touching, observing but never feeling, judging but never judged. The old man knew that this would never do, Roberto was still young—he needed to *get out more*. The boy had become trapped in life's waiting room—a place reserved only for the moribund.

"And now, such a beautiful woman should come into his life. What do you expect?" he told Nuria who was worried that her grandson would get hurt.

"He's so sensitive, he'll become disillusioned, and that would be tragic," she said.

"That's life," replied Fernando. "Sooner or later we all get hurt."

Even if he knew of their concerns, Roberto did not care, for the romance had already begun to spin its magic. He had rediscovered life, and it now seemed so much richer than before. The very essence of it reached out and touched his every thought. Colors seemed more vivid, sounds were sharper and tastes more complex. Even the very air that he breathed seemed sweeter. Love had utterly bewitched him.

Fernando sat quietly by and watched over his love-struck grandson. Often, a refugee from the turmoil of romance, Roberto would seek out the old man's company. And as they had done when he was a boy, the pair would sit on the terrace in the afternoon hours. Together they shared their thoughts and experiences until the sun had sunk below the distant horizon.

One afternoon Fernando turned to Roberto, "You are fortunate chico," he said eyeing his grandson. "A man may pass through his entire life and never understand what you have discovered today."

"What have I discovered welo?" he asked, puzzled by the old man's words.

"If you learn nothing else in your life, it is important that you know this. As each moment of our life passes, that moment becomes lost to us. But from it occurs a birth, an awakening…even a resurrection of sorts. For better or worse, as human beings, this is at the very heart of our existence.

Sadly, few of us realize it, or even understand its importance. As one door closes so another opens, as a death occurs so we are reborn. This is life in all its truth. In it there is both light and dark, good and bad, happiness and sadness. To accept this is to consciously begin your path on the journey that life has prepared for you."

Roberto did not reply, for he understood exactly what the old man meant. Instead he closed his eyes and inhaled the sweet evening air. It was October and he was in love. Whatever journey life had in store for him, he felt sure that he would cope.

An easy silence settled over the pair on that evening, and as Roberto opened his eyes again, he could see in the distance the amber afterglow suspended in the sky above the horizon. Sunsets always filled him with loneliness—even tonight. The journey that had brought him to this moment was started many years ago by a lonely and lost boy. It now made him sad to think again of that boy, for in truth, he no longer knew him.

The two men remained silent as they watched the twilight draw across the city. By now, a few of the brighter stars could be seen just piercing the dusky dome of the sky as the amber afterglow melted slowly into the horizon.

Roberto turned to his grandfather and smiled. "Thank you," he said.

"For what?" asked Fernando.

"For everything, without you I don't know what would have become of me."

"We all do what we must for those we love, that's our way—and one day you will do it too," the old man said.

As for Clara, some days, Roberto could hardly be apart from her. He was intoxicated by her; her delicate scent, the warmth of her nakedness against him, the taste of her sweetness upon his lips. For him love had now become an intense and passionate game, the rules of which he never understood nor even wanted to. Nor did he understand its reasons or the subtleties of its complicated journey—for these he could not care less. It was simply enough for him now to be a player in this sublime game of fate.

Pent-up artistic emotions too long suppressed, were now unleashed and flowed like a river of light to the very tips of his fingers. The words that fell from them onto the keyboard of his computer were lit by its creative essence. Soon that trickle of words became a torrent, and a writer was born.

To him each page was like a virgin canvas waiting for that first brush stroke, or a block of marble for that first chisel strike. He knew that writing was to be his life.

Then Clara met Antonio and as suddenly as it had begun, Roberto's romance with her was over. Life had now taken something else from him. Love he discovered was sometimes fickle and often painful. On the day that she left him, he promised himself that he would never fall in love again.

By now his writing had an audience. His Sci-fi novels were sought by readers all over Europe, and his pseudonym, Julian Verde, was now famous. Ever since his father's death Roberto had become an intensely private person; to him his anonymity was very important. Julian would become his alter ego, and publishers far and wide queued for the chance to print his works. His grandfather's quiet and unshakeable faith was now rewarded. The old man was happy. The troubled boy who had landed on his doorstep all those years before had now been resurrected.

For Roberto, the hands of time had moved on, and with them, so went his life. Soon a whole decade had passed, bland years full of dullness and tedium. If this was the path of life that his grandfather had once talked of—it wasn't what Roberto had expected. In that time, he had written more books for his legions of readers. But for him there had been little to make him happy. Boredom, failed relationships and reclusive tendencies had marred those years. He had almost come to accept this as the natural pattern of his life. He had given everything to writing and had nothing left for anything else. Then, completely by accident, he met Maya, the woman who touched his soul.

The café Els Quatre Gats, known to tourists as The Four Cats, lay on carrer Montsió. Visitors and locals alike came to soak up the modernist atmosphere and take in the Parisian air which filled its heart. A hundred years had passed since famous avant-garde artists like Pablo Picasso succumbed to its charms. It is a busy place, sometimes bursting at the seams with crowds soaking up the ambience to the accompaniment of piano keys tinkling in the background. Its style and history seemed to encapsulate everything about Barcelona. Even the name, "Els Quatre Gats," was a local euphemism for a small group of nobodies—a joke, it seems, aimed at the famous artists who once sought sanctuary there from the critics of the day.

Roberto loved this place more than any other. Like other artists, he also had succumbed to its charms.

As if by some invisible natural law, the face of the human crowd within the café reflected the patchwork of the changing seasons. Between June and August a younger mainly tourist crowd invigorated the ambience. Americans, Germans, French, all came to be where Picasso had been. Over coffee they imagined him doodling on paper napkins or pinching the bottom of a beautiful waitress. Roberto never tired of watching the chattering crowds who flocked to this place like swarming bees.

"Imagination is a wonderful thing," he once wrote. "It ensures that the idiosyncrasies of any life are available to us all."

By October, the rowdy summer hordes have taken their leave and the locals emerge once again from their summer hibernation and reclaim their barrio. The heat of summer has gone and the sweet Mediterranean breezes carry the fresh sea air deep into the city. In olden times, it was these breezes that assisted the city's merchant fleet to be dragged up onto the beaches in preparation for the approaching winter. The cooler months were now on their way, and with them would come a change of pace in the ancient maritime metropolis.

The autumn light in Barcelona had a romance all of its own—infused with refracted light from the great blue-green Mediterranean Sea lapping at the cities edges. And within this subtle fusion of differing hues radiates its special character. These qualities were renowned, and throughout the centuries, they had drawn painters and photographers to the city from far and wide. For an artist to know and capture this light as it embraced an autumn leaf was magical. To imprison it upon canvas as it entwined the sinewy bones of a gothic cathedral was a revelation. And to witness the illumination of a fleeting expression on a solitary face was to understand in a single moment why this place was special. As a writer, Roberto understood this, and was able to capture it in the words that flowed from his soul to the very tips of his fingers.

It was on one such October afternoon that he sat at a table in Els Quatre Gats. His fingers were busy at the keyboard of the laptop in front of him. He barely noticed the four new patrons enter the café. Three of them sat round a table across the room from him while the fourth person, a beautiful woman, scanned the crowded café for a moment. She noticed Roberto and walked over to him.

"Excuse me," she asked, "is this chair occupied?" her hand already rested upon the curved backrest of the empty chair.

He looked up and was at once caught by her smile.

"Yes…"

What on earth did he just say? He was confused, and for that split second had lost focus.

"I mean no…if you need it…please…be my guest."

"Thank you," she said. Her eyes met his once more, and with a smile and a nod of thanks she lifted the chair, turned on her heels, and left him. He watched her walk away. He could not take his eyes from her as she crossed the room. Moments later she rejoined her companions, two men and a woman who were already engrossed in conversation.

Two couples out for coffee, he thought. And with regret, he lowered his eyes and again focused on the computer screen in front of him.

For the next hour as he sat tapping at his keyboard, he could not stop his eyes from wandering occasionally across the room to the woman who had taken the chair. And to his delight, his eyes were always met by hers smiling back at him. Soon though, he began to feel awkward. It was obvious that she was with one of the men at the table, and he knew what it felt like to lose a woman to another man. God forbid that he should ever be the other man. And with that he decided to look no more. His mind however would not leave her. And after a while he decided to look just one more time. But when he searched again for those beautiful eyes, they had gone.

Soon he tired of his surroundings. It was time to leave; he closed his laptop and slipped it into the satchel that rested beside his chair. He signaled the waiter for the bill. A few minutes later the man arrived and placed on the table in front of him a small metal platter that held the invoice. Roberto picked it up, and to his surprise, beneath the docket lay a neatly folded piece of paper.

"What's this?" he asked, holding it up for the waiter to see.

"It's from a woman who sat at that table over there," he said pointing across the room. "She asked me to give it to you when you left."

"Thank you," he said, knowing now that he would again see that beautiful smile. He unfolded the slip of paper. Written on it was a telephone number followed by the name Maya.

He rang her that afternoon, and they met that evening in Plaça de Catalunya. From that moment they became lovers.

"Do you believe in love at first sight?" she asked him.

"No," he answered, "I believe in fate."

Maya Serrano was tall, intelligent, and beautiful—and she was American. Roberto found her utterly captivating. He had never before met anyone whose hunger for life had so energized him.

He would never forget the vision of her in Els Quatre Gats, or later when they met again that same evening. She was late, and he remembered how his heart sank almost into despair at the thought that she might not show. Perhaps she had changed her mind. But as he watched, he at last caught sight of her. She was running to meet him.

She knew that she was late and feared he may have already left, thinking that she was not coming. But nothing would have kept her from him. At last, she spotted him bathed in light standing beneath a row of streetlamps. There he waited for her. Her heart almost burst with joy when she recognized him. When finally they faced each other, both knew as they stood in the golden street glow, that what each had whispered secretly in their thoughts was true. They made love that evening in his apartment to the rhythm of their pounding hearts. From that moment their souls were forever fused.

Maya was an academic, an anthropologist who had come to Spain to immerse herself in the history of the Catalan people. Her parents were proud of her achievements. It had been a long struggle for her family, a struggle that had started when her grandparents Jorge and Evita fled Mexico for America in 1927.

Like thousands of Mexicans, they were desperate to escape the war that had engulfed their country. The Cristeros rebels had caught the government by surprise, and by 1927 seemed on the verge of taking the entire country. The battle cry ¡*Viva Cristo Rey*! echoed throughout the land and roused the populace into a bloody revolt, though not everyone took sides. Many simply packed up and fled northward, Jorge and Evita were among them. They became part of a great human tide that swept across the border into California. And it was there that Jorge eventually found work in the huge cotton farms of the San Joaquin Valley. For migrant workers in those desperate days, life was harsh. They had few rights and almost no protection under the law. The power lay firmly in the hands of the land barons who controlled their huge plantations like personal fiefdoms. Many even kept small armed forces to press labor gangs into submission and crush even the smallest hint of unionism. Oftentimes the police would simply turn a blind eye to landowner excesses. Still, as hard as life had been for them in California, they could not return to Mexico. Life there had almost no value, and the stench of poverty and violence lay heavily across the land.

Somehow through this time, Jorge managed to keep working. The hours were always long and hard, and the pay was never more than subsistence money. But he had a dream, and one day in this land of plenty, he felt sure that his dream would come true.

With the blistering sun upon his back and sweat dripping from his brow, he worked tirelessly in those cotton fields. One day he would have the money to put his own roots down into this rich soil. One day he too would have fields of his own. This was the land, he was told before he left Mexico, where dreams really did come true.

Years came and went and yet the pair struggled on. Then in 1949, Rudolfo, Maya's father was born. And just like his father before him, when he grew old enough, he too bent his back beneath the hot Californian sun, and his sweat also moistened the rich soils of the San Joaquin Valley. He toiled on the same cotton farms as his father had twenty years before, laboring like slaves alongside the sons of other men who had fled war-torn Mexico nearly four decades earlier. Time had moved on, but for these young men, life had not changed much from the days of their fathers. The hours were still long, and the pay was still meager, and the landowners were still kings upon the land.

In 1974, when Rudolfo was twenty-five years old, he met Christine Burns. They met in a bar where he and two friends often spent Saturday nights playing pool and dropping quarters into the jukebox. Who first saw who, would forever be a point of debate between them, but whatever the outcome, the attraction was mutual and thirteen months later they were married.

Christine's father Mike, a foreman in a large Los Angeles construction company, was an old-fashioned man who prided himself on being a good judge of character. He was immediately impressed by Rudolfo, whom he nicknamed Rudy. In Rudy, he saw at once a good man, an honest and hard-working man, and one who kept his word, no matter what. That was important to Mike, who believed that good old-fashioned values were being trashed by the younger generation. Rudy however, brought him hope, and it wasn't long before the two men became close friends. Within weeks he had found his new son-in-law a job as a site laborer for the same company he worked for. Soon the hard-working Rudy proved his worth and his ascent through the company ranks had begun.

A year after Rudy started work in the construction industry Maya was born. From the beginning she was special, a treasure to parents and grandparents alike—she flourished. As a youngster, there were the junior high school honors and athletic medals. Then came high school, with straight A-grades, and yet more champion medals. Eventually she completed her degree with honors at UCLA in anthropology.

But as a woman she was lonely. She had invested so much of herself into her achievements; even her own peer group had become isolated from her. She found it difficult to make friends, and even harder to meet men.

In the end though, she turned out to be just like her mother. What really mattered in her life was finding a good man and settling down. That day, when she saw Roberto in Els Quatre Gats, something about him touched her. And within an instant, in her heart of hearts, she knew that he was the one.

For Roberto, who was entangled in loves embrace, desire had no limits. Maya had consumed him entirely, and as her love blossomed she revealed to him her soul. With her help, the veil that had for so long obscured his view of life began to gradually withdraw. And like the biblical Lazarus, he too felt reborn. Eventually, in 2008, the pair moved in together. But unknown to them, Roberto's past was about to come knocking.

It was just after three in the morning, and Maya was asleep. Roberto lay beside her, his eyes were closed, but he was awake. The night air was warm and still, and he could hear the comforting sound of Maya breathing softly beside him. Suddenly, as though a door to the Other Side had swung ajar, a chill cut through the air in the bedroom. Roberto felt it and opened his eyes for he knew what it meant. Instantly he recognized the small familiar figure that crouched near the bedroom door. Its red eyes peered through the darkness. The white dog had returned.

Roberto gazed for a moment as if studying the face of an old friend. He whispered softly, "Why do you come to me now?"

There was no sound.

"I know that you have come to warn me."

Still there was no sound.

"If you can't tell me what it is, you must go," he ordered the little ghost. He was now concerned. If Maya woke up, what would she think? For years, the white dog had been visiting him, yet remained completely invisible to others, even when they were in the same room. It was certain that Maya would not see him, either. But she would see Roberto, and just one look at his face would tell her that something was wrong.

"Go now," he said. "Quickly…there is nothing for you here."

Suddenly, the white dog melted into the night air.

Maya stirred at the sound of Roberto's voice.

"Are…you…alright?" she mumbled, still half asleep.

"I'm fine," he whispered.

"I thought I heard your voice," she said.

"It was just a dream."

"Of what..?"

"It's nothing…just a dream."

Still sleepy she turned toward him and put her arm across his chest. Pulling herself close to him, she kissed his cheek and whispered, "Go back to sleep."

Within minutes, Maya had drifted off; sleep had taken her quickly.

Beside her, Roberto lay awake. Why had the white dog come visiting to-night? Over the years, he had discovered that there was a pattern to its visits. The creature appeared only when something was wrong—it was a warning to him, or others close to him. Something bad was about to happen.

But he felt fine. For the first time in many years, he was happy. Surely, it couldn't possibly be a warning for him.

He turned again and again in bed trying to get comfortable. But sleep would not come while his thoughts were crammed with worry. His head felt like a concrete mixer full of sharp-edged questions tumbling about. He was tired now, but still, he could not shut the mixer down—it churned on and on.

Did the dog's visit have something to do with Maya? Should he tell her? Would she even believe him?

Finally exhausted, he could take no more. Sleep at last took him, and willingly, he gave way to it.

When he woke the next morning, even without thinking, he knew im-mediately what he must do. Maya must know about the white dog and its visits. After all, they were living together now. She had a right to know everything about the man who slept beside her. Whether she believed him or not wasn't important anymore. Roberto simply knew that it had to be done. If not for her, he had to do it for his own peace of mind.

Later that morning, and with some anxiety, he revealed to her his secret—a secret that he had carried for what seemed to him to be more than a lifetime. Maya was the first person he had ever told of the apparition that had haunted him since his father's death.

The ghostly creature had always appeared without warning, and usually for a few moments only. Then, just as suddenly, its vaporous form would disappear into thin air. When Roberto had been young, the dog, with its piercing red eyes, had terrified him, but over nineteen years, he had now seen it many times and had grown accustomed to it.

Maya was a scholar, and Roberto expected her to be brimming with scholarly explanations—unresolved grief, for example, or repressed anger brought on by trauma. These sometimes affected the psychology of the adolescent. Such affects could manifest themselves as imaginary figures, a condition common among troubled teens—some of whom could even be afflicted by these episodes into their adult years. He had read all the theories, and he simply expected to hear them echoed again from Maya.

She questioned him closely. *Why did he think the dog visited only him and no one else? Could he feel the white dog's presence even when he could not see it? Were there any unusual circumstances prior to each visit? What were his feelings when the visit had ended?*

He answered these and many more as best he could. He was surprised by her questions. She seemed genuinely interested in what he had to say and delved even further into some of his answers. He had not expected this; nor had he expected the astonishing revelation that she was about to deliver.

Maya did not believe the apparition to be imaginary, and flatly told him so. To her, it was something else, entirely. She believed it to be a spiritual protector sent to watch over him. He was amazed and showed it in his expression.

"In many ancient tribal communities, it was normal for members of those societies to adopt animal spirits as protective forces," she told him. "Belief in protective spirits is incredibly ancient. Even today, within Christianity, the protective spirit is a powerful force underlying the very faith that Christians hold to."

Roberto understood this. He remembered back to his first Semana Santa when he was just a young boy. His parents had taken him to Sevilla at the time of Cuaresma, and the most passionate of all Holy Weeks. The memory of the golden icons and glittering images of Holy protection paraded through the packed narrow incense filled streets would remain with him forever.

"When you really think about it," continued Maya, "primitive belief systems still resonate from the depths of our collective past, and still have an effect on the way that we live, even today."

He understood her now. Perhaps the dog *was* some sort of spirit that had attached itself to him - but where had it come from and why had it chosen him? Surely these were questions no one could answer. After all this was Spain, it had been many hundreds of years, perhaps even thousands since the Spanish had been a tribal society. An animal spirit seemed truly out of place here, something so far in the past that even a memory of such a thing would be foreign.

As an anthropologist though, Maya was captivated by Roberto's white dog experiences. This was just the sort of cultural oddity that fascinated the scientist in her.

Roberto felt nervous now. He realized that it was too late to turn back. The little that Maya knew of his experiences with the ghostly dog weren't going to be enough for her. It was obvious that as a scientist she would want to know everything. He too was interested in discovering more about his ghostly visitor, but there was still a part of him that wanted it to remain a mystery. In the end though, it wasn't to be.

His belief in fate was to prove well founded. He was to learn that if there really was a line between reality and spirituality, that line could only ever be seen by someone who knew exactly where to find it.

That morning, he could see Maya was excited. But unknown to her, any plans that she had regarding his mysterious dog would now have to wait; bad news was already on its way.

Before the day had run its course she heard her father's faltering voice as he spoke to her on the telephone: "Your mother is very ill, Maya; you must come home as soon as you can."

Within forty-eight hours, she was on a flight back to Los Angeles. It was there, where her mother lay in a hospital bed, perilously close to death.

3

VALLVIDRERA, THE ANTIQUE BOX

"Why don't you visit us?" Fernando's voice echoed through the phone wires.

"I'm sorry welo, I've been so busy lately," replied Roberto. As soon as he had said it, he felt the pangs of guilt stir within him. Outside of his mother and Maya, these were the two most important people in his life.

"Rubbish!" the old man growled. "What could be so important that it prevents you from visiting your own grandparents?" Roberto knew that he was right. As he had gotten older, and without even realizing it he seemed to grow apart from the elderly couple. Even his visits to them had become more infrequent. Perhaps it was a generational thing; or maybe he really was just too busy. Whatever the reasons they meant nothing now. With his grandfather breathing heavily down the phone at him, it was time for atonement.

"I'm sorry welo. I'll come and see you tomorrow."

"That's excellent news. Your grandmother and I would love to catch up with you." Fernando's voice now rang with glee.

To those outside the family, the lives of the two octogenarian grandparents seemed happy enough. But within, a different world lay hidden. Between them were one hundred and seventy five years of collective life experience, more than enough for any couple to wrestle with.

Fernando and Nuria Hernandez were intellectually sharp, and taking into account their age, both were in good physical health. Aided in large part it seems, by two spaniels, which they simply adored. The small fluffy duo had the complete run of the large, three-storied villa. Roberto marveled many times at how the pair of little creatures kept their owners' pent-up emotions in a kind of harmonic balance. Without these two lively bundles, there was always the potential for emotional chaos between the old couple.

Born in 1921, Fernando was the youngest and now the only surviving son of three. The two older boys died fighting in the civil war. In July 1936, seventeen-year-old Jorge was killed in the Barcelona uprisings. His bullet-ridden body was discovered near Las Ramblas, the word *traidor* scrawled in blood across his forehead. *Traitor*—the very word begged an explanation, but the family never got one, and his death was to remain a mystery.

Juan was just twenty years old when a bullet found him in the battle for Belchite in August 1937. His ghost may yet still haunt the broken streets of that village which stands to this day—a bleak reminder of the futility of war. Each of Fernando's brothers had fought a different cause, one a Republican and the other for Franco and the Nationalists. But fate was sympathetic, for in battle, their paths were destined never to cross. Elena, the youngest of Fernando's siblings, married a doctor from Jerez de la Frontera—the youngest son of a sherry baron. In 1942, just a year after the nuptials, the happy couple moved to Cadiz. Emails now replace the letters which once traveled between Fernando and Elena.

The drive to his grandparents' home in Vallvidrera took Roberto about thirty minutes. He had driven this trip many times before and knew all the shortcuts that avoided the busy and often clogged main arterials.

As expected the old couple were overjoyed to see him. They fussed about as though he had been gone for decades. In fact it had been just under two months since he had last been in their company. But to Fernando and Nuria, it had seemed a lifetime.

Perhaps it was the excitement of finally having their grandson to themselves, or maybe it was just bad timing, but the day's visit got off to a bad start.

"How is your mother?" the old man asked.

"She's fine," Roberto said. But somehow, he had the feeling that this answer would not satisfy the bespectacled old man peering back at him.

"Rubbish!" scoffed Fernando. "How can she be fine? She's lonely. She needs to get out more and perhaps meet a nice man."

"Sometimes you are impossible," spat Nuria. "You think that's the answer to everything…a nice man. Listen—there is nothing wrong with Amalia. She'll do whatever she wants, and your silly old opinions aren't going to matter one bit to her."

Nuria was three years younger than her husband, and slightly built. But what she lacked in size she more than made up for in spirit. She mocked Fernando with her words and screwed her wrinkled old face up at him. She understood Amalia better than Fernando ever could and hated it when he tried to push his advice in her direction.

"The woman is lonely," Fernando countered. "I can tell that, even from here. Who does she have to talk to?"

"She has me," interrupted Roberto.

"And me," Nuria taunted back at her husband.

"No," replied the old man. "I mean *really* talk to."

"She has me," insisted Roberto once more.

Fernando paused a moment and peered at his grandson over the top of his thick dark rimmed glasses. "Does she now?" he spoke slowly, his old features verging on a frown. "You'd do better to concentrate on your own life, Roberto. Let your mother go. Let her become a woman again."

Roberto could feel a cringe coming on, but he knew better than to utter another word. His mother's wellbeing was one of those subjects that always increased the tension between his grandparents. Often these discussions took place when she wasn't even present, and that always upset his grandmother.

"He drives me crazy!" shrieked Nuria, throwing her hands up. "Why do I have to put up with this?"

Roberto noticed with alarm the savage glare she had thrown at Fernando. It even took the old man by surprise.

"Lolita!" she yelled, "I need a strong coffee."

Lolita had been the couple's housemaid for more years than anyone could remember. She was Chilean by birth and had, as a young woman, immigrated to Spain to work in the domestic service. The Hernandez household sometimes wasn't the easiest of environments to work in. But despite the challenges, Lolita enjoyed her work. Her success as a trusted employee was based on two important rules that she followed with a religious devotion. Rule one—the family came first above all else, and rule two—never, ever take sides.

"Coffee for you sir?" she smiled.

"Thank you," nodded Roberto.

"And for you, sir?" Lolita said, turning to Fernando.

"Of course," replied the old man.

"Put rat poison in his cup, Lolita. Roberto and I will gladly dispose of the body later."

Roberto was shocked; there wasn't even a hint of humor in Nuria's voice. Lolita laughed out loud as she headed for the door. She had heard it all before.

"Bring mine up to my room," Nuria called after her. "I've had enough of old man's nonsense." And with that, she stood up. "I'll see you later, in a more sensible environment," she said to Roberto, then turned and left the room.

Fernando smiled "It's good to see you, Roberto—just like old times."

"Things have changed welo," Roberto observed.

"Your grandmother needs to cool down a bit, don't you think? Old age seems to have messed with her mind. She's changed, alright."

That wasn't what Roberto meant, but he was determined not to get dragged into this conversation.

"How have you been, welo?"

Fernando paused for a moment. "I've just remembered…" he said. "I've got something to show you."

"What is it?" Roberto asked, welcoming the change of subject.

The old man eyed him for a moment, and then struggled up from the comfort of his easy chair. "Young people are so impatient these days. Come with me, since you're in so much of a hurry."

Roberto just shrugged. Growing old, he thought, seemed to be messing with *both* their minds.

Fernando had aged more rapidly in the last couple of years than he had ever done in the last decade, thought Roberto. Wispy gray hair now ringed his old head, thinning away to complete baldness on his crown. This gave him the appearance of an old and lean monk. His ripened, pale face beamed with two alert, steely gray eyes that looked out, judging the world through thick glass spectacles.

Fernando had been a collector of rare books and manuscripts almost all of his adult life. Over the years, he had amassed a formidable collection that was both the envy of his fellow collectors and worth a great deal of money. No one had seen the walls of his library for more than thirty years; they were completely hidden from view. Every square centimeter of available space was taken up by shelving which groaned under the weight of masses of books. Each shelf was piled high with tome upon tome, higgledy-piggledy, one upon another, reaching right up to the ceiling.

As Roberto followed his grandfather into the library, he couldn't help feeling that even in the tiniest of earth tremors one would be in grave danger in this room. Fernando however, had no such fears. He walked over and flopped with a great sigh into his age-worn leather chair.

"Just because a man breathes doesn't mean he's alive. Would you agree with that?"

Roberto thought for a moment; he could feel Fernando's eyes upon him. He thought he understood what the old man was trying to say and eventually nodded.

Fernando smiled, "Do you think I'm right, Roberto?"

"Why are you telling me this?"

"You're my grandson, for God's sake," he was abrupt. "Aren't I allowed to pass on my wisdom to you?"

"It's not that…" Roberto never got to finish.

"Look, I'm talking about life—that precious flash of light that appears between birth and death. I'm eighty-nine years old, and my flame doesn't burn as bright as it did when I was your age, but do you think I want it to go out? No!"

Roberto remained silent. What was the old man trying to tell him?

"I can remember everything that has happened to me in my life just as though it happened yesterday. I no longer have the strength to do any of it again, but when I close my eyes, I can see it all. It's all gone by so quickly, Roberto—eighty-nine years, gone in a flash."

For the first time in his life Roberto could see sadness in Fernando's eyes. In all of the years he had spent growing up with the old man, he had never seen him like this.

"To me the saddest thing about death is that when it comes, it is total and complete. Everything that person ever thought or knew or felt dies with them. Imagine, Roberto: all of it lost forever. You think you know someone, but when they die you realize you didn't know them at all."

Roberto nodded a little nervously, still wondering where all this was leading.

Fernando's eyes began surveying the countless books piled high around the room. "There is only one way to beat it, and that is to write. If the dead man was a writer, he would not be forgotten. We would even know his soul." A smile crept onto the old man's face as he turned to his grandson. "I have made this room a temple to writers everywhere, alive or dead. I have filled it with their souls. In this room, you will find hopes and dreams, fears and sadness, immortalized for as long as these walls stand. Look there," the old man said, pointing to the bookshelves across the room from where the pair sat. "I have all your books."

Roberto was surprised. Although Fernando had always encouraged him to write, he had never shown any obvious interest in the finished works. Because of this, he had always believed that his grandfather's reading interests lay in other, more intellectual directions. But in this, as with other things he believed about the old man, Roberto was to learn that he had been mistaken.

"Pass me that box," Fernando said, pointing toward the table nearest Roberto. On it sat an unusual wooden box; it looked old. He reached over and picked it up. Its surfaces were rubbed and darkened with age. Before handing it to Fernando, he took a moment to admire its richly decorated lid, which was covered with unusual carved images.

"There is a history in this box, and it's time you discovered it," said Fernando as he reached out and took it from Roberto. "Once, long ago you had an ancestor who chose to live his life to the fullest. He wasn't afraid of anything and had the courage to shake his fist at fate. And before he died, he wrote of his life and of his adventures. In this old box is his story, *The Journal of Francisco de Villanova*, a handwritten manuscript passed down through many generations to me. On this day, it becomes yours." Fernando held the box out to Roberto, who received it and laid it upon his lap. His fingers briefly explored the lid, and then sought out the brass latch so he could open the box.

"No," said Fernando as he reached over and placed his hand upon the lid. "Don't open it here. Take it home and discover in your own time what the box contains."

Roberto was surprised by his grandfather's action, but he smiled and nodded in response.

"Good," said the old man. "Now tell me, what have you been up to?"

The pair remained in the library for most of that afternoon, catching up and reminiscing. Their laughs could be heard ringing through the hallways of the Villa Hernandez.

Eventually the jovial commotion brought Nuria from her room. By now she had calmed down, and the jolly banter of the men brought a smile to her face. As the afternoon shadows lengthened, she suggested that the three of them move to the patio and enjoy the last remnants of the fading golden light.

For Roberto it had turned out to be another of those magical days, just like the ones he remembered from his childhood. Fernando and Nuria were simply the best two people in the world to be with. The three of them sat silently enjoying the last of the afternoon's gilded rays. With them, two small dogs, one on each elderly lap, looked skyward with growing excitement, for overhead were swirling flocks of swallows wheeling through the ever-reddening sky.

It was early evening when Roberto, clutching the beautiful old box, finally said goodbye to his grandparents. The little group stood in the doorway of the villa as Fernando wrapped his grandson in an embrace and kissed both his cheeks.

"Come back soon," he whispered. "Time is no longer my friend."

"I promise," Roberto said.

When it was her turn, Nuria pulled her grandson toward her so strongly that the pair almost fell. She clung to him tightly as he managed to maintain his balance. "We are all getting older, Roberto. Don't you forget that when you're busy making plans for your life. You listen to your grandfather and come back soon."

As he turned and stepped out onto the pavement, he caught the breeze on his face; it held an early evening chill. He walked to his car, which was parked to one side of the cobblestone driveway. The electric evening glow of Barcelona, as it sprawled across the plains at the foot of the Collserola Hills, illuminated the air above the city. Roberto could see the trees and shrubs that surrounded his grandfather's property silhouetted against the radiant sea of lights. It was a truly magnificent sight, and one exclusive to the rich owners whose villas perched along the ridge tops of the wealthy neighborhood.

The evening air was clear and cold as Roberto drove along carrer Mont D'Orsa on his way back to the city. Through the glow reflecting up from the metropolis, he could just make out the first faint stars twinkling in the dusky sky. Off in the distant harbor were the lights of cargo ships at anchor. A passenger ferry, lit up like a giant floating tiara, slowly coasted through the inky evening waters heading toward the dock.

In the city, Roberto could see the bright lights emanating from Camp Nou, home of Barcelona FC—once his father's great passion. *There must be a game in the stadium tonight*, he thought, and his mind drifted back to when he first saw a game there. He was just a boy.

It was May 12th 1982; Barcelona FC against Belgium's Standard Liége— and at stake was the European Cup. Seven minutes into the game one hundred thousand spectators inside Camp Nou were silenced when Standard Liége took the lead, 1 – 0. But just before the break, Barca struck back, 1 - 1. Roberto remembered clambering up onto his father's shoulders and remaining there for the whole of the second half. He watched as, seventeen minutes into the half, the goal scoring legend Quini put Barcelona FC into the lead, 2 - 1. Barca went on to win the European Cup with that score, and the rest was history.

Of course, he couldn't remember all the details—he was only six years old at the time. But his father had described that game so often Roberto came to know it all by heart. But that was in the past, for him, a journey with new stories now lay ahead.

The passenger ferry that he had seen earlier had now made its way into dock. Its travelers were waiting patiently to go; a journey's end for some, but for others, the journey was about to begin.

4

THE LETTER OF FRANCISCO DE VILLANOVA, 1579

By the time he arrived home, Roberto's thoughts were focused on the old wooden box that his grandfather had given him. He was eager to open it. He set it down on the dining table and sat for a moment, contemplating again the unusual imagery that covered the lid. He let his fingers brush over the grooves and swirls that faced its entire surface. The once-sharp, chiseled edges on the carved images were now smoothed with the passing of time. His fingers simply followed centuries of others, which had also explored the designs on the lid. He found and unclipped the latch. As he raised the top, a musty odor emanated from the box. He felt a slight chill on the back of his neck, as though somewhere nearby a door had been opened and a gust of cold air had blown through.

Just as his grandfather had told him, there inside the box was the manuscript, but something else was with it. Beside the manuscript lay an amulet. Roberto had never seen anything like it.

The parchment looked old. On the cover, in beautiful antique Castilian script, were the words *El Diario de Francisco de Villanova*. Roberto reached in and carefully lifted the manuscript from the box. As he turned back the cover, he noticed the stitching, which held the volume together, had loosened through centuries of handling. He pulled gently on the cover, folding it back to reveal the first page, which was a letter. A shiver ran through him as his eyes fell upon the word, *fantasma*—ghost.

Dear José,

It is obvious to me now that I will die in this prison; the sins of my father weigh heavy upon me. It seems the curse he brought upon us has finally become my fate. I did not know the Jew Josef Jimenez, who was burnt by the Inquisitor. But it was my father who had protected this man from the church. Something passed between Jimenez and him before he died. I know not what it was, but from that day, a curse has shadowed our path and seems destined to haunt us forever—and, I fear, even visiting upon those yet unborn, and seeking out generation after generation.

My father, once a strong and hard-working man, died a cripple. His body was broken, and his mind was tormented by the demons that stalked it. Was he wrong to protect the Jew Jimenez against the Inquisition? If he was, the price for doing so seems too high. He died believing that God had forsaken him, and in the moment of his death, he cried out to the ghost of Jimenez to ease his passing; and now I am fearful that the Jew will return again for the son. Like my father, I am anxious that here in this prison cell God has also forsaken me. I am adrift from the Almighty, left for the sorcerer Jew to ease my passing as he did my father.

Of the ungodly things that have been a part of my life, I confess to you now José that there is a ghost—a beast that has haunted me for many years. In these last weeks, as if savoring my demise, it now visits more frequently. I know neither why it comes nor what meaning it brings, but it has stalked me ever since the time of your birth. From that very hour, it became my unwanted ghostly companion, and a frightening secret that I have carried in silence all of my years. Your mother, Aramoana, were she with us still, would surely know the meaning of it, for it is from her world that the beast comes and not from mine.

In recent days, I have become greatly concerned for your safety. I am certain that the Inquisition will have its way with me as it did with Jimenez. But for you José, the True God will know your innocence and protect you always. You must remain hidden from these black-robed devils masquerading as priests, for they will surely bring you down into the mire that they inhabit. Do not let them find you, my son, for they will offer you up to their devils as they do me.

You were a gift to me from your mother, whom I have always loved. She died so that you might have life. From a newborn, with God's help, I raised you to manhood. I know José that I will never see you again, and that makes my memories of you all the more precious. In this prison cell, I am held captive, physically trapped, and awaiting my end. But my spirit, dear son, is with you, wandering by your side and watching over you and your family.

In all the years I have walked with you upon this earth, I have never told you of your mother and from whence she came. She has remained a mystery to you, and also a mystery to me. She died tragically when we were both young. God, it seems, in his wisdom, had taken her to him, and left you to me. But through all of the hardships life delivered to you and me, we have survived.

Now my end is close. I know the Inquisition will do its devilish work on me, an innocent man. This pack of fiends somehow believes me to be a servant of the Devil. My only mistake was to share the secret of the apparition with one whom I thought a friend. I have learned now that in troubled times, friendships fade easily. My fate has been sealed, and it seems certain that my final judgment will be upon a fiery stake. I know neither the day nor the hour of my death, but soon enough, they will come for me.

In these, my final days, I write this letter to you in consolation, and to share with you a secret before I die. I have kept a journal; it is hidden beneath the floor of the hearth. Read it, José, and you will know my life.

You were born among sailors, José, good men who gave everything so that future generations could venture safely upon the great oceans. When I am gone, do not weep for me—for I have been a sailor all my life, and now I prepare to once more sail again. This time it will be on the voyage of no return—for I go to join our forefathers. Upon my passing, offer what prayers you must to commend my soul to our Great God. But also offer prayers to commend to him those lost sailors who gave us the chance to once again walk in the land of our kin. It is to these men that we owe everything. Honor them José, those countless souls who now lay in the endless pathways that traverse the oceans of the world. It was their sacrifice that allowed me to return once more, babe in arms, to my beloved Spain. It is their voices who echo across the endless valley of time. Do not let them lie forgotten, so far from home in the silent bosom of the great abyss.

By my hand this 15th day of January 1579
Francisco de Villanova

As he reached the end of the letter, Roberto's excitement had turned to sadness. In that tangled calligraphy lay a history, bared open and raw like the scar from a red hot poker upon delicate skin. Each word that cried out from the distant past was forever frozen in script. For centuries, Villanova's parchment lay in that box like a corpse in a coffin, its unspoken words left for dead. The letter had moved Roberto; he felt a connection to its writer and a desire now to breathe voice into its forgotten words. What story lay hidden within those parchment leaves?

He closed the manuscript and carefully placed it back into the box. He knew that very soon, he would return to it again.

5

BARCELONA, MAYA'S RETURN

It was a glorious morning, and Roberto was excited as he climbed into his SEAT hatchback. Maya was finally returning to Barcelona. She had spent the last four weeks in Los Angeles at her ill mother's side. Christine Serrano had collapsed while out dining in Mid-City with her husband, Rudolfo. The worst was feared, and Maya was summoned home to LA. But after three weeks in the hospital, Christine took a turn for the better, and shortly afterwards was released to go home. The worst seemed to be over, and at last she began to regain her health. As soon as Maya knew this, she booked the first available flight back to Barcelona.

Roberto pulled out into the stream of traffic heading north along the Gran Via. The roads were busy this morning, and now that he was moving, it was hardly more than a crawl. By the time he reached the roundabout on Passeig de Sant Joan, the traffic was so dense it had come to a complete stop. He glanced at the clock on the dashboard and began to wonder whether he would actually make the airport on time.

Since getting out of bed, Roberto had felt a little disoriented, and even now, he still hadn't managed to shake the feeling. *It was just the anticipation of seeing Maya again*, he thought. He had missed her a great deal.

Reaching over, he pressed a power switch on the center console, and the driver's window slowly drew downward. The morning air outside vibrated with the sound of traffic, but it was cool and felt less claustrophobic. Just then, the car in front of him moved forward and entered the roundabout ahead. Roberto watched its right-indicator light flash as it turned into Passeig de Lluis Companys. He felt lightheaded, and for a moment, those amber flashes looked like brilliant orange stars floating in a swirling ocean of gray.

He woke up in the Hospital Nuestra Señora del Mar in Barceloneta. He had no idea how he got there.

Staff at the hospital had traced his mother through the next-of-kin details attached to his identity card. When Amalia called her parents, they insisted on traveling with her to see their grandson. Later, they were joined at the hospital by Maya, who had taken a taxi from the airport. She had called Roberto's mobile phone when he failed to show up. A nurse at the hospital answered, and she explained to Maya what had happened.

Maya hadn't met Roberto's family before, and in the waiting room, she introduced herself as his girlfriend.

Fernando at first eyed her carefully, and then gave his approval with a smile and two gentle kisses, one to each cheek. He knew instinctively that she would be good for his grandson; he could see it in her eyes.

Amalia also liked what she saw in Maya. After studying her for a moment she too, like Fernando, had decided that the girl would be a good match for her son. But Nuria was more reserved. She did not like Americans. What was wrong with a nice Spanish girl for her grandson? Fernando could see it all in the expression on Nuria's face. He turned to Amalia and shrugged. She returned his stare with a starkness that he immediately understood—*leave her alone*. He simply rolled his eyes and looked to Maya, "Welcome to the family," he said with a smile.

All the people Roberto cared for were now gathered together in his hospital room. When he opened his eyes, Amalia and Nuria began to weep. His mother leaned forward and kissed his forehead. Nuria stretched out her hand and began stroking his shoulder.

Fernando, who was seated close to the bed but on the opposite side to the pair of teary women, let out an audible sigh of relief. He reached over and rested his hand on Roberto's. Maya, who stood behind Fernando, made no sound as the tears rolled down her cheeks.

"You gave us a real fright, chico," said Fernando patting Roberto's hand.

"What happened?" asked Roberto blearily. He was pale and drawn and hadn't fully come to his senses.

"You passed out in your car. Thank the Lord you weren't moving at the time. Someone called an ambulance, and they brought you here." Amalia was still in shock, and her voice trembled as she spoke.

"How are you feeling?" Fernando asked hesitantly.

"Better, now for seeing you all," Roberto mumbled as he raised his hand toward Maya, she reached forward and gently took hold of it.

"I'm sorry I couldn't make it…" he said.

"It doesn't matter," she replied. "I'm here now, and that's all that matters."

Roberto smiled and as he turned back, he caught a glimpse of the expression on his mother's face. She had been watching the exchange between him and Maya.

It was early evening when the last of Roberto's visitors had finally left. It had been agreed that Maya would spend the night with Amalia since her apartment was closer to the hospital. That way, they could both return early the next morning. For Roberto at least, this seemed a good idea. He knew that his mother was in need of company; it was obvious that she had received a shock. Despite her trying to conceal them, Roberto noticed the tears in her eyes as she left his hospital room that evening.

That night, after the medical staff had completed their rounds and dinner had been eaten, the hospital fell silent.

"Can I get you something before you go to sleep?" a nurse asked as she leaned through the open door into his room.

"A taxi," replied Roberto. "I want to sleep in my own bed tonight."

She smiled. He looked nervous. "Of course you do," she said. "Tomorrow you have medical tests—purely precautionary, you understand—they will probably find nothing. But once the doctors are finished with you, you will be free to go home. Don't worry, and please, señor Torres, try and get some sleep. You will feel much better for it in the morning."

He knew she was right, and managed a smile, but he still wanted to go home and be with Maya.

He dozed in and out of sleep until just after midnight, when a familiar feeling began to stir within him. He knew its meaning and opened his eyes. There, in the corner of the room, sat his ghostly friend. Roberto lay perfectly still, breathing softly. He watched the white beast as it stared back at him, stretched out, as he was, in his hospital bed. Tonight, the ghost seemed more real to him than it had ever been in the past.

"Have you come to comfort me?" whispered Roberto.

The little animal sat motionless, a ghostly form shimmering in the darkness; he was a beautiful creature, even if he was a ghost. His ears sat pricked atop his long-muzzled head, and seemed to suit his intelligent face. His thin and slightly elongated body terminated in a bushy tale that gave him more the look of a fox than a dog.

But his eyes—tonight they seemed different. In past visits, the dog had done nothing more than to sit and gaze at him, but tonight, something else was to happen.

All of a sudden, the creature stood and began walking toward him.

Roberto watched in breathless silence as the beast approached; then, suddenly, just before reaching him, it simply disappeared, breaking apart like cigarette smoke caught in a breeze.

Roberto lay for a long time that night with questions churning in his head. But the answers to every one of them remained elusive. Eventually fatigue overtook him, and in the end he drifted off to sleep. There was however no escape from the ghostly canine, for since it had been so firmly embedded into his thoughts, it now invaded his dreams.

The following morning, when he woke, Roberto was still tired. He had tossed and turned most of the night, and what little sleep he'd managed to get had been disturbed by unusual dreams. Nevertheless, he was glad to finally open his eyes and see daylight. Today was the day the doctors had told him that he would be free to go home. Of course, they wanted to run some tests, but after that, he would be gone so fast that they would need the AVE bullet train to catch him.

But as the morning grew into day, Roberto became anxious. He'd had time to think about those medical tests. What might they discover? What was his body trying to tell him? He had no answers. Perhaps the nurse was right, and they would find nothing. But try as he might to convince himself that everything was okay, something deep inside of him whispered that it was not. And now he feared that even the ghostly dog's visit during the night was confirmation of the worst.

It was late afternoon when Roberto and Maya finally returned to the apartment they shared. For Roberto, the scans, surgical biopsies and seemingly endless blood tests at the hospital had been exhausting. He headed straight for the bedroom and sleep.

Around three in the morning, he woke to find himself alone in bed. As he opened his eyes, he caught a glimpse of the last vestiges of his ghostly friend as it melted away. The dog had returned. It had been silently sitting at the foot of the bed, watching over him.

A moment later, Maya entered the bedroom.

"Where were you?" Roberto asked as he pulled the covers back.

"I couldn't sleep," she said. "I've just made myself a hot drink. Did you call me?"

"No, I've only just woken up."

"That's strange, I thought I heard a voice," she said shrugging her shoulders.

"It wasn't me."

She leaned forward as he sat up and placed her hands to his cheeks. "It's so good to be here with you again." She kissed him on the lips.

"I've missed you," he whispered.

"You need a shave," she chuckled as her fingers brushed his cheeks.

"I need a hot drink, too," he grinned.

She stood up, "Come on, I'll make you one."

Later, as the pair sat in silence in the living room, Roberto noticed that Maya seemed preoccupied. He could see by the expression on her face that something troubled her.

"What are you thinking about?" he asked.

"I'm worried, Roberto."

"What about?"

"About you. Something's wrong, and we need to know what it is."

He could see now that she was close to tears.

"Don't worry Maya, everything will be okay. I have an appointment with the doctor in a few days. I'll know everything then." As he spoke, he let his eyes drift from hers, for he had not told her everything.

That morning at the hospital, the doctors had already given him their verdict—one that he had decided to keep to himself—for now at least. At this moment, he couldn't even tell his mother. The news, of course, was not what he had expected, and the deadening shock of it had hit him hard. Understandably, he was confused and even struggled to comprehend exactly what had been said. But the bottom line was clear: *Don't make plans for the future, because there was no future.* The illness was terminal—perhaps a year, maybe even less.

Right now, the facade that he had cultivated for years was still holding up—but only *just*.

Maya knew instinctively though, that he wasn't telling her everything and sadly, she had begun to doubt that he ever would. But to question him more at this moment would just push him further out of reach. Of all his idiosyncratic behaviors and his peculiarities, this was the one that upset her the most.

The conversation had now dissolved into an awkward silence. Roberto felt uncomfortable and needed to say something—anything that would get Maya talking again.

"The apparition came to me again tonight," he said thinking a change of subject a good option.

"I'm not surprised. There is something not right. I'm convinced that ghost of yours is here to help." Maya was serious, and he could see it in her face. Then she noticed his expression change.

"I have something to show you, something my grandfather gave me." Roberto stood up from the sofa.

"What is it?" she asked.

"I'll get it," he said as he left the room.

A moment later, he returned with the beautiful old wooden box and placed it on the table in front of her.

"Open it…" he said.

As she lifted the lid, she felt a slight tingle through her body. Immediately, her trained eye fell onto the small, carved amulet, and she reached for it. She could tell that it was made of bone, and by its patina she knew that it was old. She even recognized the style of the artwork. She was after all a student of anthropology from the West Coast of America. She could recognize ancient Pacific art anywhere. Her hands trembled as she held it. Drawing from her own Mexican roots, she knew instinctively that this was much more than just a piece of old carved bone. She needed to know more.

"Fernando gave this old journal to me," Roberto told her. "It was written by an ancestor of mine in the sixteenth century, the amulet was in the box with it."

He wasn't sure that Maya had heard him. She seemed completely distracted by the amulet. As she let her fingers explore its finely carved body, she knew that the curved and stylized form, with its prominent eyes, could mean only one thing. She was convinced. And now all she needed was the proof.

"What I think is disturbing," Roberto continued "is that a letter attached to the journal also mentions a ghost."

"And the amulet," asked Maya, still not lifting her eyes from it. "What do you know of the amulet?"

"Nothing, other than it came with the manuscript," said Roberto. "Why do you ask?"

"This bone carving could well be the perfect clue."

"The clue to what?"

"The clue to where your mysterious canine visitor comes from," she smiled.

Roberto was surprised. "What are you talking about?"

"I believe I know where this amulet comes from," she said. "And if I'm right, and it proves to be as old as your manuscript, there could be a bunch of upset historians on the other side of the world."

Roberto looked confused. She smiled and reached over, placing her hand on his. "I'll make you a deal," she said. "You make us another hot chocolate, and I'll tell you what I know."

Before they knew it, early morning light began stealing in through the cracks in the window shutters. The pair had been so absorbed in conversation they had not realized that the night hours had completely slipped away. And when Roberto finally opened the shutters, bright, warm sunlight came streaming through the windows into the apartment. A new day had dawned.

6

THE JOURNAL OF FRANCISCO DE VILLANOVA TO AUGUST 1525

I, Francisco de Villanova, neither knight nor serf and no more than a man of the sea, was born in the year of Our Lord 1504. In that year also, God took to heaven Queen Isabella the Catholic. A Coruña was the town of my birth, and as it had been for my father and his before him, it too became my beacon in life's tempests, and God knows there were many.

My father's name was Juanes. He was a sailor and ship's carpenter, who had spent most of his life upon the ocean. And when he was not sailing her briny waters, he toiled beside them.

He was a big man, his skin tanned dark from the years beneath the sun. I remember his hands were broad and rough, but also gentle as they wiped the tears from my cheeks whenever he left for the sea. My mother and I missed him when he was gone. Sometimes it would be years before he returned, and when he did, I embraced him tightly and nestled my face into his long black hair. I could smell the ocean in those tangled locks and could almost hear the sound of waves breaking upon distant shores.

How I loved to be with him, and when we were alone, he would tell me of his adventures. His stories were full of wonder, and sometimes my young mind would almost burst in astonishment. I still have visions in my head of the strange peoples he described, and of the lands they had discovered, and of the terrifying creatures that inhabited them. One day, I promised myself, I would go there, too.

When my father died, he did so having given over all of his life, in one way or another, to the sea. He was a good man, someone who honored his family, protected the innocent wherever he found them, and always sought the truth. And so it is hard for me to understand what led him to befriend the old Jew, Josef Jimenez, who not long afterward fell under the watch of the Holy Inquisition. It was rumored that the old man practiced magic and had visions of the future. On these grounds, he was brought before the High Inquisitor. And when his house was searched, it was found to be full of books, every one of them banned by the Holy Church. For weeks, Jimenez was interrogated, and when they could get nothing from him, he was condemned to death as a sorcerer.

Despite the warnings from his friends, my father never forsook the old man. He visited him many times in his last days, and on the day of the execution, my father was there at the foot of the pyre. As the flames reached up and seized the old Jew, he shouted in agony down to my father. He spoke in a language that no one present could understand. I know not even if my father understood its meaning, for he never talked of the incident again.

Many in the village, including the priests, believed that in the moment of reckoning, the tongue of the Devil called through the old man's throat. And in his ranting, he cursed my father for not saving Jimenez. But the villagers believed the old Jew to be none other than the Devil's agent. I do not know the truth of the matter, and can only go on my father's actions, for there I knew him to be true. I have no knowledge of what passed between him and the old Jew in the times they spent alone. And I know not what was shrieked in dying breath from the burning stake. But I do know that from the time of the burning of Jimenez, there remained unanswered questions in our lives. There was a secret, something hidden among the years, a shadow, perhaps a rumor or even a whisper, each weighing upon the other, and in turn, upon itself. For in the end, I felt sure that the shape of my life and those in my line would be fashioned by the lives of my father and that of the old Jew.

My mother was called Ana Maria, the most beautiful woman in her village. Her unfortunate fate, though she would not have it said, was to fall in love with a sailor. In time, she became his wife, and as the wife of a sailor, was destined to spend much of her marriage without him. She loved my father deeply, as he did her, and every time they parted, I saw tears in his eyes as well. Every day that he was gone, she kept vigil, watching out across the harbor, scanning the horizon for his returning sails billowing in the breeze. But each day would pass, and there would be none. Sometimes, to give her comfort, she would go out at night and sit quietly in the plaza, gazing up at the stars in the sky. She knew that somewhere in the world, her beloved husband would be gazing at them too. And so it was for most of her life—there among the stars, their yearning thoughts would entwine.

In the time of my youth, the city of A Coruña was the gateway through which young men passed seeking their fortune in lands beyond the horizon— new lands, it was said, where a man possessed of nothing in the Old World, could become a prince in the New. Men, rich and poor, from every corner of Spain and even the world, came here to this town to seek passage across the seas to find the kingdom of their dreams. Many a dreamer and adventurer alike set forth on voyages from these shores; not always did they return.

As I write these words, it seems a lifetime has now passed, yet nothing has changed from the days of my youth. Even now, the very air in A Coruña is laden with rumors of new lands and conquests across the ocean. Every day ships return with strange people and new wealth, all taken in the name of Spain. Cristobal Colón, just twelve years before my birth, ignited the hearts of men with the greatest of all discoveries. He found a hitherto unknown western route across the Ocean Sea to a new world. From that moment, the soul of every man in Spain blazed with a desire for adventure. The chance to seek out one's fortune across the Ocean Sea was all that possessed them.

It was in this atmosphere, and among these people, that I grew up. The ocean called to me from every point on the compass. There was no escape for the son of a ship's carpenter. When I was thirteen years old, my father, using what meager influence he possessed, managed to secure for me a job as a caulker's apprentice. I started work first at Ferrol, where I lived with my father's friend señor Puzón and his wife, Angelica. She was much younger than he was, and very beautiful. Often, at the market, I noticed that other men secretly watched her as she went about her business. But none would go further, for they were afraid of Puzón, who was a brute—and one who often succumbed to rages and violence for even the slightest provocation. To them, it was only natural that a man such as he should be avoided.

He and Angelica had no children, having lost both son and daughter in a terrible fire that had ravaged the old quarter of the city several years before I came to live with them. The father's grief never subsided, and he often drank himself into a stupor and then beat his wife because he blamed her for the loss of the children. She took the beatings in silence, never once uttering a sound or even shedding a tear.

Sometimes at night, when I was alone, I wept for her, for it seemed to me that her own grief had been entirely suffocated by fear. It sickened me to see her beautiful face bruised from the blows of her husband. But I was no match for Puzón, who I came to hate. Sadly, my father's honor had bound me, a boy of thirteen, to this man. A debt had existed between them, and this was my father's way of making payment. For three years, I lived with señor Puzón and his wife. And in that time, almost all of the money that I earned went to him. In return, I was allowed to eat at his table and sleep on a straw mattress near his hearth.

Señor Puzón's house was very close to the shipyard that built many of the caravels and galleons that made up the King's armada. It was a busy place, and during the day, the large docks and cranes and wooden cradles that lined the seashore near the town hummed with activity. Black smoke from pitch fires rose skyward, curling upward like mourning ribbons reaching high into the air above the docks. To the people of Ferrol, the shipyard was life, for it brought both money and work to the town.

I still remember my first days in that place. The fumes that bubbled from the great tar pans on the docks choked in my nostrils. The black tar we used on the ships clung to us so tightly that it was suffocating, and in the heat, became unbearable. In those first few days, I thought that I had stumbled into hell. But on that occasion I was mistaken. It wasn't long though before I became immune to the hard work and the fumes and the choking tar. Somehow it seems strange to me, but now that I am in my old age, I miss the adversity of that shipyard.

I had seen my sixteenth summer when I said goodbye to the shipyard at Ferrol and to señor Puzón and his sad wife. Since the debt between him and my father had now been settled, I returned to A Coruña. I know not what became of the Puzóns, and I sometimes think of Angelica and the miserable life that she endured with a brute more than twice her age. In her life, it seemed that she had been abandoned by everyone, and now, even by me. But my return to A Coruña was necessary. My father had been badly injured in an accident at the shipyard in that town: an insecure windlass had given out, releasing oak beams, which crashed down upon him. Though fortunate that he came away with his life, he lost the use of both his legs in the accident. But as lucky as I thought he was, he could see nothing but misfortune ahead and wished that the accident had taken him completely. In his darkest hours, he warned me that a curse was upon him. He blamed the old Jew for this. The curse, he said, pursued him. It seemed that Jimenez had told my father something that was not his to know and now he paid the price for this mistake. In the end my father took what knowledge he had learned from the Jew to his grave, for he did not share it with me.

It wasn't long after arriving back in A Coruña that I obtained work at the shipyard. Perhaps it was my father's reputation there that secured me the job, or perhaps it was pity at our miserable circumstance. I will never know, but to this day, I remain eternally grateful for that opportunity. At that time, the yards looked much as they still do today, a busy collection of sheltered docks and cradles lining the western edge of the harbor. And all of it under the careful watch of the fortifications of San Antón to the north.

Life was very hard then. From sunrise to sunset, we labored, often working deep into the night by the light of flickering oil lamps or to the glow from cooking fires. Many of the ships were not able to be brought into the yards and so were hauled up onto the sand into makeshift cradles. Using windlasses, ropes, and gangs of men, each vessel would be carefully rolled to one side in the cradle. Teams of workers would scrape clean the hulls, exposing the timbers and the seams. Carpenters followed; it was their job to replace wormed or rotted planks in the hulls and keels.

When the cleaning and repairing was finished, it was the turn of the caulkers to seal and make watertight the hull. We cleaned out every seam and joint and repacked each of them tightly with new oakum and pitch. Once all of the seams were dry, the entire hull was coated in tar. It was hot and dirty work. Many of us today are scarred from the boiling tar that splashed from the tar pans we carried as we scurried to and fro beneath the creaking hulls.

At the end of each day, reeking and blackened, I dragged myself along the beach in the darkness toward home. Often, I would stop just long enough to gaze out at the ships shimmering in the glow of their own lamplight, bobbing at anchor in the harbor. There always seemed to be a great many. My heart was filled with excitement at the sight of every one of them, glowing like a fleet of fireflies upon the water. How I longed to be a sailor aboard any one of those radiant vessels, floating like a dream in the darkness upon those inky waters.

When I finally made it home, there would be my parents—my father lost in sadness for being unable to work, and my mother with boiled, salted cod and eggs, set upon the table with fresh water and bread, waiting for her weary son.

In the morning, as I made my way back to the row of ships all keeled over in their cradles, I looked out to the harbor once more. The ships I saw the night before had now gone, sailing to ports in far-off lands in search of cargo and adventure. I prayed that one day, I would be aboard such a vessel, bound for ports in kingdoms yet unknown. Every morning, on my way to the shipyard, my head would fill with youthful dreams of adventure across the seas. But soon, the pungent stench of burning tar filled my nostrils and emptied those thoughts from my head.

It was around this time that I met Ramón de La Cosa. We were the same age, and like me, he was a caulker. Ramón's father had been a sail maker onboard many ships before being struck down with an illness that almost claimed his life. He was an invalid now, and so, as it had to me, it fell to Ramón to provide for his family. We became good friends, and together we dreamed of escaping the shipyard and sailing across the sea to seek our fortunes.

In those days, as it is still, it was not easy to be crewed to a vessel. A prospective sailor needed to have contacts. Ship owners and captains alike were cautious about who they took aboard. The long and arduous voyages often tested men in ways one could not imagine, and so only those with proven ability would be chosen as crew. Many good sailors had carpentry or sail-making skills, which were vital to any expedition. But even they required good contacts before being accepted aboard ship.

As fate would have it, Ramón's father, señor Luis de La Cosa, had been well thought of in his time aboard ship. And as a man of good character, he still held the confidence of many a ship's captain and even several ship owners. Thus, thanks to señor La Cosa's tireless efforts, Ramón and I finally managed to be crewed aboard a ship. In the twenty-first summer of our lives, we were finally given the chance to see the world.

I remember that day as if it was yesterday—our excitement could hardly be contained. Both of our families were to be paid a sum in advance of our departure, with the promise of the remainder being paid upon our return.

But fate is a cruel mistress, who seems always to demand supplication. And so it was for me. My happiness at the news of señor La Cosa's success lasted only until the day of my departure. It has been said that in the eyes of a mother, the truth is always revealed—I have no doubt of this. I remember the look in my mother's eyes the day that I left A Coruña. My heart trembles even to this moment, for they were the eyes of a mother who would never again see her son. Whatever she knew on that day, God must have revealed to her—for both she and my father would die before my return.

Looking back on it now that I am old, I have just one regret. In my youthful clamor to board the ship, I did not hear my mother's last words as she called them to me. And now in my dreams, she calls to me again, but try as I might, I cannot make out what she is saying. My heart crumbles when I wake, and all I can do is wash the memory of it away with my tears.

It was after Mass, on the eve of the feast day of Saint James in the year 1525, that our armada slipped from the port of A Coruña. I shall remember that morning until the hour God takes me. The light smoldered red across the horizon as the sun rose above the hills flanking the eastern shores of the harbor. A discharge of artillery signaled our leave, and our voyage to the Molluccas Isles had begun.

Great billowing clouds of sail filled the early morning sky. The flaming red sunrise seemed to bleed from the Red Cross of the Order of Christ emblazoned upon each of the gigantic foresails. A flurry of noble colors fluttered in the breeze from the tops of the swaying forest of masts. Rigging and canvas creaked and groaned as wind shifts shaped our course and sent us tacking out into the harbor and pushing us toward the open sea.

Captain General Garcia Jofre de Loaysa was in command. The first leg of our course was set for the Canary Islands. There we would provision before setting sail to the west and out across the Ocean Sea.

The armada was made up of a crew of 450 men across seven ships. Each ship was to be as precious to us as our own lives, for indeed, our lives depended on them. God willing, each caravel would keep its crew safe for the voyage, and return us once more to our homeland. I carry still their names etched into my heart. The *Sancti Spiritus, San Lesmes, San Gabriel, Santiago, Nunciado, Santa Maria del Parrel,* and, of course, our flagship, the *Santa Maria de la Victoria.*

The crews for the most part were men of Galicia, Castile, Aragon, and Andalucía. Also among our number were men from the country of the Basques and from Portugal. My companion Ramón and I were among the crew of fifty-one men aboard the ninety-six-ton *San Lesmes.* Our commander was Francisco de Coćes. As we left the harbor of A Coruña that morning, none among us was aware that fate had written her own tale for the *San Lesmes*—a tale that would see an end not as it should be, in the Isles of the Molluccas, but in an unknown land, on an unknown sea.

As the breezes carried us out of the harbor on that glorious morning and out into the open waters, we laughed at the wind and at the sea and the sky, for we were glad to be alive.

Among our number was the famous Elcano, the first man to circumnavigate the world, and second in command on our voyage. He had sailed with Fernando de Magellan, and when that famous mariner was slain at the battle of Mactan, it was Elcano who brought the flagship *Victoria* back to Sevilla. The men of the armada felt safe with him aboard. For it is men like him who have tamed the restless sea and made a highway of it for men like us.

On the 2nd of August, we anchored in the harbor of La Gomera in the Canary Islands. In ancient times, it is said a primitive, pale race of blue-eyed and fair-haired people inhabited these islands. But over the centuries, these cave dwellers gradually succumbed to later invaders who settled the land. Now, only traces of these original people have survived and can be found in the inhabitants who live in the islands today.

It is also said that on one of the islands hereabouts, there grows a sacred tree. And were it not for that tree, the inhabitants would surely die, for on that island, it never rains. The people there take the water they need from pools which collect at the base of this tree. This is a very ancient story, and one that was told to me by an inhabitant of these isles.

On his voyage, Cristobal Colón had come to the Canary Islands as well. And just as he had done before us, we provisioned our ships with wood, water, and meat in preparation for the long voyage ahead.

On the 14th of August, we left La Gomera, and keeping La Isla de Hierro to starboard we filled our sails with the last breezes of home and took our leave of Spanish waters. Like a nursing mother, the gentle easterlies carried us full square into the folds of those same fortuitous winds that pushed Colón out across the Ocean Sea and into the arms of destiny. It was auspicious, I believed at the time, for me to have been in this fleet heading the same course. Surely, God willing, these winds would carry me to my own destiny. I prayed to Him to watch over me, and when my quest was fulfilled, to return me safely to my homeland, where I would die content at having made my fortune.

Before we left La Gomera, Elcano had instructed that he alone would shape our course and that all the ships of the armada were to follow in his wake. We knew that difficult waters lay ahead, and we were happy to have him lead the way. And just as he had predicted, we were only a few days out when we sailed directly into the jaws of a furious tempest.

We took the precaution of taking in our sails and lying to for the duration. The winds were unrelenting, screaming like devils through the rigging and even tearing at the tightly lashed sails. Our ships were tossed about like small twigs as the sea smashed at them, each one struggling desperately to stay afloat.

Then we noticed that the mainmast on the *Santa Maria de la Victoria* had collapsed, and the ship was listing precariously in the tumultuous seas. The damaged mast was entangled in the rigging and swung about dangerously in the strong winds. Observing the flagship in distress, the *Parrel* came quickly to her aid. But both ships found disaster, for in an instant, they were seized by the great force of the storm and driven violently together. The *Parrel* drove hard into the stern of the *Victoria,* resulting in both ships being very badly damaged. No one was lost in the incident, and as soon as the storm had abated sufficiently, Elcano dispatched carpenters to repair both of the stricken ships.

Once the storm had passed and the ocean had become calm and clear, we noticed that the waters around us teemed with sea life. We had never seen the sea so full of fish before—so plentiful were they, we could scarcely believe our eyes. Also swimming about our vessels were large fish of the type we call tiburón; in other lands, they are called shark. These massive creatures move like giant shadows, gliding quickly beneath the waters. Their large mouths contain fearsome rows of white, serrated teeth. When they approach the surface, their black dorsal fins can be seen slicing the skin of the ocean like a knife. If by some unhappy chance, one of these beasts should encounter a man in the sea, it would devour him quickly—of that, there is no doubt. And once he is in the grip of such a creature, a man's end would be instant and frenzied. Each who witnessed these creatures from the safety of our ships crossed himself and prayed that he would never encounter such a frightening beast.

That night, I dreamed I was being pursued by one of these giant creatures. I awoke agitated and sweating. The nightmare had upset my sleeping mind. I lay awake for a long time afterwards, listening to the night sounds aboard the ship. It is only while you are awake that you realize nights upon the ocean are so densely black that even visions in the mind can become reality if one is not careful. And care upon the ocean is what must guide every sailor, lest he become its victim.

7

THE JOURNAL OF FRANCISCO DE VILLANOVA TO

MAY 1526

It was about forty days' sail from La Gomera when we sighted our first ship. Immediately, we thought it to be French, because upon seeing us, the vessel turned and took flight. The *Santiago,* the fastest ship in our fleet, pursued the running vessel, and sometime later, returned with a Portuguese carrack under grapple. It was brought alongside the flagship and lashed securely to her.

The Captain General, who was eager to show Spanish hospitality, lavishly entertained the Portuguese crew, who were on their way home. In return, they agreed to take letters back to Spain when they departed the following day.

Several weeks later, we crossed the equinoctial line and soon after lost sight of the Pole Star from which our navigators had been charting our course. From that time, we relied on the constellation known as the Southern Cross. For Ramón and me, it was to be our first sighting of this small cluster of stars. I am led to believe that the cross does not sit at the south celestial pole, as does the Pole Star over the north, but merely points to the pole—the bright star positioned at the foot of the cross being the actual pointer. It seemed to me somehow fitting that the success of our journey now depended on a holy sign in the heavens. From the moment we sighted the constellation of His holy cross, we knew that our journey was now, more than ever, in the hands of God. That night, we celebrated Mass beneath the very stars that He had arranged to light our way.

We were all excited about entering the southern waters, for they were different from those that we had previously known. Even the air was different, seeming heavier and moister than the air about the northern oceans. And of course, the southern waters teemed with much fish life, the likes of which we had never before seen. Great shoals of albacore glistened in the waters around our ships, some of the shoals so thick that they looked like banks beneath the sea. We caught many of these fish, and they were wonderful to eat. Flying fish, too, rose out of the sea in such great numbers that at times, they blacked out the sun. Many would drop from the sky onto the decks of our ships, and in doing so, ended up as a meal upon our table. Their tender, sweet flesh is delicious. But as eating fish go, their single disadvantage is a row of fine bones along the midline. These can set a thorny trap for the reckless diner.

It had been many weeks at sea for us now, and some of our provisions were running low. The Captain General decided to make for the nearest port, which was called San Mateo. Here, we took onboard more fresh water, stocks of fowl, potatoes, and sweet fruits. We also obtained baskets of fish and bartered for quantities of meat cut from an animal the locals called the Anta. I remember the flesh of this animal to be very good to eat, being much like that of the cow.

The port of San Mateo was, for us, a most-welcome break from the monotony of the rolling sea. I remember fondly my time ashore, and in particular, the many good bargains that each of us made. For a piece of ribbon and a looking glass at San Mateo, Ramón bought an entire basket of fish. Not to be outdone, the captain, for the price of a comb, purchased two fat geese. Some of us even used our playing cards for trade. For the queen of hearts, I received eight fowl, and the vendor later boasted that he had received the better deal. Soon, however, we had provisioned fully, and despite the local inhabitants' wanting to trade further, we could not.

Before we sailed from San Mateo, we took onboard a number of Indians who longed to journey with us. We would teach them to become men of the sea. They gave us no trouble, and once we were at sea, seemed completely at home onboard the ship.

After passing the Rio de Plata, we again ran into terrible weather. This time, it was so bad that the whole fleet was blown off course. We lost sight of the flagship, and for a full day, the remaining ships searched in vain for her. That night, under the cover of darkness and in the midst of the raging storm, Ramón was attacked by Enriquez the Portuguese. The man was crazed and full of anger, falsely accusing my friend of stealing a woman from him while the armada was in port at San Mateo.

Ramón, who was strongly built, fought back hard. In the end, Enriquez was mortally wounded, and shortly afterwards, death took him. Later, when the opportunity presented, his lifeless corpse was dropped unceremoniously into the sea, which greedily swallowed him. After that, no one spoke again of the dispute. Enriquez, we had decided, was a victim of the violence of the storm and had been washed overboard and taken by the sea. My friend Ramón remained quiet for many weeks after this unfortunate incident. For he knew that to take a life, even in such circumstance, was something for which God alone would judge. And when the Day of Judgment arrived, Ramón knew that before God, fear would be his only companion.

The day after the Portuguese's death, the storm abated, and Elcano decided that the fleet would make haste for the Rio de Santa Cruz near the strait that Magellan had discovered. We would wait for the flagship there. As we headed south toward the mouth of the river, we lost sight of the *San Gabriel*, but because time was against us, we did not wait. Her navigators knew the course that had been set, and we were confident that she would eventually reach us at Santa Cruz. By late afternoon, we had arrived at the mouth of the river. The winds, at this time, did not favor us for entering the river under sail, and the tide was also against us. So we lay anchor for the night to windward off the northern shore, just out from the river mouth.

That evening, all the captains were summoned aboard the *Sancti Spiritus* for a council with Don Elcano. After some discussion, it was agreed that the *Santiago,* commanded by Don Guevara, would sail when tide and wind were favorable, into the Rio de Santa Cruz. There they would find an island, and on the shore of that island, they were to erect a large cross; one that could easily be seen by an approaching ship. At the foot of the cross, in a container, they were to place a letter. Once this was done, the *Santiago* was to make all haste to the Strait and thence to the port of Sardinas, where the rest of the armada would be waiting. When the captains of the two lost ships found the letter, they would know that we awaited their arrival at Sardinas.

It was early the next morning when we prepared to sail for the Strait. Even now, I remember vividly that dawn, anchored in those waters of half river and half sea. Our sails gently fluttered in the light northerly breeze as the sun rose above the watery eastern horizon. It lit the barren lands to the east of us with amber light, unfurling slowly across the hills, and sliding silently into the dry and rocky ravines. By the time the shadows quit the shoreline, we had already raised our anchors. I will always remember that abandoned and barren place. Never since have I felt as alone as on that morning off the mouth of the Rio de Santa Cruz.

Soon the armada was under full sail. We tacked southward, following Don Elcano aboard the *Sancti Spiritus,* for he had been this way before. The great navigator Magellan had charted this passage for the very first time only a few years ago, and it was fortunate for us that Don Elcano had been with him on that voyage.

Less than a day had passed before we discovered what the pilots believed to be the entrance to the Strait. However, to us, it looked more like the mouth of another great river. But the pilots were sure that this was the opening to Magellan's strait. So it was that on their advice, the armada entered the inlet. It wasn't long, however, before we realized that they had made an error. By then, it was too late, for within minutes of discovering their mistake, the lead ship, the *Sancti Spiritus,* had run aground. Don Elcano ordered a skiff to be launched from the stricken vessel. The crew's orders were to proceed further into the inlet and ascertain if this was indeed the opening to the Strait. The rest of the fleet waited a safe distance further out in the bay and watched the skiff as it was rowed from the grounded *Sancti Spiritus.* By that afternoon, the skiff still had not returned. The tide had now come back, and the *Sancti Spiritus* was again afloat. She soon joined us out in the bay as we waited for the returning skiff. It was later that evening, and in the glow of lamplight that the skiff finally showed up. The men aboard reported that the inlet was not the hoped-for entrance, so it was decided that we would sail at first light further down the coast in search of the elusive entrance to Magellan's strait.

That night, at around midnight, a terrible tempest blew up. Our ships were tossed mercilessly about in the fierce wind and mountainous seas. The storm was so violent that despite laying its heavy sea anchors, the *Sancti Spiritus* was driven into the shore and dashed violently against the rocks. We tried several times to make our way to her, but each time, we were beaten back by the fury of the storm.

Shortly afterwards, it became clear that we also were in danger of being wrecked upon the shore. We found ourselves struggling hard to hold the *San Lesmes* from being dashed to pieces. Thankfully, our sea anchors held, and we were saved from being driven ashore. But that night, the *Sancti Spiritus* was completely ripped apart on the jagged rocks, and with her went the lives of nine of her crew. Don Elcano and the remaining men made it to the shore and were saved. They were in a miserable condition the next day when the storm had passed, and we were finally able to rescue them.

There remained only three ships of the original fleet of seven—the *Nunciado,* now commanded by Don Elcano, the *Santa Maria del Parrel*, and the ship that Ramón and I were crewed aboard, the *San Lesmes.*

However, the weather had not finished with us. And as we reconnoitered further south along the coast, eventually finding the true entrance to the Strait, another violent tempest blew up. This one was so powerful, it completely scattered the remaining fleet before it. The *San Lesmes* was blown by the howling winds deep into the mouth of the Strait. The weather was so bad, we could do nothing except commend our souls into the hands of the Holy Father in the hope that He would keep us safe. Miraculously, during the storm, we were able to lay out sea anchors, which prevented us from being dashed into the rocks on the shoreline. The violent seas lashed us relentlessly for four days before passing. And in that time, we were completely isolated from the rest of the fleet. Once the tempest had abated, we discovered that most of our provisions had been lost into the sea. Mercifully, this time, no lives were taken.

On the fifth day, we were able to make some repairs and later begin searching for the rest of the armada. Soon, we were full of joy as we rounded a headland and saw before us the *Santa Maria del Parrel.* She was a picture to behold, anchored in the calm waters of a sheltered sandy bay. We joined her, and together praised God for sparing us all. She had weathered the worst of the storm in this small bay, and when it had passed, the Patagonians who inhabit this land came down from the hills to greet them.

These Patagonians are a wild and hardy people who have made do with what little the land here offers them. The men are very tall and are strongly built. They go about clothed in goatskin and wear plumage in their hair and metal hoops about their ankles and wrists. When they dance, the hoops on their ankles clang out loudly. The men stomp about and chant rhythmically and wave their weapons about wildly. These untamed giants are indeed a fearsome sight, cavorting wildly about in their savage finery. The huts they live in are covered with goatskin. It is in these constructions that the women and children reside. There are no beasts of burden in this land, and when the Patagonian clan leaves one place for another, they take apart their huts and carry them on their backs. The women, children, and weapons, are also carried in this manner. This is a sparse and bleak country, and the people who inhabit it seem always to be hungry. We took pity and shared our food with them. But unlike us, it is their custom to eat meat uncooked. It is difficult to see how a people can survive in a place that is so unforgiving.

For several days, we stayed with the Patagonians in the hope that other ships of the armada would discover us there. And on the seventh day after the storm had passed, our prayers were answered. Just as we were about to give up hope of ever seeing Don Elcano again, we saw the *Nunciado* sailing toward us from the mouth of the bay. Our hearts were filled with joy, for we thought we had lost them all.

The following day, Don Elcano sent a party of fifteen men to travel overland, returning to where the *Sancti Spiritus* was lost. They had orders to establish a camp at the site and recover as much of the provisions, cordage, and tackle as possible. They were to take particular care in salvaging any ammunition, artillery, and rigging that might have survived the wreck. These things would be needed in the future, for it was to the future that Don Elcano had focused his thoughts. We now had too many men and too few ships in which to transport them. So the salvage party had to set up camp and remain there, keeping the rescued store safe for when we returned on our voyage home.

We remained in the Patagonian bay for two more weeks, making repairs and gathering what provisions we could for continuing our voyage.

I remember, at the time, it seemed to me a sad fate for such a large armada to have been reduced to just three ships. God knew what perils lay ahead. Would any of us complete the journey? However, my concerns were unfounded, since on that very afternoon, we were all amazed to see a caravel sailing toward us into the little bay. It only took a moment to recognize it as the flagship, *Santa Maria de la Victoria*. After the joyous reunion, the three remaining captains were summoned to a council with the Captain General, whereupon he ordered that all ships return to the wreck of the *Sancti Spiritus*. It was there that he happily advised us that the other two ships, the *San Gabriel* and the *Santiago,* awaited us.

Once all of the ships had gathered at the site of the wrecked *Sancti Spiritus*, a Mass was held to remember the sacrifice that had been made there. Later, the Captain General ordered that the *San Lesmes* be sent further southward along the coast on a mapping expedition. According to him, Magellan had not sailed any further south than the mouth of the Strait in which we were now anchored. The task had fallen to us because of all the ships in the fleet the *San Lesmes* was the least in need of repair. Before we departed several crew were left behind to make room for another navigator and a mapmaker who joined us from the flagship.

We set sail at first light the following morning leaving the rest of the armada at anchor in the mouth of the inlet. We headed south for many days following the line of the coast. We passed many small islands inhabited entirely with geese and sea wolves. These geese are black and white and are covered all over with short feathers. They have no wings but can move very quickly once they are in the water. We found them to be easily caught and excellent eating, being both fat and tasty. But to cook them, they first had to be singed because their feathers were so short it was impossible to pluck them.

Eight days after we left the armada, a tempest blew up and forced us further seaward away from the coastline. The violent winds and freezing rain raged for a full two days. We could do nothing but keep our sails under ratchet the whole time. When the fury had subsided, we found we had been blown much further south than we had intended to go. This was a cold and miserable place, and even though the worst of the tempest had passed, the freezing rain and wind did not cease. I felt sure that we were near the end of the earth. By night, we could make out fires along the shores, and by day, smoke rose in many places about the terrain. We did not dare to land anywhere along the coastline, for there we knew resided the anthropophagi, who consume the flesh of other men. These cannibals must surely belong to the Devil to be able to survive in such an inhospitable place. By now we had seen enough and were greatly relieved when the captain finally ordered a course be set northward to rejoin the armada, which awaited us in the Strait.

It was a full two weeks before we again saw the other ships. Gladness filled our hearts as we rounded the headland and looked down into the inlet to see the armada at anchor. The crews were still busy carrying out the necessary repairs to the ships. The weather was generally bad now, and the temperature had dropped to near freezing. Winter had set in, and working in the cold waters was a great hardship for the men. The keel of the flagship was badly damaged during the storms and had to be repaired before we set sail again. The hulls of the other caravels needed to be cleaned and made watertight for the coming voyage. Teams of men had been made busy catching and drying fish, and collecting firewood and water—all to be carefully stowed aboard the ships. Some of the men, including myself, were dispatched to hunt the sea wolves that came to bask on the rocks in the nearby coves. Once killed, the flesh of these creatures was smoked and dried. In this way, it could last for weeks aboard ship. They are unusual animals, and look like they might make easy prey, but they were more difficult to catch than we imagined. In our first attempt, we only managed to kill one small sea wolf. But with better planning and the use of nets and firearms, we were able to supply the necessary quantity of dried meat for the voyage ahead.

Finally after many weeks, it was time for us to take our leave. After the ships had been rigged, Mass was celebrated, and we set our course through the Straits of Magellan. Perhaps it was the excitement of finally being at sea once again, or perhaps it was just a restless mind, but that night, I dreamt a dream that frightened me. The men of the *San Lesmes* were in grave danger.

When I woke the next morning, I kept the dream to myself, knowing that many aboard ship take such things seriously. Sailors are a breed of men who believe that all is possible, and where it is not, then magic will make it so. Had they have known of my dream, none would have ventured further than the Strait itself. So quietly, I sat and kept counsel to myself.

On the 30th of May 1526, we finally entered the Pacific Ocean, and as we did, we penetrated into the very jaws of hell. I have never experienced such a storm before or since. We quickly lost sight of the fleet as we struggled for days to hold the *San Lesmes* afloat in the tempest. Our last glimpse of the flagship was on the 1st of June. It was late in the day, and she was far out off the starboard bow. We could do no more than to look, since we still struggled hard against the roaring seas. That was the last we would ever see of her or her crew. As for the other ships in the armada, we had not seen any of them since the day we left the Straits and entered the Pacific Ocean. Sadly, I know not what became of them or their crews, and it is possible that we may be the only survivors of that fateful expedition. But had we known what lay ahead of us, we would surely have prayed for the sea to have taken us all, as we believed it had our companions.

8

BARCELONA OCTOBER 2009

Roberto looked up from the pile of papers in front of him, all strewn across the dining room table. His interest had been drawn to something else. Outside, he could see Maya through the glass doors that led to the patio. The autumn air was cool as the last rays of afternoon sun settled across the beautiful old city. Silhouetted against the light, Maya was seated on a chair, reading. Roberto knew that the book she held was one of his—his first attempt at a sci-fi romance, and written before he had met her.

His attention once more returned to the pile of papers on the table, an unfinished manuscript, and a stack of research notes he had pulled from a cardboard box that sat on the floor beside him. He felt numb as he leafed through the pile; there seemed no point in keeping any of it now. The manuscript would never be finished—his illness would see to that.

Just then, the phone rang; he got up and answered it.

"Good morning," said the husky female voice on the other end. "May I speak to Maya?"

Roberto turned toward the terrace and pointed to the phone in his right hand, "It's for you..." he called.

Maya got up and came inside, closing the doors behind her.

"Who is it?" she mouthed as she took the phone and raised it to her ear.

"Don't know," he shrugged.

"Maya speaking."

"Maya, I received the photographs you emailed."

Her puzzled expression now became a smile. Even though it had been years since she'd heard that authoritative English tone, she recognized it instantly. Professor Bourne—or Gabriella to her friends—had been Maya's anthropology tutor in LA. During that time, they had become good friends. As a tutor, Maya had found her disciplined, academically rigid, and at times uncompromising. But as a friend, she was loyal and sincere, and to Maya's delight, she was also great fun.

"It's good to hear your voice Gabriella. What do you think of the little treasure I sent you?"

Maya had emailed photographs of the amulet to Professor Bourne several days earlier. She knew when Roberto had first shown her the mysterious little object, that there was only one person who could identify its origin. And her hunch was right.

"Definitely Polynesian," replied Gabriella. "But more specifically, it's an indigenous piece from New Zealand, carved by the ancestors of the Maori. The artwork is very distinctive, and your *manaia*—that's what it's called—is everything that one would expect from its period."

"New Zealand…" Maya exclaimed, "…that far south."

"Yes indeed—that far south. Where did you find this little artifact of yours?" Gabriella sounded excited thought Maya.

"A friend of mine here in Barcelona was given it by his grandfather."

"That's interesting. Of course, even you know," chuckled Gabriella, "that Spain was in the north Pacific from the early sixteenth century. But there is no record of them ever making it south into New Zealand waters until the eighteenth century. The archaic style of that manaia suggests it's a lot older than the eighteenth century."

"I'm with you on that," agreed Maya. "It has a patina and feel to it that seems much older than just one or two centuries."

"There is no doubt that it's from New Zealand," interrupted Gabriella. "The style is unmistakable. The Maori used *manaia* just like that one as a kind of supernatural talisman. A sort of spiritual guardian, if you like. That piece would have been very important to its original owner. From the design, it should be possible to find out exactly where in New Zealand that little bone pendant originated. Unfortunately, I'm out of my depth there. You will need a local expert to help you sort out that mystery. You're in luck though—I just happen to know someone."

"Perhaps later," said Maya. "First I want to find out more about how it came to be in Spain."

"You understand that, as an academic, you have certain responsibilities in matters like this," Gabriella said, rather impatiently. "This is a rare find. Sooner or later, you're going to have to do something about it."

"I understand what you're saying—but not yet," replied Maya. "I need a little more time at this end. Don't worry; I'll get back to you for the name of your expert."

"Good, make sure you do. I guess I'll be hearing from you then?"

"You will—and Gabriella thanks for everything."

Roberto had been listening to Maya's side of the conversation, and when she hung up, he wanted to know more.

"What did she say?" he asked.

"As I suspected, it's a Polynesian piece, and a very old one at that. As to its origin, Gabriella believes it to be a Maori amulet from New Zealand."

"New Zealand—but how is that possible?"

"I don't know," replied Maya. "But we need to find out—it's important."

Roberto shrugged, "I guess so." He sounded vague and almost indifferent.

For Maya, not being interested wasn't an option.

"You don't sound convinced…" she was abrupt.

"It's not that," he was puzzled by her terseness. "But is it really *that* important?"

"This is what I do, Roberto. As an anthropologist, I'm constantly on the lookout for cultural enigmas, and this amulet of yours is just that—an enigma. Ask yourself this question—what is a bone carving from New Zealand, which could be at least five hundred years old, doing in Spain? It's a mystery, right? The answer to that question could open a completely new chapter in history. Now that's important, don't you think?"

"Okay," he replied. "I guess you're right—it's important."

"Good. Now the next question is simpler. Is there a connection between the amulet and the journal?"

"I don't know," he shrugged.

"Have you finished reading it?"

"Not yet." As he spoke, he realized something which hadn't previously occurred to him. He had lived with his grandparents since he was thirteen years old, and in that time, Fernando had told him much about the family history. But he had never once mentioned the manuscript or the amulet. The first Roberto knew of them was the day on which, without any real explanation, he was presented with the old box and its contents. Why had the old man not mentioned them before?

That evening, Roberto decided to turn in early. Over the last few years, he had developed the habit of rising around four-thirty to write. He found that his mind was much more alert in the early hours of the morning. This meant that by the evening, he was quite often tired much earlier than everyone else. In recent weeks, he seemed even more tired than usual.

Maya kissed him goodnight; she wasn't ready for bed. The call from her old anthropology professor had heightened her excitement. All she wanted to do now was troll the Internet for anything she could find on Maori manaia.

It was after midnight when she finally decided to retire. As she entered the bedroom, she found Roberto sitting on the side of the bed. He seemed dazed and not fully conscious.

"Are you alright?" She reached out and touched him. His skin was clammy and cold. "What's the matter?" she asked as she sat down beside him.

"It was a nightmare," he mumbled. "And when I finally woke up, that wretched dog was here with me."

Maya pulled the bed covers up around his shoulders, "Are you okay?" she again asked.

"I dreamt that Fernando had died. His body had somehow turned to a fine gray powder that was scattered like ash across the ground in front of his house. Suddenly, a wind blew up, whipping the powder into a giant cloud that swirled around me. I closed my eyes and could feel the fine particles striking my face. Within the cloud, I could hear an old woman's voice calling. I didn't understand what she said. Suddenly, the swirling air became cold, and the cloud left me and swept away out over the city and toward the sea. I stood and watched from the terrace of my grandparents' house as the gray mass drifted across the water and eventually disappeared far out over the horizon. When it had gone, I felt happy for Fernando. I don't know why, but in my mind, it seemed as though he was returning home. When I thought it was finally over, I turned around and saw that I wasn't alone. The white dog had also been watching. It was then that I woke, only to find the dog was sitting here in this room with me."

Roberto looked disorientated, as though he was about to lose his mind. Maya put her arms around him and pulled him close to her.

"What's happening to me?" he whispered. "I feel like I'm going mad."

"You're not going mad, Roberto." She pulled back and looked him in the eyes. "There's an explanation for what's happening to you, and I'm going to find it."

He could see the look of determination in her eyes, but he was too tired and confused to discuss it any further.

"Now lay down," she whispered.

He reached back, pulled himself fully onto the bed, and lay back. She removed her clothing and climbed in beside him. She drew her naked body close to him, and he wrapped his arms around her.

She kissed him, "I love you, Roberto. Don't forget that."

His eyes were closed as he lay quietly beside her, and she felt the tension in his body slowly drain away. She stroked his forehead with her right hand. Maya had suspected for some time that he was unwell, but could not bring herself to ask him outright. She knew him well enough to know that he would simply clam up. She didn't want to put him into a position where he felt forced to tell her anything. When the time was right he would tell her—she knew that. His breathing had slowed now, and she could tell that he was asleep. "Good night my love," she whispered softly and kissed him gently on the forehead.

9

VALLVIDRERA—FERNANDO ESTÁ MUERTO

The ringing woke Maya. As she attempted to get out of bed, she discovered that Roberto was already up. She heard him pick up the phone in the next room, and could hear his voice. She glanced at the bedside clock—it was just after seven.

A few moments later, he came into the bedroom, and from the expression on his face she knew immediately that something was wrong. She waited for him to speak, and in the silence searched his face for a hint of what it might be.

"Fernando's dead," he was trembling as he uttered the words.

Maya was shocked, and hesitated for a moment—then she reached for him, "My God," she gasped.

"He died last night," his voice strained. "I dreamt about it."

"What are you saying?" she asked.

"It's crazy, but I dreamt that Fernando had died—and now he's dead." Maya could see that he was struggling with the very thought.

"Listen to me," she said trying to calm him. "That was just a dream, and nothing more than an awful coincidence."

He took a deep breath and nodded. Then his expression changed, he looked concerned.

"I have to meet Mama at the house. Nuria isn't coping."

"What about you Roberto?" She asked as she took his hands in hers.

"I'm alright." He looked pale and in shock, and Maya could see it.

"I need to go, Maya."

"Do you want me to come too?" she offered.

"No, wait for me here." His hands fell from hers, and he turned away.

As she sat down on the bed and watched him walk slowly toward the door, tears began welling in her eyes. Suddenly, he stopped and turned back. "I love you Maya, but I don't know how I'm going to get through this. I need you here. I need someone to come back to."

Maya stood and walked to him. She wrapped her arms around his neck and kissed him on the lips. Her tears moistened his cheeks.

"I'll be here, Roberto." She felt her heart melt as they held one another close. Then they parted, and she watched him turn and go.

Her whole body now felt numb; it was only her heart that still held feeling—and it ached for him. He seemed so tragically alone. After he had gone, she sat on the bed and wept.

It was late afternoon when Maya heard the sound of the front door. Roberto came into the living room, his face pale and drawn. Their eyes met momentarily; then he turned and slumped down onto the sofa. Maya walked over and sat in the chair opposite him. She leaned forward, took his hands, and held them in hers. She kissed them and pressed them against her cheeks. Roberto looked as though he had been crying.

"How is your grandmother?" she asked.

"She was sleeping when I left. God knows she needs it. They were married sixty-eight years, and in the last few, did nothing but bicker and squabble with one another. Anyone would think that they no longer cared for each other, but they did. And now she misses him terribly."

The pair sat facing one another; in the moments silence Maya's eyes searched his weary expression. "How are *you* coping Roberto? It must be tough for you."

"It's been tough," he said, "but I'm alright. It's my grandmother I'm worried about. She's in a real mess. I'm not sure what she's going to do without Fernando in her life."

"And your mother, how is she?"

"She's taking it hard," he answered, "but she'll get through it—she's strong enough."

Maya already knew this. She remembered back to the night her and Amalia had spent together when Roberto was in hospital. They'd become friends that night. And they'd come to understand one another as only two women who loved the same man could.

Amalia emanated pure serenity from within, and those who found themselves in her presence could not help but be touched by her warmth. Her eyes, those mirrors to the soul, held a strength that seemed to threaten life itself. But beneath it all—behind the facade, there were wounds. Life had exacted a toll. For her the hands of time had been busy, and like the hands of a potter creating a beautiful and delicate vessel, they had fashioned the life of this complex woman.

In Roberto, Maya had come to recognize the same attributes. And although he also hid himself behind a facade, through the windows of his soul, she had seen the truth. She knew at that moment, with him, her life would be complete.

Since 2001, Amalia had lived alone in her apartment on carrer de Llull. There she was close to the Parliament de Catalunya, where she worked as an archivist. At sixty-four years old, neither the passage of time nor the vagaries of life had diminished her radiance. She was still graceful, straight backed, and resolute. Her dark, insistent eyes and determined features gave her the look of a politician as she came and went from the parliament buildings. But nothing was further from the truth. Life had revealed to her the mysteries unique to her journey, and she, in her own way, had made good with what had been given her. She carried regrets, of course—particularly about her husband's demise. A part of her still blamed herself for not recognizing the signs. She still believed, even now, that she could have prevented his death. If only she knew what had driven him to do such a thing. But now—and more than she would ever admit, those regrets had shaped her life. She had never married again after Sebastian died—and probably never would.

Three days later, under a dark and threatening sky, they laid the old man to rest in the Cementiri de Montjuic. It had been his wish. This was the perfect place, from which his spirit could forever keep vigil over the Mediterranean. A cold wind blew in off the water, sweeping through the port below and funneling up toward the somber little gathering. Entangled in its chilly gusts were fragments of sounds from the vehicles and port machinery operating in the docks below.

The bitter wind made Maya's eyes water as she held Roberto's hand. She could see the tears rolling down his cheeks as he watched his grandfather's coffin finally disappear from view. Nuria's mournful wailing grew louder, drowning out the priest's final offerings, as Amalia attempted to comfort her. Rain soon began to fall. Some in the gathering started to walk back to the parked cars. Others remained, their tears mingling with the cool autumn raindrops.

After a while, the drizzle had stopped, and Amalia motioned to her son, "Help me," she said.

He came to her aid and took his grandmother by her left arm. The old woman's body was cold and limp, and her head hung as she leaned heavily into him. She was exhausted. Roberto glanced at his mother, who steadied Nuria by her right arm; she nodded toward their car. He took his grandmother's weight, and the sad little procession made its way up the slight incline toward the waiting vehicles.

Later that evening, Roberto and Maya arrived back to their apartment on the Gran Via. As they passed by the mailboxes in the lobby, Roberto noticed a large envelope protruding from theirs. He collected it, and they continued on up the stairs.

"Finally!" whispered Maya as she closed the door behind her. "It's so good to be home."

Roberto did not hear her; he was too busy examining the envelope and the unfamiliar handwriting on it. He opened it and pulled out several large black-and-white photographs. What he saw almost stopped his heart. The note accompanying them simply read:

Your father was not the man you thought he was.

Roberto stood staring at the photographs in his hands.

"What's wrong?" Maya asked.

Without a word, he held out the contents of the envelope. She took them and examined them.

"Who are they?" she asked.

"That's my father," Roberto said pointing to one of the men in the photograph in Maya's hands. "I don't know who the other man is."

"But who sent them? And why?"

Roberto just shook his head, "I've got no idea. My father's been dead twenty-two years, so whatever this is about, I'd say it was a bit late."

"And the note," asked Maya. "What do you make of that?"

Again Roberto shook his head. "I don't know."

She looked at the envelope again. "There isn't a postmark or stamp. This envelope was hand delivered."

By now Roberto had found a seat and was staring blankly at Maya, not really knowing what to say. Of all days, this mysterious letter had arrived on the day of his grandfather's funeral. *But why?* he wondered, *and who sent it?*

"Tomorrow," said Roberto, "I'll show these photos to my mother. Perhaps she'll know who the other man is. She may even know who sent them."

The more Roberto thought about the mysterious correspondence, the more it disturbed him. But what bothered him most was the brief note that implied that his father had been leading a secret life. It seemed now, that whatever he had previously thought of his father, all was about to change. The well dressed, slightly balding man with the big smile and neatly trimmed moustache? The man who'd play-wrestle with him—who'd take him on long walks in the park and to the beach? *That man* had somehow led another life? Did Amalia know? Roberto needed to find out who had sent him this bombshell. Perhaps, with his mother's help, they could even track him down.

The following day, Roberto and Maya caught up with Amalia at the villa, where she had been staying to comfort Nuria since Fernando's death. When they were alone, Roberto showed Amalia the photographs and the note.

She examined everything carefully, at first not saying a word. Then, after she finished, she handed them back to Roberto.

"What do you make of them?" he asked.

"The man pictured with your father is Henri D'Anjou. He is French. That's all I can tell you." Her voice was cold, and her unblinking eyes seemed to look past him, off into the distance. He had not seen this side of his mother before, and it surprised him.

"And the note?" he asked.

"I have no idea about the note."

"Who could have sent such a thing?"

"I don't know."

"Aren't you in the least bit concerned about this?" Roberto asked her.

He was worried; she seemed to be confused. And why did she seem so distant? After all this was important.

"Look Roberto, let me remind you of something you seem to have forgotten." Amalia appeared defensive. "Your father has been dead a long time. If someone wants to play games with that, let him. We have nothing to hide. So don't give them the impression that we do by acknowledging their tedious little game. Just ignore them. They will soon tire of us and go and bother someone else."

"It upsets me to know that someone out there has something to say to us but won't come out into the open with it," replied Roberto.

"Don't worry about it, hijo. Just do as I say and ignore it. Your father was a good man—that's all you need to know. My advice to you is to toss that envelope and its contents into the fire where they belong."

Roberto knew what his mother was trying to say, but something inside of him just couldn't let it go. As for tossing the photos into the fire, he'd have to think about that. Surely it wouldn't hurt to hold on to them for a while longer.

He would take his mother's advice on one thing, though—he would ignore the note. After all, she had known Sebastian better than anyone else, if there was anything to be told, this was exactly the right time to tell it to her son. Her silence led to only one conclusion. There was nothing to tell. Sebastian had indeed been the man that Roberto had always thought him to be.

That evening, after he and Maya had arrived home, he put the envelope and its contents safely away and tried to forget about them. Later that night, he settled down in his favorite chair and began to read more from the journal of Francisco de Villanova.

10

THE JOURNAL OF FRANCISCO DE VILLANOVA TO
FEBRUARY 1529

For more than a week, we were at the mercy of the freezing winds and battering seas, which smashed in every direction around our little caravel. Every man aboard was exhausted and survived only from one breath to the next, fearing at any moment that it would be his last. Above deck, the icy wind howled like a raging beast through the rigging and clawed ferociously at the tightly fastened sailcloth. Somehow, we had managed to lash the sails in an effort to keep them from being flayed in the tempest.

Day after day, the *San Lesmes* was tossed about like a leaf in a gale. From the highest ocean peaks to the lowest watery valleys, our ship rode the tumultuous seas. Despite the endeavors of the angry waters, she stubbornly remained afloat. But there was a price to all of this, and within days, we would feel the sharp edge of it upon us all.

Then, as suddenly as it had come upon us, the storm was gone. God, it seemed, had heard our prayers, and through his mercy, had spared our lives, and we were glad of it. But an uncertain future now lay ahead. We had been blown well off course and could see neither ship nor land—though in our bosoms, each of us still concealed a nervous hope that the armada would soon come to the rescue. The wind in this new ocean had an uncertain and cold edge to it.

We had lost most of our food to the storm, and what drinking water we had was now contaminated by the sea. The mainmast was damaged, and a good part of the rigging needed repair if we were to sail our way to any land that might lie nearby. We were also taking on water, and at least one pump had to be worked day and night to prevent the ocean from swallowing us all. After several days and only with the greatest of difficulty, we were able to complete repairs to the mast and the rigging. Once this was done, we again hoisted our sails. Our mission now was to seek out land, and from that day onward, our eyes searched the horizon for any glimpse of it. This was to become our main occupation.

A week later, our rations had almost gone. What remained of the biscuits was nothing more than a mixture of dust and worms. Our hunger drove us to ignore the stench of rat urine upon this disgusting combination. Hunger also drove us to cut away the leather from the main yard. It was so tough that we soaked it for days and then boiled it so that we could eat it. We even ate sawdust, which some of the men actually fought over. But in the end, the very worst of it was being reduced to eating the rats. It is hard to believe now, but on that ship, a rat could sell for as much as one ducat a piece.

To live was important, and each day, we fought with everything we had just to survive. But our greatest misfortune was a malady in which the gums blackened and swelled so large as to hide the teeth. It was this sickness, more than starvation that claimed most of the men who perished. In those awful days, death stalked the *San Lesmes* like a vulture. And soon we began to see him everywhere. To have the affliction was to have a death sentence; there was nothing more certain. The entire body of the victim succumbed quickly, and in the final stages, his gangrenous limbs and swollen gums meant that he could neither carry himself nor even eat. He simply rotted until death came to him through starvation. Each man in his own fashion would perish in silence, curled pitifully behind a chest or barrel. And all the while, the rats gnawed at his gums or the soles of his feet—indignity upon indignity, until, at last, the release. Each would eventually find his salvation—his soul to Our Father, and his body to the deep.

We saw many brave men depart this life on our ship of death. And each would end up in the currents of a foreign ocean, far from the succor of his native land. I watched my friend Ramón die in this way. It sorely pains me to think of it even now, though decades have passed.

Death was an indiscriminate master, and from among us, he claimed his victims at will. Thus, the captain was among those who perished. Gaspar De la Puente, the only one of the lieutenants to have survived, now took command of the vessel. It was our new captain who brought something interesting to our attention: When a Christian corpse was placed into the sea, it always floated with its face turned upward to heaven. However, the Indians among the dead always floated with their faces turned downward, into the water. Further proof, he suggested, that God takes care of his own.

"Have no fear, for it is God in those final moments who smiles upon the face of his child before receiving the soul and committing the body to the deep abyss."

But for those still alive on the *San Lesmes*, weakened by storms and starvation, a starker reality held true. On that ship of ours, there were indeed only two types of people—those awaiting death's grip, and those who had already found it. Which aspect the eventual floating corpse presented was of little importance to any of us.

For many days, we sailed about aimlessly, always hoping that land would soon be discovered, or another ship would be seen. Day after day, we saw nothing but the endless ocean in every direction, and all the while, men were dying around us. By now, what remained of the fresh water was so putrid that many had resorted to drinking their own urine.

Day after day, our spirits sagged; ocean and bare horizon were all that could be seen. Soon enough, as we knew it would, the time had come when the flame of hopeful spirit flickering within our hearts could no longer be sustained. Every man aboard felt certain now that all was lost; the caravel christened the *San Lesmes*, which began her life as a coastal trader, would now become a floating tomb.

When she is found, we thought, *nothing but the rotting carcasses of her crew will be aboard. None will be left to tell her tale or speak the heroic deeds of the brave men who numbered her crew.*

That evening, a storm blew up, surely the last we would ever see in this world. It raged violently throughout the night. We knew not the hour at which God intended to call us, but felt sure that before this night was done, we would all be in his heavenly care.

But all, it seemed, was not lost. For a reason known only to Him, God had decided that this night was *not* to be our last. He sent a sign of hope— knowing that without hope, in a storm, no man will ever survive. (How true it is that we will never understand the mysteries of Heaven.) Suddenly, and there for all to see, at the very peak of the storm during the master's watch, was hope ablaze—the glorious lights of Saint Elmo's fire played atop the masts of our ship. Its brilliant light shone for almost two hours during the most violent part of the storm. Every man aboard knew Saint Elmo had been sent by God to watch over us. And when the lights were gone, the storm abated. We knew then that we were saved.

The sun rose the following morning, and by degrees climbed its way into the endless blue sky. And as it did, a cry gave up from the masthead lookout riding above us—the call we had waited eight long, perilous weeks to hear: "Tierra…Tierra!"

Voices were raised in cheer; tears were shed in great relief. Those men able to walk came to the starboard side to examine the distant smudge upon the horizon. Every heart was united once more in hope. At last—we had been saved.

The toll upon us in this new ocean had been a heavy one. We had been reduced to just nineteen men from the original crew of fifty-one. In truth, we all should have been dead—so miserable was our condition. But the expectation of setting foot once more upon land stirred within us an excitement and energy that we had not known for many weeks. From that moment, our course lay to the west, and nothing could sway us from it.

By afternoon, the land we desired so very much had changed from a shadowy sliver lying low upon the surface of the ocean to a dark, mountainous form. Sometimes it was hidden completely by the clouds that hung about it. It was still light when we sailed close by, and from the ship, we could see that in places, the seacoast was high, and the land was hilly and heavily wooded, with a lush greenness that clothed it completely.

As we drew nearer, we could see mountains looming in the distance, with clouds resting about their peaks. Soon we were reconnoitering up the coast in search of a place to come ashore. And as we did, we could see smoke rising from small villages dotting the hills. Shortly after rounding a narrow headland, we noticed a bay ahead. Captain De la Puente ordered the ship to enter it. The bay was small—at least a cannon-shot deep, and twice as wide. It was here that the captain decided we would anchor and make for shore in the skiff.

As we lay anchor, we could see a group of people gathering upon the shoreline. And even before we managed to launch our skiff, we noticed that those onshore had launched three longboats and were rapidly paddling toward us. We did not know what land this was, or anything of its people. Desperation, however, left us little choice. We must make ourselves known to the inhabitants of this land in peace, and place ourselves at their mercy. And if they be Christian, we would be saved. If not, we would place ourselves in God's hands and theirs. Some of the crew brought armament to the deck in alarm at seeing the oncoming longboats, but the captain gave orders that the arms were to be stowed, and those too weak to stand were to be taken below. None of the sick should be visible to the approaching Indians.

As the longboats neared, we could see that each carried around fourteen men. Suddenly, the boats stopped—about a spear's throw from the ship. The rowers raised from the water their paddles—which to our eyes looked more like baker's shovels. They began to shout and wield these in the air, shaking them as though they were weapons. Their commander, a strongly built man wearing a white cloak, stood at the center of the largest of the three vessels—the one nearest our ship. He raised his right arm, and his men fell silent. He then addressed us, but we could not understand what he was saying. As he spoke, the longboats began drifting closer to our ship. Captain De la Puente hailed the Indians, holding his arms aloft. He told them that we were Spanish subjects under the protection of the King of Spain, and that we came in peace. We were on the business of the Spanish Crown, and we sought from them supplies and assistance to refit our damaged ship. He explained that we were willing to trade what we had for their help. Their commander, whose dress appeared more that of a chief than of a captain, seemed not to understand what De la Puente said. However, as the longboats floated nearer, it became clear by the expression on his face that he had noticed our condition. He gestured, saying something to his men, who were now silent. He turned and waved to the men in the other two longboats, shouting to them. Both boats turned in the water and made for the shore.

The chief noticed our skiff, which was hanging from the windlass out over the starboard side in readiness for launching. He pointed to it and indicated that we should lower it into the water. He then ordered his boat to be turned in the direction of the shore. They waited as we lowered the skiff. The captain picked a small crew, which included me, and we climbed into the skiff. The rest of the men waited on the ship.

Once we were lowered into the water, we made for the shore, following the men of this land, who in some ways resembled the Indians we had seen in the land of Brazil. As we reached the sandy beach, many more Indians had come down to the shore. Some waded out into the water to pull our skiff up onto the beach. By this time, their chief had landed and was waiting for us. Large numbers of men, women, and children crowded around us, touching us and pulling at our hair and beards.

The chief pushed his way through the jostling crowd. He seemed annoyed and motioned to the people to stand back. He waved his staff and struck out at those who were slow in obeying his commands. He said something as he approached the captain, but we could not understand him. The captain bowed his head, then raising himself up, he again explained that we came in peace, seeking only protection and assistance. The chief carefully examined each of us. Many in the crowd pushed and elbowed one another to get a better look at the strangers who had arrived, unannounced, into their land.

Suddenly, without a word, the chief took the captain by the arm and helped him from the skiff. He beckoned for the rest of us to follow. As we made our way up the sandy beach, more Indians came out to see what the commotion was. In a short time, we had arrived in the village, and the chief signaled us to be seated upon the woven mats, which had been spread out upon the ground. Women brought baskets of food, which they gave to us. But before we could eat any of it, the captain ordered us to hold until the chief had given his permission. We sat quietly, desperately awaiting his word. Every one of us was starving, and could not lift our eyes from the food. It took all of our strength to control the desire to devour every morsel we could see. The chief, clearly a shrewd man, once again carefully studied each of us. Then, with a wave of his hand, he indicated that we should eat. Our eyes went to the captain, seeking his approval. He gave it with a nod.

Our hunger was so great that we fell upon the food like starving animals. At that time, none of us noticed that the captain would not eat what had been set out for him. The chief indicated that he, too, should eat. But instead, De La Puente pointed to the ship out in the bay. The chief smiled, nodded to him, then turned and said something to a man standing to his right, and pointed to one of our crew. The captain seemed to know what was in the chief's mind.

"Go with him," he said to Juan. "Tell the men aboard that these are friendly people. Tell them that they must do as they are bid. See to the sick, Juan—bring them all ashore."

By now, baskets of food and containers of fresh water were being gathered together and carried to the skiff. A party of Indians boarded several longboats and lashed the skiff behind one of them. Juan climbed into our small boat still clutching his food, and as we watched, he was towed out toward the waiting ship. The chief smiled to the captain and passed a container of water to him. The captain drank from it and passed it on. Each man drank, as more water was brought. The captain, now happy in the knowledge that the men on the ship were to be cared for, picked up the basket of food set before him and began to eat.

The chief seemed impressed by De la Puente's loyalty to his men. He could easily have given in to his great hunger and forgotten about the men waiting aboard the ship. Though neither man knew the other's name, that moment was to mark the beginning of a friendship between the two.

We were to remain in that land for almost three years, and in that time, we cleaned and repaired our ship and made ready for the day when we would finally sail her home. The country was called *Uawa* by the Indians who lived there. For the most part, they were a friendly people, tall in stature, well built, with tanned skin and dark hair. The Uawan men were physically strong, and generally went about during the day undressed except for a loincloth or a kilt made of a type of long grass. They wore their hair long, often tied in a topknot and adorned with the feathers of forest birds. In the morning or evenings, when it was cooler, the men wore a type of cape or cloak made of skins, or platted cloth, woven with feathers from an unusual bird, which they called *kiwi*.

The kiwi was larger than a fowl, brown in color, and unusual in that, though a bird, it could not fly. Its wings were but short, useless stubs attached to its sides, but its legs were strong, and it could run swiftly when pursued. This unusual creature had a long, curved beak that it used to probe about the forest floor during the night hours, searching for food. When captured, the bird was eaten after first being roasted on the fire or cooked in earthen ovens. The feathers of the kiwi were soft and had an almost fur-like quality. They were highly prized by the Uawan people, who used these feathers for making cloaks, and a decorative cover for the loins, which were worn by both men and women of rank.

Cloaks were also made from the skins of the small dogs that these people kept as domestic pets. They called these little dogs *kuri,* but by the time we left that land, some of the Indians had begun referring to them as *perro,* because that was what we called them. The perro were small in stature and mainly black or white in color. They had bushy tails and howled like wolves. These little beasts did not bark like the dogs of our country, and the Uawans often used them for hunting the kiwi. And as with the kiwi, the people also used the dogs for food. They were best eaten when young; their flesh was tender and tasted similar to that of the wild fowl. The Uawans cooked them much in the same way that they cooked the bulk of their food—in earthen ovens. These were simply holes dug into the ground that contained rocks heated by fire, and similar to other ovens we had seen in the land of Brazil. Once the raw food was placed onto these hot rocks, it was then completely covered with large leaves and then with soil. When the food was cooked, the soil oven was opened, and its contents were shared among the people of the village.

The weapons of the Uawan warrior are simple, consisting usually of a wooden staff shorter than a pike or even a spear, and a club made from hardwood or stone. The staff is used for close combat, much as we would use a staff for defense. But the Uawan staff has the added value of having a sharp wooden blade at one end and a spearhead at the other. It is both a defensive and an attacking weapon, and can be used to cut and stab an opponent at close range.

They do not use the bow and arrow, and in fact, it is not known at all in this land. There is neither use of metal nor pottery that we observed in Uawa. There is a special stone, though, highly prized for its beautiful green color and which the Uawans fashion into a flat, sharp-edged club. These weapons were reserved for use only among the high-ranking warriors. This green-colored stone is obtained by trade from the people of another land called Wai-Pounamu. This land is many days' travel to the south of Uawa. We were told that the country of Wai-Pounamu was a vast land that contained great snow-capped mountains, and could only be reached by a sea voyage.

The Uawan women are lighter in color than the men. Many of them go about during the day with their breasts exposed, and like the men, wear simple grass kilts or loin coverings to clothe their lower regions. They also wrap themselves in cloaks when it is cold. The women are generally handsome, particularly when they are young, and while we were there, it was difficult for Captain De la Puente to keep the men in check, for it would have been extremely foolish of us to abuse our host's hospitality. These people were friendly toward us, and we were ordered to give them nothing but friendship in return.

The village spread along the north bank of the river mouth. Farther north along the seacoast stood cliffs, upon which were situated more dwellings, and at the highest point was a fortress, protected by a stout, wooden palisade. I remember the whole region to be beautiful and well situated for the people who lived there. The surrounding forests were rich in food and bird life, and the ocean bordering the eastern shore teemed with sea creatures. To us, this place seemed nothing short of paradise.

I remember now that there was a species of tree in that country that the Indians called Pohutukawa. These trees can grow to a very large size, and are to be found mainly along the coast or within sight of the sea. They flower only in the warm season, and we were led to believe that they can live to a great age. The older trees of this species are venerated by the people of this land, and one such tree grew on the southern bank near the mouth of the river, opposite the village.

The Uawans held this particular tree in great reverence. It was at this site that we witnessed an unusual ceremony. A huge tiburón, a fish they called Mangō-ururoa, was caught in a large fishing net that was in use for the very first time. Although this particular creature is highly prized by the chiefly class of this land, the first catch is always hung in the branches of the Pohutukawa tree as an offering.

The very next fish to be caught in the same net was cooked in the shade of the tree and eaten by all of the people who had gathered for that occasion. The Uawans believe that cooked food has an opposite spiritual force to uncooked food. And by offering the first fish to the Gods uncooked, and hanging it in the tree that is the guardian of such rites, a harmony of spirit was initiated. The fulfillment of this harmony was, in turn, guaranteed by everyone who ate the cooked fish, sitting beneath the tree. Thus they shared in the feast with their sacred Gods, and thereby, they became sacred too.

Some months before we left Uawa, a serious incident occurred that had an effect on our relationship with the Uawan people. By that time we had been accepted into the community and had even learned some of their language. A number of women in the village had been living with Spanish men and several half-caste children had already been born to these couples.

One day, a beautiful young woman called Aramoana, the daughter of the paramount chief, was attacked by Yñigo de Salinas, who attempted to rape her. I discovered them and fought with him. Several of the Uawan men, hearing the commotion, arrived and took her away. She was taken by them back to the village. When the captain discovered what Yñigo had done, he had him tied to a tree and flogged.

When the chief of the Uawans heard the news of the attack on his daughter, he became enraged. He had her brought before him and made her kneel at his feet. In a tearful fit of rage, he struck her heavily with his staff, almost knocking her senseless. Captain De la Puente quickly intervened, attempting to protect the young woman who now lay at their feet. He tried to explain to the chief that she was innocent of any indiscretion and that he had already punished Yñigo, who was the real culprit.

Although the chief was angry, he respected the captain enough to refrain from any further violence toward the girl. In the eyes of the Uawans, though, what had happened to Aramoana was a bad omen for the tribe. They believed that nothing but misfortune would come of it. It was disastrous for a person of her rank to be careless enough to leave herself open to such a shameful attack. Her potency as a woman of high status had been stripped away, and in their eyes, such a thing, once taken, could never be regained. For them, the shame was her father's for not protecting her. We were told that in olden days, he would have killed her on the spot. Indeed, as I think of it now, on that day, if the captain had not intervened, I feel sure that the chief would have taken her life.

But fate was hers, for in the confusion, a moment of fortune smiled upon the girl as Captain De la Puente stood between her and her father. Though still delirious, Aramoana realized that her moment had come. With blood streaming from the wound in her head, she crawled piteously from her father like an injured animal.

The large crowd that had gathered remained silent as the bloodied girl dragged herself into the surrounding forest. It was a miserable sight, and one that I shall not forget. That was the last any of the villagers ever saw of her, and at that time, none believed that she would survive the night.

The chief made it clear that his daughter was beyond help and that any further intervention by anyone would be punished severely. We were sickened at his decision, but this was his land, and the laws by which it was governed were his laws. We could do no more.

Several days later, I was walking in the hills surrounding the village when I chanced upon a stray dog. Though it wasn't uncommon to discover strays in the surrounding forests, there was something unusual about this particular creature. It seemed different from the others. The small white beast examined me carefully with its wild red eyes. He seemed intelligent, and I got the distinct feeling that he wanted me to follow him—and so I did. I followed him some distance through the dense forest; crossing a small stream before finally arriving at the base of a cliff.

There before me was a shallow cave, as I approached the entrance, I noticed a body curled up within it. I called out and saw it move slightly. It was then that I recognized Aramoana.

She needed immediate help. She had very little strength and had lost much blood. Her eyes were glazed; her lips were dry and cracked. Even though she lay close to a stream, she had no strength to crawl to the water.

It must be said that the Uawans are a hardy people, and many have survived the depravations of hunger and severe injury to become healthy again. If I helped her now, I was confident that Aramoana would do the same, but the thought of her father's anger flashed through my head. I knew that, should anyone find me with her, the consequences would be dire. But who would I be if I did not help this wounded girl? I had spent too many months battling storms, savage seas, and watching men die of disease and starvation to now let even the slightest flicker of life go without a fight.

I brought water to her and made her drink. It was obvious that she had not eaten for days. As I had learned from the Uawans, I collected fern roots, washed them in the stream, and scraped the skin away with my blade. I bruised them with a stone and mixed the juice with a little water. She sucked weakly at the liquid. Later, I cut the mashed roots up and fed her as much as she would take, which was only the amount a small bird would have eaten.

The whole time I was with Aramoana, the dog that had brought me to this place sat quietly watching as I tended to her. He obviously had a connection to the girl.

I had learned from the Uawans how to dress a wound with nothing except that which the forest provided. As a dressing they make use of a certain type of moss that grows on the rocks hereabouts. After cleansing the wound with water they apply the moss directly, binding it in place with long slender leaves taken from a plant that grows wild in the forests. This application, I hoped would help her wound heal. I did not know what else to do to help the poor woman.

The rest of that day, I collected dried fern leaves to make bedding for her and, using sticks and vines I constructed a better shelter, which I hoped would keep out the cold and damp should it rain. That afternoon before the light disappeared I left her and made my way back to the village. I had already resolved to return to her in the morning with food and clothing.

At dawn the next day, I set out again into the hills, making sure I wasn't followed. I did not know what would happen to the woman if she was found by her own people. The sun had risen a full two degrees above the eastern horizon by the time I arrived at the small shelter where the young woman hid. The dog had met me halfway along the trail and led the way back to the cave.

When I arrived, Aramoana lay awake in the fern leaf bed, which I had made for her the day before. She heard me approaching and could see me through the gaps in the shelter that lay across the front of the cave. At first, she was hesitant. I could see a mixture of fear and helplessness in her large brown eyes. My heart was full of pity for the poor girl.

From the bag that I carried, I removed some cooked food—a vegetable the Uawans called *kumara*. Along with the roots of particular ferns, the kumara is a staple among the people of this land, who also eat fish, shellfish, and birds. I also brought some dried shellfish, which she ate hungrily.

I saved a few morsels for the dog, who sat a little distance off, watching my every move. He ignored the food that I had carefully laid out for him, and Aramoana smiled when she noticed this. That was the first smile I had seen on her face since finding her in the cave. I knew a few words of her language, and thus, with a mixture of these words, combined with gestures and expressions, we were able to communicate.

I visited her almost every day for weeks. I brought her food, and things that would make her life there more comfortable, and it wasn't long before she had regained her health.

One morning, as I crossed the little stream on my way to the cave, I saw Aramoana bathing in a pool a short distance away. Her naked form glistened as she stood in the dappled sunlight flickering through the forest canopy. The sight of her beauty caught me, and for an instant, I was robbed of breath.

At that moment, she turned and saw me watching her. She smiled, and then calmly sought to conceal herself within the deeper water of the pool. I felt embarrassed and quickly walked on to the cave and waited for her to arrive. It wasn't long before she entered the small clearing. Her long black hair was wet and dripped water down onto her back. Droplets of water glistened in the sun as they trickled down over her bare breasts, and in those moments, her eyes smiled as they met mine.

That morning, we became lovers in the warm confines of that small cave. A lonely boy and a lost girl fused together as one, melted by desire, oblivious to the world. Her scent mingled with that of the forest and filled my nostrils. We both hungered for satisfaction, and when it came, we sought it again. The sounds of unrestrained passion echoed from the cave that was to become our home, and blended into the orchestra of birdsong that rang out through the forest.

Finally, in the warm afterglow, we both lay naked and exhausted on the spongy fern leaf bed, covered with a soft, woven cloak that I had brought to keep her warm. From where I lay, I could look out through the gaps in the shelter wall across the front of the cave, out into the little clearing. The white dog, which had been a constant companion to Aramoana and a constant observer of me, was sitting with his eyes fixed intently in our direction. It was obvious that the sighs of ecstasy that had earlier filled the air had alerted him.

I wondered why he had attached himself so faithfully to Aramoana. I had learned since we came among these people that they are very religious, though they were not Christians. Their Gods lived in the forests of their land, and inhabited the sea that surrounded it, and dwelled in the sky that covered it. They also believed that their dead ancestors had the spiritual power and strength to protect the living from harm, sometimes taking animal form to do so. I could only imagine that the white dog that had attached itself to Aramoana might be such an animal, for it was certain to me that the dog was her protector. She looked upon it with a special affection, addressing it as though she were talking to a relative. She also sang to it and uttered what appeared to be prayers to it late at night.

Several months had passed, and I found myself spending most of my time with Aramoana. The cave where she lived had now become one room in a small hut that I had constructed against the cliff face. Now more than ever, it was important for me to make her comfortable, for she was pregnant with my child. And because of this, I looked upon her as my wife.

It was during these days that I had made an important decision: The time had now come, I believed, for me to confront her father and her people. I wanted them to accept her back into the tribe for her protection and the protection of our child. I could see no other way for the two of us. And if her father commanded that she be struck down, then I would let that be my fate, too. For in truth, I had decided that there would be no life for me without her.

But fate's ways are completely unpredictable. Within a few days of me making my decision, Captain De la Puente had also made a decision. And his was to become far more important to us than mine ever was. He had decided that the *San Lesmes* and her crew were now ready to set sail for home—and that this would occur as soon as we had gathered together the necessary food provisions.

It is fair to say that many of us were very excited at the prospect of seeing our motherland again. But I knew that the captain would not accept a pregnant woman on board and especially one who was the chief's daughter—a woman who was a fugitive from the tribe, condemned—unjustly by our standards, but nevertheless condemned. He would not have it. So it was upon my shoulders now to see to it that my wife and unborn child somehow made it onto the ship. I resolved to smuggle her aboard two days before we sailed, and, once at sea, to tell the captain. By then, it would be too late for him to do anything; he would have no choice but to accept her presence on the ship. What else could he do? But sadly, fate was again to play its capricious hand, and this time, there was no coming back.

11

THE MEETING, CAFETERIA NUDIVEL, BARCELONA

The thud of the car door shook the languid afternoon air and startled into silence a pair of cooing doves hidden in the leafy surrounds of the Villa Hernandez. Roberto had been summoned by his grandmother. Stepping from the car, he paused briefly and took in the view. A few fleeting memories from his childhood teased his thoughts as he gazed at the villa now before him.

What was so important that Nuria had demanded to see him today?

The phone call he'd received from her that morning had been short.

"Roberto, I need to talk to you urgently, you must come at once."

"Are you alright?" He asked. There was tension in her voice.

"Of course I'm alright," she replied rather bluntly. "I must talk to you—it's important. What time should I expect you?"

"Can it wait until this afternoon?"

"Three o'clock, and don't be late."

The urgency in her voice rang in his ears, even after he had hung up the phone.

Throughout the day, Roberto's thoughts drifted occasionally to the question of why his grandmother wanted to see him. Something had clearly spooked her—but what?

The hours passed, and all too soon he stood in the portico of the villa. He pressed the doorbell and waited anxiously for the door to be opened. Finally the sound of the main bolt being drawn echoed from within and the grand old door slowly swung ajar.

"It's you señor," smiled Lolita. "Come in—she's waiting for you in the patio."

"How is she?" he asked, a little anxious.

"She's fine, but she misses Don Fernando greatly."

Roberto nodded. He missed him too. He left Lolita as she closed the door and he made his way to the patio. As he emerged from the subdued light of the hallway, he could see through the arched doorway into the rectangular space that comprised the patio. It was open to the sky, and the warm afternoon sunlight streamed in. Potted plants in large, multicolored terracotta pots decorated the private area. Roberto could see Nuria seated at a small table toward the far end of the courtyard.

Her diminutive frame cut a forlorn picture as she sat by herself. She and Fernando had lived in the villa for more than thirty years—and now she was alone. To see her in that moment was difficult for Roberto, she seemed completely out of harmony with the tranquility that surrounded her.

Roberto's heart saddened as he remembered the countless times he and his grandparents had sat together in this same patio and enjoyed many similar sunny afternoons. Without Fernando, nothing would be the same again. He missed those wonderful balmy days.

As Roberto entered the courtyard, his footsteps echoed against the cobblestones and caused Nuria to turn.

"There you are…I thought you'd never get here," she said as he neared her.

Roberto glanced at his watch. "You said three p.m."

"Come and sit with me," she pointed to the other chair at the small table. "I want to talk to you."

He walked over, pulled the chair out, and sat down.

"Your mother has told me that you received a package in the post—one that contained photographs of your father and a man called Henri D'Anjou."

"It's true…" Roberto said.

Nuria eyed him carefully. "Do you know this man—Henri D'Anjou?"

"No," said Roberto.

"Good," she sounded relieved. "You would be wise to have nothing to do with him. He is a dangerous man."

"What do you mean?" asked Roberto.

"Your father was involved with that man, and no good came of it. Your grandfather also became involved with him, and how he wished he had never set eyes on him. He's dangerous, I tell you. Keep away from him." The old woman's eyes narrowed as she fixed her stare on him.

"If he's so dangerous, how did Sebastian and Fernando come to be involved with him?" Roberto was keen to find out. If there were unpleasant secrets lurking in the past, now was the time for him to know.

"I'll tell you," she said lowering her voice a little, "but you might not like what you hear."

"Why not?" he asked.

"Because there are things at play here that not even I understand."

"Go on…" he prompted.

"D'Anjou is a spiritualist, and he believes that he is in touch with the 'other side.' Many years ago, here in Barcelona, he established a group that met and practiced certain ancient rituals. Your father was a member of that group, and through him, your grandfather became one too. As you know, Fernando was an intellectual, so it was obvious that dabbling in such things would fascinate him. He was always keen to learn about the mysteries of life. Your mother and I let them get on with their secret meetings, thinking no more of it."

"So you didn't mind them being involved with D'Anjou?"

"At the time, we knew no better. We thought it was harmless. To us, this group was just another men's club. This country's crawling with them. One more wasn't going to deprive women of their husbands any more than the others had already done. Over time, however, we became concerned. We started to see changes in the two men—particularly in Sebastian. Soon it became serious. You see, your father started believing that he was possessed by some sort of spirit or curse…something like that. We were never sure whether it was one or the other, or whether it was his mind playing tricks on him. Anyway, his personality changed dramatically, and he eventually became quite unstable. By now, Fernando, who had become concerned about him, had had enough, and he left the group. He tried hard to convince Sebastian to do the same, but the hold D'Anjou had over your father was just too strong. In the end, we became helpless spectators watching Sebastian's sanity dissolve, as he eventually gave way entirely to the belief that he was possessed by a curse. This was the ultimate cause of his death."

"What do you mean by that?" asked Roberto.

"I mean that your father's precarious mental state at the time drove him to take his own life." As she spoke, she carefully studied her grandson's expression.

Roberto seemed even more confused now. "I don't remember any of his behavior being out of the ordinary…"

"Of course you wouldn't—you were young. You didn't see what we adults saw. Your mother saw it, and it affected her so badly that in time, she simply blocked it all from her memory. It was the only way that she could cope. Even today, there are things from that time that she refuses to remember. In the end, she was forced to recreate in her mind her own story, one that helped her cope with everything that happened. And thank Our Holy Mother for that, for it has given her the space to move on in peace. You see, she couldn't cope with the truth."

"What is the truth?" asked Roberto.

"The truth is that your father took his own life because he got mixed up in the occult. It's a deadly concoction if you're not strong minded. He should have left it alone, and he would still be alive today." Nuria's voice now sounded as harsh as her words.

"How can you know that?" he asked.

"I *know* it!" she dismissed his question with a flick of her hand.

Roberto glared at her.

"Well you asked for the truth," she said, "and there it is."

Roberto simply shrugged and looked away.

Nuria's voice softened: "Since receiving those photographs and that note, it has become important that you know all of this. D'Anjou is obviously sniffing around for something, and that makes him dangerous as far as your mother is concerned. You must not let him near her—you must protect her from him. There is no telling what memories will be awakened if she comes into contact with that man. You understand this, don't you?"

Roberto faced the old woman again. He heard the concern in her voice. "Yes," he said, "I understand. But why didn't someone tell me about this earlier?"

"If you're referring to your grandfather, when he left D'Anjou's group, he never breathed another word about the whole episode—people make mistakes you know. The entire thing became a silent chapter in his life. I'm telling you now because things have changed. D'Anjou has returned.

I don't want you to be sucked into the same trap as your father. You keep away from all of that occult stuff—it's dangerous."

That afternoon, sitting in that serene and sunlit courtyard, his grandmother's words had been a shock. The thought of both his father and grandfather being tangled up with a spiritualist group seemed almost unthinkable. And the thought of his mother and what she had been through filled him with anguish. He understood now why she had always been so protective of his father's memory, why she never liked to talk about the past, and why at times, she even feared the future. All this of course, she had neatly concealed behind a wall of determination. But now Roberto knew—scratch the surface, and her fears would be revealed—tangled and uncertain as they are.

He realized he had to do something about D'Anjou, whatever he was up to the man had to be stopped. And the first step in reaching that goal was to meet with him. Just the thought of it sent a shiver through him. But for his mothers sake it had to be done.

Only a few days after the visit to his grandmother, Roberto received another note. He immediately recognized the handwriting on the front of the envelope, and like the last one, it too had been hand delivered. His hands trembled as he tore open the sealed flap. Inside was another note. And even though he was apprehensive, he knew that this was the opportunity he had been waiting for.

Señor Torres,

I have something for you. Meet me at noon tomorrow at the Cafeteria Nudivel on carrer de Ribes. Please come alone.

Henri D'Anjou.

If Roberto had been honest with himself; ever since receiving the photographs of his father and D'Anjou, he'd always known this day would come. After all, why would D'Anjou have sent such a tantalizing package in the first place? It was obvious that he wanted to meet. So despite his unease and the warnings from his grandmother, he knew that to refuse this invitation would not put an end to D'Anjou's determination. He had to meet him, and he had just one day to prepare to come face to face with the spiritualist Henri D'Anjou—the man who was responsible for his father's death.

Cafeteria Nudivel was quiet. Four men sat talking in hushed tones at a corner table, and an elderly couple stood leaning against the bar sipping coffee. Roberto walked in and sat at a table near the back of the room, one that gave him a clear view of the entrance. The barman made a beeline for him and took his order. Even before his coffee had arrived, Roberto noticed the tall man, elderly and distinguished, enter the café. He instantly recognized him from the photographs. Henri D'Anjou had aged a lot since they were taken, but the resemblance was unmistakable. D'Anjou noticed Roberto and approached him.

"Thank you for coming, señor Torres. It is good of you to make the time to meet with an old man such as myself." He smiled politely as he pulled a chair from the table and sat down. Before another word could pass between them, the barman had returned with Roberto's coffee.

"What can I get you?" The waiter's large eyes scanned D'Anjou.

"Coffee with milk please" replied D'Anjou. The waiter nodded and headed back toward the bar.

"What is it you want of me?" asked Roberto, cautiously eyeing D'Anjou.

"Please, permit me to introduce myself…"

"I know who you are."

"Of course you do," smiled D'Anjou. "I expect your mother has told you everything, but let me explain—"

"Explain what? That you're a spiritualist who, through some sinister means, had a hand in my father's—"

"I had no hand in your father's death." The old man's expression hardened. "You'd better be very sure of your facts, young man, before firing that allegation about."

The barman returned with the coffee and placed it in front of D'Anjou. He looked up and nodded politely to him.

"Anything else?" inquired the barman.

"Nothing," replied Roberto shaking his head. The man nodded and left them.

Roberto was quiet now; he watched as D'Anjou picked up his cup and carefully sipped the hot coffee. The old man seemed content to just sit for the moment, but the silence that hung between them was too much for Roberto.

"What do you want of me?" he asked again.

D'Anjou calmly looked up from his coffee and smiled, "I want nothing from you."

"Then why am I here?"

"Because your fate is here…" replied D'Anjou, completely unfazed by Roberto's sharpness.

"Get to the point, man. Stop playing games."

"Oh, there are no games here. It all makes perfect sense."

"You haven't answered my question. What is it you want?"

The old man took another careful sip of hot coffee. His expression began to soften. "I liked your father, Roberto, and when he died, I was overcome with grief. He was a good friend to me. I always promised myself that one day, I would look in on his son."

"So you waited twenty years? And on the day of my grandfather's funeral?" snapped Roberto.

"I'm sorry for that, but I needed to know something."

"Know what?"

"I needed to know that what had taken your father's life had ended with him. But I see it did not."

"What the hell are you talking about?" demanded Roberto.

"Like your father, you have been cursed. I can see it on your face. Your life is running out."

Roberto was shocked—at first, he could not respond.

"But for you, there may be hope," continued D'Anjou. "It appears that you do not travel alone. You have a protector in your midst, though I have not seen this one before."

At that instant, as if a light had suddenly lit a darkened room, Roberto knew what D'Anjou was talking about.

"The white dog…" he whispered.

"I see him," said D'Anjou. "You may be fortunate to have him, but he alone will not save you."

"How do you know all of this?" By now, Roberto was struggling to keep his composure.

"I am, after all, just as you have said, a spiritualist. But for me, I much prefer the term *seer*. It seems so much more appropriate, don't you think?"

"Are you satisfied now, seer? Have you seen enough to make you happy?" snarled Roberto—he suddenly felt extremely vulnerable beneath the old man's gaze. What else could D'Anjou see of his life?

"Yes, I have seen enough, but I am neither happy nor satisfied. I prayed that the curse your father carried had followed him to the grave. But alas, it did not, and you, señor, do not deserve to carry it now."

"Well then, it seems you know everything," shrugged Roberto. "What do you suggest I do?"

D'Anjou lowered his eyes. "I was not able to help your father, and as much as I want to now, I cannot help you."

"What good are you, then?" scoffed Roberto.

"Your anger is completely understandable. But you are misguided to aim it at me. I'm simply the messenger." D'Anjou picked up his coffee and took another sip.

"I've heard enough," spat Roberto as he stood up. He reached into his pocket, drew out some coins, and dropped them onto the table for the coffee.

Just as Roberto was about to leave, D'Anjou smiled. "It is quite possible that we may never meet again, señor Torres," the old man said softly. "Your fate delivered you here today, and by its power, it will take you to whatever end it holds in store. I wish you luck, for I can see that you will need it."

Roberto looked blankly at D'Anjou for a moment, and then turned to go.

"One more thing, señor—I have something for you." D'Anjou extended his arm toward Roberto and opened his hand. Roberto turned back to see what the old man held. His heart almost stopped when he saw what it was. The item was distinctive, and he recognized it instantly. His father's missing signet ring—the ring that the police had failed to find—lay in D'Anjou's hand.

Roberto was staggered. He could not take his eyes from it. "Where did you get that?"

"Your father gave it to me just days before his death. He made me promise that someday I would pass it to you. He knew that only by that means would you come to know the real truth about his death."

Roberto took it and held it in his hand. He fought back the lump rising in his throat. He looked at D'Anjou for a moment and studied the expression on his face.

"What will you do now?" he asked the old man.

"Tomorrow I return to France, where I have been living for many years. It is the land of my birth, and I am pleased to be among my own people. I am not well, señor, and it is there that I hope to spend what is left of my life. I have returned to Spain this time only to see you. I sensed that the time had come to tell you what I know. So there you have it. I will trouble you no more."

Roberto eyed D'Anjou, trying hard to read his expression.

"You know that your name is not welcomed in our family."

"I do," replied D'Anjou. "And now that you know the truth, will you ever mention my name again?"

"Never…" said Roberto as he met the old man's gaze.

"Good. Everything is as it should be." A smile of contentment appeared on D'Anjou's face.

Roberto held out his hand, "Thank you…for everything."

D'Anjou took his hand and gently held it for a moment. "You have a long journey ahead of you. Make the most of it, for your salvation may well be in it."

Henri D'Anjou lingered for a while in the café after Roberto had left him.

He's so much like his father, thought D'Anjou, *lost and desperately wanting to be found. What will become of Sebastian's son?* D'Anjou closed his eyes for a moment, and in his mind, he could see a small ship tossed about, lost upon the great ocean of time.

Who will rescue it from certain disaster?

As Roberto made his way back to his apartment, he thought about D'Anjou. The old man had seen everything—even the white dog. The very thought of him being able to mysteriously paw through his life as though it were an open book unnerved Roberto. Part of him was also suspicious of the old man's motives. *Was D'Anjou telling the truth about the death of his father?* He wasn't yet fully convinced. He knew though, with D'Anjou's departure to France, he may never know the truth. *Perhaps it's all for the best,* he thought, *some things are better left in the past.*

That night, before he settled down to read more of the journal his grandfather had given him, Roberto burned everything that D'Anjou had sent to him. He watched as the fire consumed the photographs. A chill shot through him as he caught sight of D'Anjou's eyes peering up through the dancing flames. The heat blistered and contorted each of the pictures before the fire reduced them to ashes. When there was nothing but embers left, he finally felt relief. It was as though a new chapter in his life was about to begin. He picked up the journal and retired to his favorite chair.

12

THE JOURNAL OF FRANCISCO DE VILLANOVA TO

DECEMBER 1532

During our time with the Uawans, their chief had shown us nothing but friendship. He was an intelligent man, always eager to learn what he could of our ways, and willing to pass on to us knowledge of his. We valued and returned his great friendship. For in truth, it was he who ensured that we had survived happily in his land. Without him, I feel certain that we would have perished at the hands of a lesser man.

Even so, when it came time to finally leave the land of Uawa, there was a great jubilation among us. The desire to again see our homeland had at times been so strong as to become a torment. And those whom we had left behind missed us also; their mentations sought us out and discovered us in our dreams. So on the eve of departure, only the old chief and certain of his tribe mourned, for none among us shared the sadness.

The night before we sailed, I smuggled Aramoana aboard the ship and hid her in the hold. There among the barrels, sacks, and chests, she concealed herself. I remained aboard that night and checked on her whenever I could.

The red sky the next morning, daubed across the eastern horizon, would be the last sunrise we would ever see in that land. The time had come for us to leave the Uawans. It had been almost three years since we had come to their shores, and in that time, we had been treated like friends. We would not forget them. Some of us had even begun families. A few men sought permission from the captain to remain behind with the women who had become their wives. He granted their requests, but in their stead, sought agreement from the chief to take with us six Uawan men when we departed. This the chief agreed to, personally choosing the six young men himself.

Soon, the hour of departing was upon us. We said our goodbyes, and the Uawan chief embraced the captain warmly. As he did so, many women in the large crowd that had gathered upon the beach began wailing and scratching at their faces and pulling at their hair. Some began to bleed as they tore at their hair and cheeks. The scene was unsettling, and some among us felt that it conjured up bad omens for our journey. But to the Indians, this was both a parting gesture to us and a final farewell to the men of their country, should they not see them again. The Uawans are a seafaring people and know only too well the dangers of the ocean. A sailor's return, though always expected, was never certain.

Before climbing into the skiff, the captain made one final gesture of kindness to his friend, the chief of the Uawans, presenting him with a sword, breastplate, and helmet, in recognition of the generosity and protection he had extended to us. It was a gift of great honor and surely without precedence, for the sword had once belonged to the captain's own beloved father.

The chief, for his part, was overjoyed by the gift, which he had long coveted. But at the same time, he was also deeply saddened by our departure, and as the remaining crew and the captain boarded the skiff, he wept openly. He had attempted many times to persuade the captain to remain with him and his people, but this was not to be. The captain, like the rest of us, had his heart firmly set upon returning to Spain and to the loved ones who waited there.

Once aboard the *San Lesmes*, we made ready to sail. Our course was to be northward, in the hope that there, we would find winds to carry us home. But no one among us knew that such winds existed. Nor did we know for certain that such a course would take us anywhere near our homeland. But in this adventure, we could do nothing but place ourselves before the winds of fate and in the hands of God.

As the ship tacked away from the shore and into the breeze, I watched the Uawans gathered along the beach. We could hear the grieving women wailing across the water as we headed away from the shore. The men in the gathering stood in silence. My eyes searched for the chief, but I could not see him among the crowd. His sorrow had obviously driven him back to the village.

As we made our way out of the little harbor toward open water, I noticed an outcrop of rocks north of the village that ran right down to the water's edge. It was there, amongst the rocks, that I saw a small flash of white in the sunlight. I looked again, this time searching to see what could have created that brief burst. Then I saw it. Sitting on the shoreline was the white dog that had been Aramoana's faithful companion all those many months. Even though I could not make out his face, I felt his eyes upon me, and my heart was heavy for him, for it was certain that he knew his mistress was aboard our ship.

As the *San Lesmes* tacked into the wind, I looked back and saw the white dog enter the water. His head rode just above the waves as he began swimming toward us. I felt the ship lift into the wind as the sails caught the salty, open sea air. She was happy once more to be free upon the ocean. Far behind us, I could still see the little white head bobbing heroically in the water. No one but I saw him, and my heart was seized with pity for the little creature as it struggled in the choppy waters.

The people on the beach were slowly fading into the distance, and the cries of the women had now almost completely dissolved into the breeze. But still, the little dog kept on, now just a tiny bobbing white dot in the water far behind us. For almost thirty minutes, I watched in amazement, praying at every second that he would give up and swim for shore.

But he did not. Instead, the valiant little creature labored on, pushing his tiny frame hard into the beating waves. I remembered his little face that first day he found me in the forest surrounding the village. I remembered his eyes as he sat in the clearing outside the cave the morning his mistress and I had first made love. For me now, seeing him in the water like this had become almost impossible to watch.

Then, suddenly, he was gone, sunk to the deep. I stood with heavy heart on the afterdeck, my eyes searching the choppy waters. The faithful little creature had succumbed to the sea. In that moment, I resolved that I would never reveal to Aramoana her companion's fate.

That night, and far from land, I brought Aramoana from the hold and presented her to the captain. As I expected, he was furious. And when he discovered that she was pregnant, he had me flogged and chained to the mainmast for two days without rations. His reason was simple: *I should have left her with her people.* At least there, she could have sought her father's mercy.

But her father's laws would never have permitted reconciliation. I felt sure that she would have perished, along with our child, at his command—or even by his hand.

The captain, though, was clear: A sailing ship, on an uncertain adventure, was no place for a pregnant woman. I took my punishment and then begged the captain's mercy in the hope that God would help him accept our situation as it was. And in time, Captain De la Puente proved once more to be the good and merciful man we all knew him to be. The day after I was released from the chains, he called the crew together for an announcement. He had decided that Aramoana and I would have to share my food and water rations. There was no alternative. Our journey, as far as we knew, was one that had never been made before, and for that reason, we had to be cautious with supplies. The ship had been carefully stocked according to the number of crew, and now one more mouth to feed put those calculations at risk.

Secretly, I made a decision to eat only half rations every other day. Had the captain known this, he would not have tolerated it. He needed a strong and healthy crew to man the ship. But I could not let Aramoana survive only on meager rations; she was now eating for two.

The six men that we had brought aboard from Uawa at first treated Aramoana with great suspicion. None of them would acknowledge or talk to her, and two of them would not even look at her. It was clear that they were fearful of the wrath of her father. But soon, they realized that, like their land and their kin, we had also left their laws in our wake. And the laws aboard ship were now those of our country, and for us, Aramoana had committed no crime. She was innocent of that for which she had been charged, and in this community of men, she was now someone to be cared for. It did not take long for her countrymen to treat her as we did.

And soon, just like the rest of us, they too began saving water and small amounts of food for her. Everyone aboard took care to keep her warm and safe below deck in bad weather and did what they could when she was ill. It was obvious why the men cared for her in this way. She was pregnant and reminded them of their own mothers and wives and sisters—not one of them forgotten, but all of them very far away, and for years, unseen. To the men, Aramoana had only brought the best of memories, and she had given us our reason to keep the wind in our sails and our bow searching for home.

We were a month at sea, having seen neither land nor ship, when tragedy struck. Late one night, a fierce storm blew up, and for days, we struggled hard to hold the *San Lesmes* afloat in high seas and heavy winds. But in the end, our fates were sealed. On the night of the third day, in complete darkness, our ship was lost. Dashed furiously into jagged rocks, the raging sea tore her belly clean apart.

God must have been with us that night, though, for not a soul among us was lost in the tempest. Every one of the crew made it safely to shore. By the time I dragged Aramoana from the sea, she had almost no strength left to fight the waves that had tried so hard to claim her. It was her feeble and exhausted voice that led me to where she lay, hammered by the wind and water on a short stretch of sandy beach. I stumbled about in the darkness until I found her lying near the shoreline, washed about like a rag doll in the tumultuous waters. She shook uncontrollably as I dragged her from the grip of the ocean and up onto the beach.

The night's icy wind cut through everything it encountered. I shielded her from its teeth and wrapped my arms around her shaking body in an attempt to warm her. But it was cold, and soon I, also, began to shake.

That night, all that we could do was huddle into the hollows that we had dug into the sand hills, our pitiful attempt at shielding us from the piercing wind. On that blackest of nights, we lay in those hollows and grieved as we listened to the raging sea tearing our ship apart. Though we could not see through the darkness, we could hear her death throes. She groaned pitifully under the fury of the water pounding down upon her. We wept that night, for we knew without the *San Lesmes,* all hope of ever seeing our homeland was lost.

Tears fell as we remembered that day in July 1525 when we sailed from A Coruña—we'd been happy then. Every one of us had been thankful to be aboard a ship that we believed would carry us to the Spice Islands and to our fortunes. And now, as far as anyone could reckon, it was February 1529. And here we were, on an unknown coastline in the middle of a storm, somewhere in an uncharted ocean. On that darkest of all nights, we wondered whether this was to be our eternal resting place. As I dried the tears from my eyes, the howling wind cut like a sword through my wet clothes. In the hollow that I had fashioned from the sand, I lay over Aramoana to shield her from the tempest.

How we made it through that night without freezing to death is a mystery, but with the sunrise came a clear and bright day. During the night, the storm had abated, and come the morning, our first instinct was to see how the ship had fared. We were not prepared for the grim sight that greeted us. She lay as a butchered whale cast against the jagged rocks. Her belly was ripped open, and her ribs protruded into the air—picked clean by the fury of the sea. It was a sight that broke even the heart of the strongest among us. If ever we were to be tested, that time had arrived.

Cargo, timber, tackle, and torn-and-tangled sail lay strewn across the beach. Barrels of fresh water and food stock had been washed ashore; some of them had burst open and lay empty and half buried in the sand. Fortunately, our arms, which had been sealed in boxes and hidden aboard ship from the Uawans, had survived the storm intact, and now the crates littered the shore. Some of the powder and shot, which had been sealed in watertight canisters, now lay strewn along the sand. The task to recover what remained began immediately.

Later that morning, the captain called us together and chose from the assembled group three lieutenants. Under each, he organized teams, to which he assigned tasks. A group of men were to remain on the beach and continue the salvage that we had earlier begun. The second and largest group was to set about clearing a site where a makeshift camp would be established. They were also to forage for food and water and begin the construction of a shelter large enough to accommodate everyone. The third and smallest group was to explore our new home. The captain led this group, of which I was a member. Our main task was to discover whether this land was an island or part of a mainland. We were also keen to know whether it was inhabited.

Soon after the other two teams had set to work, we armed ourselves and left for the forest. I said goodbye to Aramoana, who had recovered well from her ordeal the night before. She smiled and waved to me as we departed.

Once we left the beach, it was hard going. We cut our way through the tangled vegetation that grew thickly all around us. As we traversed deeper into the forest, we discovered several small, freshwater streams that flowed toward the sea. The sweet, clear water was home to many large, black, shrimp-like creatures that wandered idly over the submerged rocks. We drank from these cool little streams, noted their positions, and then moved on.

Before we'd left the beach that first day, we had observed a hill that stood conspicuously above the surrounding landscape. It was this hill that was to become our main objective. From the summit, we hoped to get a better understanding of the shape of this new land. Several hours later, and after much effort, we had finally achieved our goal. But for us, unhappiness waited there. From the summit, we were heartbroken to see that our ship had been gutted upon the rocks of an island. In silence, we searched with our eyes the vast open space that confronted us. We were completely surrounded by ocean, right to the horizon, in every direction.

It is said, though, that even in adversity, there is always a little luck—and so it was true for us. Although we had landed on an island, it was one with both food and water in abundance. At least it seemed likely that we could survive here for some time without much trouble—or so we thought.

It was the captain who first sighted it. His attention had been drawn to something in one of the distant gullies that ran from the main range of hills down to the sea on the far side of the island. A moment later, we all saw it—a wispy thin trail of smoke that swirled, almost invisibly, into the still air. Nervous tension gripped each of us as we realized that we were not alone on this island. The captain decided that we should start back and join the rest of the crew. Tomorrow, he would send a party out and attempt to make contact with the inhabitants on the other side.

It was on the cusp of nightfall when we arrived back to join Aramoana and the others. The camp was slowly taking shape, and a basic shelter made of material from the *San Lesmes* had been erected. The sea had remained calm, and there was almost no wind during the day, which made the salvage of the ship's remains easier. Much had been brought ashore, including four cannons that had once protected the ship, though they had never been fired in anger. Would we now need them to protect us? This was the question that was never far from our thoughts.

The men in camp greeted us with relief when we told them that good, fresh water was to be had close by. We all knew that in order to survive here, we would have to secure food much as the Uawans did, harvesting from the sea and hunting in the forest. There were many small animals and birds in the forest, and the ocean around us teemed with sea life. We would not go hungry.

But there was another serious issue that needed to be discussed that evening. The news that we had seen smoke rising from the other side of the island was greeted with an uneasy silence from the men. But the captain had already decided that in the morning, an armed party of ten men would set out in an attempt to make contact with the people who had lit the fire. It could be several days before the armed party returned, so those left behind must continue the work that had been started. Everyone in camp, however, was to remain armed and vigilant. The captain also ordered that tomorrow, a large cross was to be erected on the beach. Any passing ships would then see that Christians were in need of assistance on this island. That night, armed guards were posted around the camp, each to be relieved twice before the morning.

I was selected as a member of the party ordered to establish contact with the mysterious people on the other side of the island. It was an early start for the group the next morning, and as was entirely proper, the captain was in command. We armed ourselves fully, including firearms. One of the Indians who sailed with us from Uawa had also been selected for the overland party. The captain hoped that he might be able to communicate with the people that we would encounter. Soon enough, we were ready to take our leave.

I kissed Aramoana and told her we would be back in a few days. As we left camp, I could see the tears pooling in her eyes. There was also something else in them that caught my attention—fear dwelt there, too. This filled me with unease which, at the time, I did not understand. Looking back on it now, perhaps she had some forewarning of the events that were to unfold. But whatever the truth of it, my life would never be the same after that journey across the island.

We marched all that day through dense and almost impenetrable jungle. It was very late when we came out of the thick forest and up onto an outcrop that overlooked the valley where we had seen the smoke the previous day. From where we stood, above the heavily forested gorge, we could see no sign of people or habitation. After surveying the scene, the captain decided we should set up camp just over the brow of the ridge. The following morning, we would make our way down to the floor of the valley. Guards were posted on roster, and the rest of us settled in and waited for darkness to descend. That night we lit no fires, ate cold rations, and remained as quiet as we could.

Early the next morning, we made our way down into the gorge. It was steep going, and the thick vegetation made it difficult at times to make headway. As we neared the bottom of the valley, we could hear the sound of water surging and splashing over rocks. The stream was clear and fresh, and when we reached it, I knelt and cupped my hands to the brim with the cold, refreshing liquid. As I brought it to my lips, I looked up and was astonished to see a group of Indians standing a hundred or so paces upstream. I turned to raise the alarm, but quickly realized that the rest of the party had seen them too.

The captain bid us all to be on our guard. For a moment, there was a tense silence. Then Mahaki, the Uawan who had accompanied us, called to the Indians in his own language, telling them that we meant no harm. As he spoke, more Indians came down into the stream.

One of them called back, but Mahaki could not understand what the man had said, and when he attempted a reply, they did not allow him to finish.

A wooden spear was thrown. It struck a rock near him and glanced off, ricocheting away and burying itself, point first, into the riverbank. At this, the Indians, who had up until that time remained quiet, charged forward, screaming and hurling spears at us. We readied instantly; the first volley of shots was fired, and several of the charging Indians fell dead. The sound of the firearms and the sight of the falling men stopped the others in their tracks. They were taken by surprise and examined the dead bodies. This gave us time to reload, and when the next charge came, we were able to fire again. This time, though, the Indians did not stop to inspect the fallen, but kept coming and met us head-on. The battle was one-sided. Their wood and stone weapons were no match for our metal armor and steel blades. By the time the Indians had given up and fled, we had killed and wounded at least twenty-five of their number.

We all knew that it would have been much better not to have killed anyone, but sadly, that choice had been taken from us. Once we had dispatched the wounded, we moved quickly down the valley, pursuing the remaining Indians. Within the hour, we had them cornered on the beach. We discovered them frantically trying to make their way back to their longboats, which sat in the shallows just offshore.

We now realized that, like us, they also were visitors to this land. We could not let them leave, for they would surely bring back many others and eventually overwhelm us. And so we set about killing every last one of them—none escaped our blows.

When the day was nearing its end and the sun hung like a blood-red globe upon the horizon, I lay exhausted on the ground. My body was numb, and my heart felt like stone. When I closed my eyes, all I could see were the tears in Aramoana's eyes when I had left her the day before. In my mind, they fell like rain to wash away the blood that now stained my hands. I could not be sure, though, whether such a thing was possible. The blood that was spilt on that day had also stained my conscience and my faith. These were people just like us, just trying to survive and make do with what they were able to fashion from that which they had found around them. And now they were dead for doing nothing more than trying to live. There was cruel irony in this lesson for me, and one that I never forgot.

The following day, as the sun came up, we buried the dead in a pit that we dug out of the sand hills. Although none were Christian, we gave them all a Christian burial and commended each one into the hands of God. It somehow seemed fitting, since only He could sanctify what we had done to these people in order that we should survive. Later, just before high tide, we boarded two of the Indians' longboats, having burnt the rest, and rowed them round the island until we came to the bay where the *San Lesmes* was wrecked. Here we landed, much to the amazement of the men in camp, who came jubilantly down to the water's edge to greet us. After that battle, we became much more vigilant on our little island. And in the weeks that followed, we built a small fort in case we were attacked. But in the end, we were to have no more trouble from the Indians.

We remained on that island for almost a year. To many of us, however, it seemed much longer. After five months had passed, I lost my beautiful Aramoana. She died giving me a son; the ordeal having almost claimed his life as well. But José—for that was his name—was a spirited baby, and he fought hard for his little share of life.

Everyone in the small community of men looked upon him as a miracle child. And they believed that if God was prepared to grant us this miracle, He would surely grant others. On the night of his birth, when it was all over, and I had finally closed my eyes, I thought of Aramoana. My heart was full of pain. With her passing, she had taken a piece of my soul, and nevermore would it be whole again.

I tried hard to sleep that night, but all was not yet done. An unwelcome visitor was to come to me in the midnight hours. For the first time, I was to see the ghost that would haunt me even to this very day; and as I write these words, I saw him but an hour ago. The white dog, which I last saw in the sea following the *San Lesmes,* had come into our village on the night of Aramoana's death. Whimpering forlornly, it crawled upon its belly to Aramoana's body, whereupon it rose and gently laid itself across her chest.

I was terrified at the sight. However, none but I could see this apparition, for no other who was present made comment of it. I felt sure that it was the work of the Devil, and prayed for Aramoana's salvation in the hope that God would hear me. The dog remained with her all night, and in the morning, it was gone.

We buried Aramoana near to our little village, and as we lowered her body into the sandy grave, I noticed the ghostly dog sitting at the edge of the forest. It remained there while we said our prayers. Then, just before we left, I looked back, and it was gone. From that time, I cleared it from my mind in the hope that I would never see it again, since its mistress was now dead.

Aramoana's death changed my world forever. When she died, I took the amulet that she had always worn around her neck. I hoped that it would forever keep her in my memory. In her religion, she believed that it would protect her from evil. Perhaps now that she was gone, it would protect me, but I hoped also that it would protect our young son. After all, he had his mother's blood flowing in his veins. Surely her religion would protect him, as would mine.

When José was just six months old, a passing Portuguese caravel came to our island, attracted first by the smoke from our fires, and then by the large cross we had erected on the beach. We watched the ship lay anchor in our small bay, and shortly afterwards, welcomed the crew ashore as heroes. Within a few days, we were taken aboard the ship that was headed to La Java. From La Java, we eventually managed to barter passage back to Europe.

It was Christmas 1532 when I finally made it home to the town of my birth. I had not seen A Coruña since setting sail for the Indies seven years earlier. With me was my son, José, a boy who had not yet seen his third year. The journey had been a very long and difficult one, and it was a miracle that my son had survived it. Caring for one so young when journeying across land and sea is not easy. On the day of my return, I sought out the chapel to thank God for his blessings and for allowing me to see my homeland once again.

Much time has passed, and I am an old man. José has grown up now, and he fills my heart with gladness. And the land I so longed to see again when I was young and lost at sea has also grown old. It is a land now filled with suspicion and dangers, a land under the spell of the deadly Inquisitor.

What of the friendly Uawans? How have they fared in their land? Here in mine, the people are drowning as the black robe of darkness and fear covers all. Now even a whisper will send a man to his doom. What is it that they want of me? I have given them everything. All I have left is the breath in my body, and now it seems they have come even for that. I am old—their task will be easy.

13

THE JOURNEY BEGINS, BARCELONA

The first thing that Roberto noticed when he entered the room was the smile on Maya's face. She was seated at the dining room table and her attention was centered on what appeared to be an email on the computer screen in front of her.

"Good news?" he inquired as he pulled up a chair and sat down beside her.

"I've received this email from Gabriella back in the States. She's just sent me the name and phone number of one of her anthropology contacts in New Zealand—a Dr. Daniel Potae. He's a curator at the country's national museum, and since receiving the photos from Gabriella, he's keen to talk to us about the amulet."

By now, Roberto had finished reading the journal; nowhere in it could he find any mention of New Zealand. He was the first to admit, though, his knowledge of the place was limited. In fact, if he was honest, besides being able to point to the small country on a globe, he knew little else about it. How, he wondered, could these anthropologists be so sure that they were on the right track? And even if they were right, what difference would it actually make?

But more importantly, there was nothing here that interested him anymore. His life was on a timer—and to him that was far more concerning. Everything had to be rendered down now to fit into the smaller window of time that fate had allowed him. How big that window was, he did not know—nor could he. The *not knowing* had become a torture all its own. Some days, he felt as if he was wearing a leaden straightjacket. So right now, searching out the history of an amulet was right at the bottom of his to-do list.

But it was clear that Maya had other ideas. The mystery of the amulet was the perfect fit for her anthropological curiosity.

That evening, the sight of her at the computer as she typed away gave him the jitters. He could tell from the tone in her voice when she read the email from Gabriella that she was excited. The question he kept asking himself was, *do I have the strength to keep up with her?*

"Well, what do you think? Should we call him?" she asked, her voice was full of excitement.

"Do we have to call him now?" Roberto asked, attempting to stall. "Let's think about it a little more before we jump into this thing."

Maya seemed oblivious to what he had just said as she continued to rap away at her keyboard. "Roberto, I've just pulled up the world clock. It's nine-fifty a.m. in Wellington, New Zealand. This is all so exciting! I think we should call Doctor Potae now and see what he has to say."

Roberto went to interrupt, but before he could, Maya was already dialing the number.

"Daniel speaking…" said the voice on the other end.

"Good morning, Daniel, my name is Maya Serrano. I'm calling from Barcelona. I understand you received some photographs from a friend of mine—Gabriella Bourne."

"Yes I did," replied Daniel. "Thank you for calling, Maya. Is the manaia yours?"

"It belongs to a friend of mine…perhaps you would like to speak to him." Without warning, she held out the phone to Roberto. He glared at her in utter dismay. The scowl on his face said it all, but Maya simply smiled and gestured for him to take the receiver.

He snatched it from her, took a deep breath, and placed it to his ear. "Good evening. It's Roberto Torres speaking."

He had a strong Spanish accent but his English was good, thought Daniel.

"Good morning Roberto! I'm very pleased to be talking to you. My name is Daniel Potae, and I'm curator of the Maori collection for the National Museum of New Zealand. I've been studying the photographs Professor Bourne sent to me from California. You have a very old Maori manaia in your possession. How did you come by it?"

"My grandfather gave it to me several months ago. It's been handed down in the family for generations, along with a journal that was written in the sixteenth century by an ancestor of mine."

"You have a journal as well?" Daniel's voice rose with obvious excitement.

"Yes." replied Roberto.

"Have you read it?"

"I have," he answered.

"And…does it say anything about the manaia, or where it came from?"

Roberto told him the story of Francisco de Villanova, the *San Lesmes*, Aramoana, and the amulet.

"You can't begin to know how exciting this news is to me," replied Daniel. "I would love to see both the manaia and journal sometime. Any plans to come to this part of the world?"

"None at all. I'm sorry," replied Roberto.

"Well, if you ever want to come to the antipodes, you call me first. I will be waiting for you at the airport. That's a firm promise, Roberto. I would love to see you and your family treasures."

"Do you think they're that important?" Roberto asked.

"I'm serious," replied Daniel. "Those two heirlooms of yours could potentially knock a hole in the established history of the European discovery of this country. You think on it, Roberto. Come and visit me in New Zealand. I promise you won't need to worry about a thing. I'll take good care of you and make sure you have the time of your life. This is a great country—come and check us out."

"You make it sound hard to resist."

"Think about it. You'll have a great time here."

After he hung up, Maya was eager to know everything.

Roberto told her about Daniel's interest in the historical importance of the pieces.

"He asked whether we wanted to go to New Zealand," he admitted, rather hesitantly.

"I've always wanted to go there," interrupted Maya. Her voice sizzled with excitement. "It looks so beautiful in the travel advertisements—don't you think, Roberto?"

"We can't just drop everything and head off to the other side of the world, Maya," Roberto was now alarmed at the direction that this discussion seemed to be heading—and fast.

"Why not? Besides it would only be for a couple of weeks. It'll be fun. Come on Roberto! Where's your sense of adventure?"

"I don't want to just drop everything and jump on a plane to New Zealand," he said, glaring back at her.

"Look…" she told him, attempting to contain her excitement "let me do a little research—see what I can come up with. After that, we'll talk about it again."

"I'm not agreeing to anything Maya."

"Yes, I know," she smiled. "I just want to see whether it's possible—that's all."

Roberto had known Maya long enough to recognize the signs. She had made her mind up on this one, and her only problem now was how to convince him. Although he had tried to make it obvious to her that he wasn't interested, he knew there was a battle ahead of him. She would move quickly now. The softening-up process would begin immediately. He silently braced himself for the onslaught. There would be the beautiful tourist pamphlets that would somehow find their way into the apartment. Interesting facts and figures about New Zealand would also be inserted casually into conversations. And of course, there would be the You Tube video clips paraded on the computer at every opportunity.

Maya was so full of energy and passion that some days, for Roberto, she paled everything around him. That was why he loved her. She was everything that he wanted to be. But his awful secret, the one he would not share, was beginning to catch up with him. Right now, the last thing he needed was a trip to the other side of the world. His body had begun to whisper to him. Things were not okay anymore. He tired easily now, and had also begun to lose weight. He tried desperately to hide all of this from Maya. He knew, though, that sooner or later, the time would come when he would have to tell her. When that time would be, he did not know. But he could feel in his heart that it was close, and he dreaded even the very thought of it.

In his life such as it was, he had never felt like being a martyr for anyone or anything. But this evening, watching Maya, he realized that his love for her was an inescapable force—a force that even now, he still did not fully understand. If he told her of his illness, he felt that he would be robbing her of an adventure that was a part of her destiny. But by not telling her, he could well be endangering his own life. What was he to do?

Tears began welling in his eyes as he realized that the answer to that question already lay within him. It did not matter how many times the question was asked—the answer now would always be the same. He was tired and sick, there was no doubt of that, but he knew that if he pushed himself hard, he would make it. And if she really wanted to go, he would go with her. *In the end,* he thought, *whether we like it or not, love makes martyrs of us all.*

14

The Boeing 747-400 shuddered as its wheels met the tarmac, releasing a cloud of metallic blue smoke into the warm breeze. Roberto glanced at his wristwatch as Maya slipped the magazine she'd been reading back into the seat pouch in front of her. It was just after nine in the morning, and Auckland International Airport loomed in the windows along the left side of the aircraft as it cruised along the runway toward the disembarkation gates. It had been a long flight, and there was excitement among the passengers as the aircraft finally came to a halt.

As he stepped from the plane into the air bridge, Roberto was relieved—at last he could stand on something that did not have 30,000 feet of air beneath it.

Maya smiled as she took him by the hand. "I'm so excited," she giggled. "It's like a dream come true."

By the time the pair entered the immigration hall, the queues at the kiosks were beginning to thicken. The thud of passports being stamped echoed above the passenger chatter.

Finally it was their turn. "Welcome to New Zealand," smiled the immigration officer as he struck entry stamps into both their passports.

"Thank you," replied Maya, her American accent mingled with the mêlée of other accents that filled the immigration hall. "We're very pleased to be here."

After passing through customs with their luggage, the pair were relieved to make their way out into the arrivals hall. A sea of expectant faces beamed as they came through the automatic doors and walked fresh-faced out into the waiting crowd. There was a buzz of excitement and laughter around them as families greeted returning loved ones. Off to her left, Maya spotted a man holding a sign: *Welcome Roberto Torres and Maya Serrano.*

"That must be Daniel," she nodded. Roberto had spotted him too.

He was younger than they had imagined, a tall man, not at all the museum-curator type. He looked Hispanic with his olive complexion and wavy, shoulder-length, jet-black hair.

By now, Daniel had made eye contact with the pair and had begun making his way through the crowd.

"Kia Ora," he beamed as he held out his hand. "You must be Roberto."

Roberto returned the smile and shook his hand, "I'm pleased to meet you, Dr. Potae."

"Call me Daniel," he said. "And you must be Maya."

"It's a pleasure to meet you," she said. He leaned forward and kissed her on the cheek.

"Welcome to New Zealand. You must be exhausted after such a long flight."

"Exhausted yes, but very excited to be here," said Maya. "We've been looking forward to visiting your country."

"Good," replied Daniel. "We've lots for you to see and do, but first let's get you both out of here. You must be sick of airports by now. A friend of mine has an apartment in Newmarket, near the city, and he's kindly allowed me to put you two up in it while you're in town. I've got relatives up here in Auckland; I'll be staying with them."

"You've gone to so much trouble. You must allow us to compensate you for this," offered Roberto.

"Not at all," Daniel shook his head. "My friend owes me. I'm simply allowing him to pay me back this way."

"Please," Maya pressed, "you must let us pay something."

"I won't hear of it. It's not every day I get to welcome guests from as far away as Spain. And besides, you have something to show me later that will be payment enough. You brought the manaia and the journal, right?"

"Of course," nodded Roberto. "We couldn't leave them behind."

"Good, let's get you out of here and into your apartment."

Two days before leaving Barcelona, Roberto had buried himself in books; his mission had been to find out as much as he could about New

Zealand. He had almost no knowledge of the country, and most of what he did know was from school geography lessons many years ago.

New Zealand, he discovered, was a small island nation in the South Pacific, roughly the same size as Great Britain. For some reason, he had always thought of it as being much smaller—a little archipelago in the middle of nowhere.

It was the *antipodes* of Spain. That meant that if he were to dig a hole from his country straight through the center of the earth, he would emerge somewhere in New Zealand. It was an interesting thought, but there was no question—flying there was a much easier option.

The little South Pacific country was made up of two larger islands and a smaller one. All of these were washed by a vast ocean that completely isolated the nation from the rest of the world. Rolling in along its western shores was the Tasman Sea, across which Australia lay more than two thousand kilometers away. The South Pacific Ocean battered the eastern shores, and beyond that horizon, almost ten thousand kilometers distant, lay Chile. Two thousand, six hundred kilometers to the south lay the frozen continent of Antarctica, and fifteen hundred kilometers to the north were the romantic isles of French Polynesia.

Roberto learned that the first man to discover New Zealand was Kupé, a Polynesian mariner who arrived in the country around 925 AD. Since that time, a branch of his people, the Maori, had populated the country, which they called *Aotearoa*. The ancestors of these people had left the shores of the Persian Gulf around five thousand years earlier. This was the beginning, for them, of an epic journey that would take them through India, Asia, and finally to the Malay Archipelago. About three thousand years ago, these early pioneers had launched themselves out into the uninhabited vastness of *Te Moana-nui-a-kiwa—the Great Ocean of Kiwa*, in search of land.

By the time they set sail across *Kiwa's* vast ocean—the Pacific—these hardy Polynesians were expert mariners who possessed considerable experience in star navigation. They were also keen observers of the natural world around them, and as a result, built up a wealth of practical oceanographic knowledge. With the help of these skills, they discovered and settled the remote and scattered islands of the Pacific. In their large catamarans, these great but now almost-forgotten mariners sailed from west to east across the entire breadth of the Pacific. They established a settlement on *Rapanui* or Easter Island near the coast of Chile. And now modern science has discovered that they also made landfall on the South American mainland. In the North Pacific, they settled east as far as Hawaii, and many archaeologists believe that there is evidence to indicate that they also made landfall on the western seaboard of the North American mainland. Roberto could identify with these audacious seafaring feats, for he too came from a once-great maritime nation—a nation which, in the fifteenth and sixteenth centuries, became a world superpower based on its dominance of the sea.

History recorded the first European visit to Aotearoa in 1642. The commander of that voyage was a Dutchman named Abel Tasman. It was he who gave the land its first European name—he called it Staten Land. Later, the name Zealandia was used by mapmakers to describe the beautiful South Sea islands. Finally, around a decade after Tasman's visit, the name New Zealand was given to the land that the Maori had known for centuries as Aotearoa. Though initially, the new name caused some confusion since it had already been given to another island off the coast of New Guinea in 1606, it wasn't long before the name New Zealand became permanently associated with Tasman's Staten Land. Tasman himself never actually landed in the country. After a seaborne attack by the locals, which claimed the lives of four of his crew, he sailed away, never to return. The bay where his crewmen were killed is now known as Murderers Bay.

Today, Roberto read, the country was a modern and independent democracy, and Auckland, with almost 1.5 million inhabitants, was its largest city. Sprawling in all directions along the narrowest part of the upper North Island, the city was bathed by the Manukau Harbor on one side and the waters of the Waitemata on the other. People had lived in that region since 1350, when the place was known as *Tamaki-makau-rau*. The modern city of Auckland was only founded in 1840, making it—by European standards—a young city. Roberto noticed the differences immediately. Maya, on the other hand, had seen similar cities in the United States.

The drive into Newmarket from the airport was slower than expected. "The roads are always busy in the mornings and afternoons," said Daniel, sounding a little frustrated. "The public transport system in this, our biggest city, is third world, and expensive, so everyone uses their cars to get around. One day, we might finally get a government with some real vision, but until then, we just sit in traffic."

"It's warmer here than I thought it would be," Maya commented.

"We're in the middle of summer, and this one's been a scorcher."

"In Spain we know all about hot summers," said Roberto.

As the car wound its way through the suburban streets, Roberto noticed the lack of stone as a building material for houses. Most buildings seemed to be constructed of timber, and there was a distinct lack of large apartment blocks, something he was familiar with in Spain. It wasn't until they finally got to Newmarket that he found some similarities with the cities that he knew back home.

The apartment that Daniel had arranged for the pair was located on Carlton Gore Road, a few minutes' walk from the beautiful parkland the locals called the Domain. For the people of Auckland, this place is a haven of tranquility in the center of a busy city—a place where picnics and Sunday strolls were enjoyed or friendly games of rugby, cricket, or football were played. Kite-flyers and concertgoers, wedding parties and lovers, bikers and joggers, all who came, worshiped the open jewel of greenery and sunlight. Its oaks and kiosks and Old-World architecture provided a welcome escape from the bustle of city life outside of its borders.

The Domain was also where the Auckland War Memorial Museum was situated—its grand, neo-classical building having been opened in 1929. It was to become not only the main regional museum, but also a place to remember the sacrifice of New Zealand blood upon the battlefields of Europe—*Lest We Forget*. Today the museum is home to the most important Polynesian artifact collection in the world. And it would be here where Daniel would confirm the age of the manaia that Roberto had brought all the way from Spain. He already knew, from the manaia's stylized carvings, the region that it had originally come from. All he needed now was a confirmation of its age.

Once the trio arrived at the apartment, Daniel helped the pair with their luggage. Inside he found a map of the city on a shelf in the living room. He opened it out onto the dining-room table and gave the pair a quick map tour of the immediate environs. They would be fine here for a day or so, he thought to himself. Then he would take them south out of the city. That journey would be to a place where Roberto would finally be able to touch the past. There, he would meet the descendants of the people who, many centuries earlier, had carved his manaia. So far, he had not mentioned the trip to the pair; he preferred to save that news until after he had examined the manaia in detail.

As excited as they were at being in a new land full of fresh experiences, it seemed on that first night they could do nothing else but sleep. Exhausted, the pair turned in early. The long journey had taken its toll. That night, Roberto dreamed that he was standing at the rim of a vast hole in the ground. Gazing down, he could just make out the tips of his shoes protruding ever so slightly across the edge of the rim. Into the abyss, his eyes were drawn, but he saw neither shape, nor even a single molecule of light. There was only blackness—nothing else. No sound or smell or feel, just the sheer weight of the abyss that seemed to be pulling him ever closer, right into its blackest of hearts.

It was just after ten-thirty the next morning when there was a knock on the apartment door. Daniel had already phoned ahead.

"Are you ready for some sightseeing?" he asked.

"We didn't come all this way to sit in an apartment," replied a beaming Maya. "Let's go."

Roberto was quiet, but smiled and nodded in agreement.

A quick glance told Daniel that his new Spanish friend looked unwell. He was even paler and more drawn in the face than he had been yesterday after such a long trip. Daniel knew that whatever ailed him was none of his business, and he took no more than a glance and left it at that.

It was a beautiful morning in the city as they left the apartment. Daniel had sketched up a rough itinerary that he shared with them as they climbed into his car.

"Whatever you think, Daniel—you're our guide," said Maya.

They weren't to be disappointed. The view from the observation deck of the Sky Tower on that crystal clear morning across the metropolis and the harbor was breathtaking. Neither Roberto nor Maya had ever been near an extinct volcano before. That morning, they stood on the rim of Mount Eden, and gazed down into its long-dormant crater bowl. They walked up Mount Hobson, once an ancient Maori fortress, and discovered parts of the old earthwork defenses. After lunch, they sauntered around the Viaduct precinct, taking in the sights and sounds of a people in love with the sea. Roberto also loved the sea, and it never went unnoticed by him that wherever you were in this city, you were always close to it. It reminded him of Barcelona. Both were maritime cities, one as old as the wind itself, the other as fresh as a newborn's first breath.

It was after five that evening when the trio finally made their way back to the apartment. Roberto had promised Daniel that when they returned, he would show him the journal and the amulet. Daniel was full of excitement when Roberto finally produced them both for his inspection. He was awestruck as he held the bone manaia in his hands. The scientist in him was now convinced of the age of the amulet. He could easily judge this from the patina of its smooth and yellowed surface. He could also reasonably assess the history of the piece from the stylized carvings and markings that decorated it. From this information, he knew that he was right in his initial assessment. It had come from the region of Tolaga Bay on the East Coast of New Zealand.

"Why does this thing interest you so much?" asked Roberto as he watched Daniel carefully examine the artifact.

"According to the recorded history of this country," he said, "the first Europeans to arrive here came in 1642. However, they left the country within days, and did not return. There are tribal histories that exist among Maori people that the first Europeans may well have arrived much earlier than 1642 and stayed longer than a few days. Maori along the eastern seaboard tell stories of Spaniards visiting their shores in the 1530s. But there is no real evidence to confirm this. To date, there are only unconfirmed finds and tribal stories."

"What do you mean when you say unconfirmed finds? Roberto asked.

"At the turn of the twentieth century, a piece of Spanish armor and several cannon balls dating from the 1500s were discovered in a southern port on the North Island. Then there was the skull of a forty-five year-old European woman found exposed in the bank of a river, and carbon-dated to the late 1500s. There has also been the discovery of what are said to be the remains of a caravel in the far north of the North Island. All of these have been discounted by so-called serious researchers. But for me, I prefer to keep my options open."

"So I guess now," suggested Roberto, "you think these things that have been in my family for generations have a good enough provenance to be accepted by the skeptics."

"You've got it," grinned Daniel. "According to accepted history, it wasn't until 1769 when the British arrived here that Europeans first set foot in this land. If I'm right, your family treasures are a serious challenge to that."

"But surely," asked Roberto, "if sailors from my country came here in the 1500s, they would have left more than just stories behind. Where is that evidence?"

"Now that's a tough one—no question. But there are some intriguing anomalies that make investigating history in this area very interesting. For instance, it's believed that red hair in Maori made its first appearance in the population in the 1500s. And there have always been questions about the construction of Maori food storehouses called *pataka*. Why do they so closely resemble the old Galician food storehouses, the *hórreo*? And of course, there are a number of Maori words that seem to have a Spanish origin. For example, Maori have two words for dog; one is *kuri*, and the other is *perro-perro*. The latter, you will no doubt recognize as being similar to your own Spanish word for the same animal."

"You raise some interesting points," interrupted Maya, "but as a scientist, you know that without attribution, none of it constitutes real evidence."

"Agreed, and that's why this manaia is so important. Along with the journal, which provides its provenance, it could be the catalyst for other scientists to take a new and more serious look at history before Captain Cook. At present, the popular history clock in this country seems frozen on the year 1769. Before that year, only myth and legend existed. That's not true, of course, but when you have a social and educational paradigm that tells you it is, it becomes hard to refute. Ask any white New Zealander who discovered this country, and many will mistakenly tell you that it was Captain Cook. Ask a Maori the same question, and he will tell you that it was Kupé. Almost eight hundred and fifty years separate those two men, and that, I'm afraid, is about the size of the gulf that needs bridging. As a people, we need to know and understand the collective history of this land as one long and continuous story, and not one that starts in 1769."

"I see," said Roberto. "So you're convinced that the country of Uawa mentioned in the journal is right here in New Zealand."

Daniel smiled. "There is no doubt of it. Uawa is the ancient name for Tolaga Bay, and tomorrow, the three of us will take this amulet of yours back to the place where it was carved five hundred years ago."

Early the next morning, the trio left the city and headed south along State Highway 1, eventually making their way out into the countryside. The first rays of sun illuminated the dew-laden, early-morning stillness. There had been a lot of rain last night, the first in many months. Wisps of light morning mist draped like translucent veils across yawning valleys. A fleeting rainbow glittered unexpectedly through the dewy mist, catching the eye as the car sped by. The low angle of the morning sun backlit the dew drops that hung on the fence wires framing paddocks of grazing cows. Each droplet sparkled like a diamond, millions shimmering in the wind.

Roberto marveled at the beauty of the country. Mile upon mile, in every direction spread the manicured land of an agricultural people. Small settlements dotted the landscape on the trip, occasionally warming travelers with coffee or a snack as they took pause along the way. Finally, after what seemed to be hours, they had arrived in the small settlement of Tolaga Bay.

For hundreds of years, people had lived on the fertile flats that surrounded the Uawa River as it snaked its way to the Pacific Ocean. There had been a village near the mouth of the river for as long as anyone could remember. Navigable by canoe, the Uawa River was used by early communities as a transport artery into the hinterland. Upon its gentle waters, food and trade goods were ferried inland from the Pacific Ocean, which lapped incessantly against the golden sands of the beautiful and sheltered bay. Since time began, the sweet waters of the Uawa had mingled into the brine of the bay, creating a rich microenvironment, where throughout the ages, the local inhabitants had drawn sustenance. This was their heartland. They knew that at this very spot, the Gods had brought the river, the forest, and the ocean together to form the cradle of their society.

Daniel pulled over to the curb, and while the vehicle idled he began rummaging in his jacket pocket.

"I've got an address here, somewhere," he muttered.

The evening before they left Auckland, he had made a phone call to Tolaga Bay. The old lady he'd spoken to was called Hinetitama. She was the senior village elder, and therefore, the single-most important person in the little community. Daniel knew that if he wanted to know anything about the history of the area, she was the one he first had to consult.

"Found it," he announced as he unfolded the slip of paper.

He studied it for a moment. "Good, not far now. Just a few minutes up the road on the right."

A moment later, they were back on the road, cruising slowly through the little village and across the bridge over the Uawa River. A short while later, they pulled up outside a rundown old house.

"This is it," said Daniel. "We're here."

Roberto and Maya looked out at the view through the car window. The overgrown hedge bordering the road in front of the house hadn't been cut in years. Flowers grew wild in the front yard between old and gnarly fruit trees, some bleached with age and others dressed with lichen beards, which fluttered in the gentle breeze.

The old homestead sat forlornly surveying the unkempt gardens that surrounded it. All had seen better days. Paint was peeling off the timber cladding, and in places, long, streaky rust marks stained the wall where the old, galvanized roof spouting had rotted through.

Daniel got out of the vehicle, "Come on," he said. "She'll be waiting for us."

As they followed the footpath toward the house, they could hear the pitiful voice of an old woman chanting. To Roberto, it sounded like a desperately sad flamenco canto, though he did not understand the language. The voice whimpered sadly at times, and then scaled high and quivered, almost chilling the air about him. He felt the hair on the back of his neck rise.

The wooden stairs that led up to the front door looked frail. Daniel glanced back and nodded a caution with his eyes. One at a time, they carefully ascended to the front door. Daniel was in front and knocked. The chanting from inside immediately ceased, and a moment later, the door swung open to reveal a skinny young girl no more than six or seven years old. Her brown urchin face was partly hidden by a wild mass of curly, chestnut-colored locks that dangled down to her shoulders.

"Yes?" she demanded, aiming her large brown eyes up at Daniel, then swiveling them to carefully scrutinize the pair who stood reticently behind him.

"I'm Daniel Potae, and my friends and I have come to see Hinetitama."

"Wait a minute." Without taking her eyes off the trio, the little girl yelled, "Nana, there's someone here to see you. He said his name is Daniel Potae."

"Show him in, girl," echoed a raspy old voice from within.

Roberto immediately recognized the voice as that of the eerie vocalist they had heard as they approached the house.

"Take your shoes off before you come in," ordered the little girl, pointing to their feet.

"It's the custom here," said Daniel, almost apologetically, as Roberto and Maya began removing their shoes. Daniel attempted to soften his young host with a smile, but her big eyes stared relentlessly, and her little face remained expressionless.

When she saw that all shoes had been removed, she turned and walked down the hallway, stopping for a moment and glancing back to make sure the trio was still with her. Then she stopped and pointed toward the living room. "She's in there."

It was a gloomy and cavernous space; unwashed, gray net-curtains drooped from the windows, across which hung half-drawn, sun-bleached drapes. Almost everywhere Roberto looked, he could see decades of old paraphernalia piled up and cluttered about in dusty and unorganized heaps. Through the gloom, he spotted a large bookshelf leaning against the far wall of the room; it seemed to groan under the weighty stack of books crammed into its shelves. *The inhabitant of this lair is a reader at least,* he thought to himself, as he ran his eye along the book spines that filled the shelves. History, geography, and esoteric—unusual, he thought.

Up on the ceiling, cobwebs stretched taut across the corners of the room. Several resident house spiders with long fine legs were suspended, waiting patiently near their gossamer flytraps. As he entered, Roberto felt nauseous. A claustrophobic quiver seized him, and he was forced to pause. He took in a deep breath to steady himself. His head felt light, and for a moment, he thought that he would faint, but the moment passed.

Maya noticed his instability and reached for his arm, but he managed a smile and nodded that he was all right. His eyes now searched the room, trying to make sense of the surroundings; a space full of lost memories and silent echoes trapped within its confines. There must have been light and happiness here once, in a place where now only gloom and sadness seemed to reside.

The plump figure of the old lady they called Hinetitama loomed ahead of the trio like a ghost seated on the sofa in the corner of the room. The only color on her was a patchwork blanket that covered her old legs; otherwise, she was dressed completely in black. Her wiry gray hair had been neatly contained by a black silk scarf that was tied beneath her chin. And although her face was wrinkled with age, her eyes took the three visitors by surprise. They sparkled brightly and brimmed with a cheeky and almost youthful vibrancy.

The old woman remained silent after Daniel finished the introductions. She had already thrown a welcoming glance and a smile to Maya. But all the while, she had been silently studying Roberto.

Soon he began to feel uncomfortable. *What's wrong with her?* he thought.

Finally, after what seemed to be an eternity, she spoke. "Why have you come here?" she asked. Her eyes were fixed firmly on Roberto.

Daniel went to say something, but Hinetitama held her hand up to stop him.

"I know why *you've* come," she said, fixing her eyes on Daniel for a moment. Then she turned back to Roberto. "But why have *you* come to see me?"

Right now he was out of his depth. Something unusual was happening, and whatever it was, he was ignorant of it. Why was this old woman eyeing him as though she were the Grand Inquisitor? It hardly seemed fair. After all, he had just traveled halfway round the world. Was he now to be interrogated by this old woman? He could have saved his money and gone to visit his grandmother instead. She would have done it for nothing.

It was then that Roberto heard the voice: "I am here to see you, old woman, and I bring home he who casts no shadow."

He turned in complete surprise and faced Daniel, who he thought had made the utterance. But Daniel stared back, completely dumbfounded. Maya, too, was wide-eyed in astonishment. The look on both their faces told Roberto that something was wrong—but what? Suddenly, he realized that they both thought it was he who had spoken to Hinetitama. However, he had no recollection of saying anything. What in God's name was happening to him?

The look on Roberto's face caught the old woman's eye. She smiled, "I see you now, young man. Don't worry. Come and sit here beside me." She gestured to him and patted the cushion beside her.

Daniel and Maya looked on in astonishment. Roberto smiled reluctantly as he approached Hinetitama and warily positioned himself on the couch beside her. The old woman smiled back at him and took his right hand in hers. She held it to her cheek, and he could feel her warm and soft wrinkled skin against his fingers. Suddenly, to his amazement, tears began to stream down her cheeks.

The old lady seemed to recognize him. Roberto knew, of course, that this was not possible. She was clearly confused, and perhaps even senile. Maybe she had become befuddled by the small group of strangers in her house. Whatever the case, he had never seen this old woman before, and he was absolutely certain that she had not seen him. She had obviously mistaken him for someone else. If only the light in here was better, perhaps her old eyes would see that he was not who she thought he was.

The young girl who had greeted them at the front door glared ferociously at him as she hurried over with a handkerchief for the old woman.

"Thank you dear," she said to the girl as she took the cloth and mopped her eyes.

"Are you alright?" asked Roberto as Hinetitama released his hand.

"Yes, thank you, boy—I'm alright now." She leaned back on the sofa and gently pulled at the blanket covering her legs. "By the way, this is my great-granddaughter, Kahu. Among other things, I am trying to teach her how not to grow old before her time, but she doesn't understand. Young people these days listen with their eyes and think only with their stomachs. I ask myself every day: 'What is this world coming to?'"

Roberto had no idea what she was talking about. After all, they were strangers. He couldn't possibly know.

"Not very talkative, are you?" the old woman said as she studied Roberto's bewildered expression.

"No."

Daniel had been quietly observing with interest what had happened between Hinetitama and Roberto. Carefully choosing his moment, he stepped forward with the amulet in his hand and held it out to the old woman.

"Roberto has brought this manaia all the way from Spain to show you. It has been in his family since the sixteenth century."

The old woman glanced at it lying in the palm of Daniel's hand. She dismissed it with her eyes and didn't even attempt to pick it up.

She turned to Roberto and smiled. The wrinkles on her old face seemed to glow softly as she spoke. "That trinket," she said, nodding toward Daniel's hand, "was your guide. It brought you here on the most important journey of your life. And now that it's done its job, it's nothing more than a piece of old bone. Let those anthropology types play with it to their hearts' content. It has no more value to you, my young friend."

Roberto was surprised at Hinetitama's response, but not as surprised as Daniel. The look on his face said it all. "What do you mean by that?" Daniel asked.

Maya looked askance at him, surprised by his tone.

"He has returned to us. I never thought I would live to see the day," the old woman's voice trembled as she spoke.

Roberto eyed Daniel closely, struggling to understand what was happening. He could see that the anthropologist was also confused.

"Tonight Roberto, you and I will sleep in the wharenui next door. Everything needs to be done properly from now on."

"What are you talking about?" interrupted Daniel. "What needs to be done properly?"

"Roberto doesn't know it yet, but he is on an important journey, and it is essential that we acknowledge this in the proper manner. We must honor it using the old ways."

"I don't understand," replied Daniel.

"And you may never," interrupted Hinetitama sharply. "But that doesn't matter. What matters is that this young man is living proof that there is more to life than we could ever understand in a hundred lifetimes. And tonight, he will stay with me in the Meeting House."

Daniel went to butt in, but Roberto beat him to it.

"It's alright, Daniel," he said. "I'm happy to do as she says."

Hinetitama turned to Maya. The old woman couldn't help but see the concern in her eyes. "It's alright, my dear. Your man is in good hands. Tonight he will sleep with the ancestors, and tomorrow, he will be yours once more. You can stay with my daughter tonight. She will be back soon. She will look after you at her place. It's not far away."

Maya's expression remained unchanged, and she looked to Roberto.

He smiled. "I'll be fine, Maya—don't you worry now."

"As for you," the old woman said, turning to Daniel, "Two doors up the road is my son. You can stay with him tonight."

"We didn't come here to impose on anyone. We can take care of ourselves," replied Daniel firmly.

"Now you listen to me," the old woman's voice was raised. "You're not going anywhere until I've quite finished with this young fella. It's all for his own good. Without my help, he doesn't stand a chance. So you might as well get used to the idea and make yourselves comfortable. You hear me?"

This wasn't at all what Daniel had planned when the trio had left Auckland all those hours ago. But the sheer determination in those old eyes told him that arguing with Hinetitama simply wasn't worth it. *Better* he thought, *to just give way to her.* After all, it was only for one night. Besides, though Roberto might not realize it now, he was lucky. Very few strangers would ever get the chance to spend the night in a wharenui, the most important house in the village. And even fewer would ever have the chance to spend any time with such an important elder as Hinetitama. Daniel couldn't really deny Roberto this privilege—not that he had any real choice in the matter. But he did wonder why the old woman had singled out the Spaniard and what she meant by saying that, without her help, he didn't stand a chance. It was a puzzle, and one that he had now become interested in. Daniel also knew that time spent with an important elder like Hinetitama was a learning experience reserved only for those worthy by virtue of noble birth or special deed. And so the time the old woman sought to spend with Roberto confused him. In the hours they would spend alone in the wharenui, the old woman would teach Roberto the secrets of her world, sacred knowledge meant only for those chosen by rank. There was something here that he clearly did not understand. For a woman such as Hinetitama to pass on knowledge was indeed an honor, for the very name *Hinetitama* was associated with the dawn. And it was always at the dawn where one found a beginning, new light, new life, and new knowledge. The old woman, a chieftainess in her own right, had been aptly named. For in this small community, she *was* the path to the light.

15

TOLAGA BAY FEBRUARY 2010

The late afternoon air hung warm and still over Tolaga Bay as Roberto and Maya sat in the sand, silently gazing out to sea. To the south of them lay the village's pier, stretching out like a long wooden finger into the rippling blue waters of the harbor. There were no boats tied up at the wharf, and none at anchor in the bay. The only sounds were those of the small waves rolling in along the sandy beach and the squawking gulls that cruised in the balmy air currents above.

Maya spoke first: "You must be a little nervous about spending the night cooped up with that old lady?"

"No," Roberto answered, "I'll be alright."

"I don't mind admitting," said Maya, "as an anthropologist, the whole thing fascinates me no end. But you have to agree, there are some rather creepy overtones to the whole thing. Why do you think she's doing this?"

"I've got no idea," shrugged Roberto. "Perhaps she's confused—I know *I* am. Anyway, don't worry about it—it's just for one night."

"I guess, by tomorrow, we'll know a little more," said Maya. "But I have to say, it's still creepy."

By now, the sun had started its descent into the west, and early twilight had begun to lie upon the land like a gossamer veil. Soon, the red evening glow settled like an endless craggy ribbon, draped roughly along the distant ridge tops that formed the westerly horizon. As the early evening chill crept down into the bay, the pair made their way back up toward Hinetitama's house.

Maya took Roberto by the hand as they crested the last rise of dunes, "You're cold," she said softly, as she rubbed his hand.

"I'll be fine," he said. "We'll be inside soon."

From the top of the dune, they could see Hinetitama's house a short distance away. As they walked along the track that led to it, they could see, in the dusky light, Daniel talking to someone in front of the old building.

"This is Hōne," said Daniel to the pair when they finally arrived. "He's Hinetitama's son."

Hōne grinned as he shook Roberto's hand and then kissed Maya on the cheek.

"Pleased to meet you, bro. Not every day we get foreigners down this way, aye."

"It's a very beautiful place," replied Roberto.

"The bro here," said Hōne gesturing with his eyes toward Daniel, "tells me you two are from Spain."

"I'm from Barcelona," nodded Roberto. "Maya is American."

Hōne smiled, "Some people along this coast will tell you stories of how Spaniards came here, hundreds of years ago. Yep! They sailed right into this little bay of ours, aye. Some of these people think they've even got Spanish genes. Can you believe that, bro?"

"Interesting," Roberto answered. "Maybe there's something to it. Perhaps one day DNA tests will show it to be true."

"But for now," Daniel replied, "Roberto's brought something with him from Spain that might prove those stories true."

"You don't say," Hōne answered as he eyed Daniel.

Turning to Roberto, he asked, "What proof you got there, bro?"

"I guess we shouldn't get ahead of ourselves here," Daniel said. "At the moment, it's all still up in the air."

"Yeah, right," Hōne grinned; his tone was skeptical. "Let's get inside, aye? See what the old girl's got planned. She said something about sleeping in the wharenui tonight. She's a handful that old *kuia*—full of ghosts, aye. It's a big job taking care of that one. Which one of you poor buggers is up for the treatment tonight?"

Daniel nodded to Roberto, "He is."

"What? You, bro?" coughed Hōne. "Shit," he muttered.

"That's what she wanted," Daniel said.

"C'mon, let's get inside, aye." Hōne nodded toward the house, and pointed the way to Roberto and Maya, who began down the path. As the pair walked away, Hōne turned to Daniel, looking slightly alarmed. "Is that a good idea, bro?" he whispered. "Letting the old girl scare the shit out of the Spaniard? You know he'll be on the first thing that moves out of here tomorrow."

"I don't know," shrugged Daniel. "It's up to him. He seems fine with it. I think he'll be alright."

"I hope you know what you're doing, bro," Hōne grunted, shaking his head. "Poor bastard's gonna leave here thinking we're a bunch of bloody nutcases."

It was almost pitch black outside when Hinetitama led Roberto to the old building everyone in the community knew as the wharenui. It was situated less than twenty meters from her house and had stood on that spot for more than a century. Before that, another wharenui had occupied the same piece of land for a hundred years prior. This had been the way of it, right back to the very dawn of the community. And when each wharenui, in its turn, became too old and run down to service the community's needs, what remained was carefully dismantled and solemnly buried. A funeral was held for the old building, just as a family might mourn the loss of a beloved member, for the Maori believed that these buildings were much more than mere timber structures—they were the spiritual embodiment of the tribe. They gave form to tribal history and life to the sacred genealogies, and within their power, they firmly anchored every member to their place in the clan. Thus, it was within the hallowed walls of the wharenui that all ceremonies and special gatherings were destined to take place. For it was in this environment that the breath of the past blew life into the yet-unborn future.

After removing her shoes at the front door of the Meeting House, Hinetitama indicated to Roberto to do the same. When he straightened up after he had finished, the old woman opened the door and bid him enter into the building's dark interior. "Come on, young fella—we haven't got all night. It's too cold out here for us oldies."

As he passed through the door, Roberto heard a match strike behind him. He turned to see Hinetitama lighting a candle. She handed it to him and proceeded to light another, which she had taken from the woven bag hanging by a strap slung over her shoulder.

As they entered the single, large, rectangular room, Roberto heard Hinetitama mutter something in her own language. He never understood what she said, but guessed that, since this was a special place for her, it was probably a prayer. He remembered back to when he was a boy; when he accompanied his grandmother to pray at the Catedral del Mar. They always crossed themselves when they entered, and he felt the urge to do the same now. Hinetitama closed the door to the wharenui behind them.

The interior of the building was spacious. The heavily decorated ceiling peaked in a central ridge high above their heads. It ran in a single spine the entire length of the building, just like the strong backbone of a man. The light from the two candles they held played out into the gloom that filled the space. At first, Roberto couldn't see much within the dimly lit room, but as his eyes became accustomed to the soft, flickering light, his blood chilled. To his astonishment, the walls surrounding him seemed to writhe with grotesque figures as the soft golden light played across the heavily carved facades. Terrifying, luminous eyes bore down upon him like spotlights reaching out from the spiritual world. At another glance, he could see fierce, gaping mouths with great protruding tongues quivering as the weak light floated in and out of the shadowy recesses. All he could do was hold his breath, for at that very moment, none of it made any sense to him, and he doubted that it ever would.

Suddenly he gasped, and his whole body jolted with fright. Someone had nudged him from behind.

"Come on," Hinetitama muttered. "They won't bite you. Nothing in here will harm you." She seemed annoyed at his hesitancy and began ushering him toward the rear of the room, where he could now see two mattresses stretched out on the floor. A pile of pillows sat against the wall at the head of each mattress, and a stack of blankets had been neatly folded at their feet.

"Sit down," she mumbled, pointing to one of the mattresses. She placed the candle she was holding upright onto the floor and put the woven flax bag she was carrying beside it. Then, with a great sigh, she bent her old frame further and eased herself down onto the other mattress. Stretching out, she dragged several pillows from the pile toward her and rested herself against them. Her elbow dug deep into the padding as she rested her chin in her right hand. Taking a deep breath, she lifted and curled her legs up off the floor and onto the mattress. Meanwhile,

Roberto had made himself comfortable on his. He kept a watchful eye on the old lady, who groaned and puffed as she sought to make herself comfortable.

"Why are you here?" she asked, still puffing from her exertions.

Roberto was puzzled by the question. They had already discussed that one earlier in the day.

"Don't answer that," she finally said. "I'll tell you why you're here. But if I'm wrong, we'll be in big trouble."

"What trouble?" Roberto asked.

"Don't worry about that now. You just listen to what I have to tell you, and then maybe we'll discuss the trouble bit later."

"Tell me Roberto—are you aware that you have a spirit following you?"

"A dog," replied Roberto. "It has white fur and red eyes. It's been following me ever since my father died."

"It's good that you know he's there," nodded the old woman, a sly smile adding more creases to her already wrinkly features. "I am right—you are the one."

"What do you mean?"

"I mean," she answered frankly, "that I'd be wasting my time talking to anyone else. That's why you've come to see me."

The look in the old woman's eyes frightened him a little. He had no idea what she was talking about or why she had singled him out. Only she knew that.

"The white dog that follows you is what we Maori call a *kaitiaki*. In your country, you'd probably call him a guardian angel. He originally came from this place, and is with you because a part of you came from here too. Centuries ago, an ancestress of yours once lived in this land, and that dog belonged to her. The reason the white dog now follows you is because something in the spirit world is trying to harm you. That small creature has been sent by your ancestors to watch over you and do whatever it can to protect you."

"I already know of that woman…and of her dog. Does that surprise you?" asked Roberto.

"No," she said. "All these things are revealed in their own good time, and for reasons that may not be immediately apparent. It's no surprise to me. Sooner or later your ancestors would have wanted you to know about something as important as that."

Roberto had earlier felt reluctant to enter this old building. The very thought of it had left him feeling uneasy. But hearing the old woman's words tonight somehow seemed to calm him.

"You've done the right thing by coming to me," she smiled. "I know the history of the little beast that follows you, and that makes me the only one here who can help you."

"And how will you do that?" asked Roberto.

"Don't worry about that at the moment, young man. We'll get to that in good time."

She could see the questions looming in his eyes. Whether he understood what she was saying or not was immaterial to her at that moment. She knew, though, that he would eventually understand everything. He had to—there was no other way for him.

"Look around you and tell me what you see?"

Roberto peered out into the large room. The shadows from the carvings that adorned the walls swayed in the flickering candlelight. The room was devoid of furniture, not even a chair or a shelf or even a stool could be seen. But it wasn't empty. The ghosts of long ago were present, filling the room with the smothering weight of the past—unseen yet overpoweringly at hand. History oozed from every niche, every breath was filled with its odor, and every caress was chilled by its touch. And Roberto could feel it all.

"I see a room full of the past…" he answered hesitantly, "but the future lives here also."

The old woman smiled. She had heard what she was waiting for. "You needn't be afraid," she said. "It is in here that your learning will begin. Your spirit may now be Spanish, but when your learning is complete, you will no longer be bound by borders. That is the only way you will ever become true to who you are. You will be like this candle. See how it fights back the darkness and struggles to illuminate this large room? Imagine if we had a hundred or even a thousand such candles in here, how much better this room would be lit. It is the same in life. This world is full of darkness in need of light."

"But why should you care?" Roberto asked. The old lady was beginning to sound like a preacher.

"Why do you not care?" she countered. "In the end, not caring is the only thing that will finish us all. So let's ask the question again—why have you come here? It is because I am your candle, and because I care. And when you leave, it will be me who has struck the match that ignited the fire within you. In this world, we are all candles in search of a light. I am giving you my light."

"I know nothing of your culture. What good would I be?" Roberto attempted to finish, but Hinetitama held up her hand and shook her head.

"You don't need to know anything of my culture. It's true that tonight I am your teacher, but you haven't come here to learn our tribal ways. When you are seeking freedom, why would you step from one confined space into another? No Roberto, me and my culture, such as it is, are only the lens through which you will see your pathway. What you make of it after that is up to you. I will have done my bit."

"I don't understand," he said, there was a little frustration in his voice.

"Listen to me—when Aristotle explained the laws of nature to the ancient Greeks, he told them that if a stone and a pea were dropped at the same time from a tower, the stone would hit the ground first because it was heavier. This was the divine law of nature, he said, and everyone who heard it simply accepted it without question. It took almost two thousand years before a man called Galileo actually climbed a tower and dropped the stone and the pea. To his astonishment, they both hit the ground together. This discovery turned out to be important, and it was only forty years after Galileo's death that Isaac Newton came up with his universal law of gravity—a law that, as we know now, is at the very heart of the universe itself.

"What I'm saying here is simple: don't get caught up in other people's beliefs just as the ancient Greeks did. By doing that, you will only ever know as much as they know—and nothing more. You must be like Galileo and Newton, free thinking enough to find your own answers."

Roberto eyed the old woman for a moment, and then nodded. He let his eyes drift into the dim candlelit surroundings. Hinetitama was unlike anyone he had ever known. She seemed so full of wisdom that at times she looked as if she might burst. Part of him was flattered that a person such as she would take the time to spend with him. Another part, however, was concerned. What was he doing here? And what did it all mean?

At that moment, in his head, Roberto heard the echo of a voice not unfamiliar to him *"You have a journey ahead of you, make the most of it for your salvation may well be in it."*

He had come on a journey alright—half way round the world. Was this the journey that D'Anjou had spoken of at Cafeteria Nudivel?

"Do you like stories?" asked Hinetitama, her broad face lit with a smile.

"Only if they have happy endings," he joked.

"Oh this one will end happily; I'm absolutely sure of it," she answered. Her smile had dissipated, and for a moment her dark eyes studied Roberto's expression. Then she leaned back against a pile of pillows in an attempt to make herself more comfortable. "In olden times," she began, as she boxed the top pillow into shape to better support her, "my people had no form of writing. This meant that all tribal history, knowledge, and genealogy had to be passed down orally through generation after generation. The same process applied to our spiritual practices: all passed down in the same way, by word of mouth and by application. In order to make certain the oral transmission of information was accurate, only special people were selected to learn and retain this knowledge. To ensure a smooth transition from one person to another, the elder who held the knowledge would begin training his successor from a very young age, just as it had been for him. This process went on for a very long time. Then Europeans came, and with them, they brought writing. From then on everything changed. And now it is our turn—all of those histories and genealogies have now passed to us. Those who understand them—and there aren't many of us left—know their value. People who do not understand them refer to them simply as myths and legends. It is from this history that I know of your ancestress and of the white dog that was last seen swimming out to sea after a departing foreign ship. The people of those times knew that dog well, and when they saw it in the harbor swimming after the vessel, they were in no doubt that its mistress was aboard. Her name was *Aramoana—the path to the ocean*. The people of that time believed that the bearer of such a name was important. She was forever connected to the twilight world of spirits that existed between the realm of the land and that of the sea. The name, they believed, had given your ancestress special powers."

"And did it?" he asked, enthralled by the tale.

"Oh yes. For centuries after the dog was last seen, nothing more was heard from her or the animal. But the legend continued right to this day. It spoke of the woman called Aramoana and how she and her dog would one day return. And now it is true, for you have arrived, her descendant—and you bring with you the white dog. I am the only one left who can put the pieces of this puzzle together. All the others have gone."

"So that's how you knew me, even before Daniel had introduced us this afternoon," said Roberto.

"As soon as I saw that dog I knew who you were," replied Hinetitama. "It is truly amazing what has happened here. To think that five hundred years have passed between you and this place, and yet half a world away, just a few days ago, you decided to come and see me. How did that happen?"

"Maya made it happen. And now when I think back, it is incredible just how determined she was. Perhaps she has been looking out for me all along," he said.

"Oh I know she's looking out for you, boy, because by bringing you here, she has saved your life," smiled Hinetitama. "Do you believe that, Roberto?"

"Yes," he said quietly. "I believe that now."

"Good," she grinned, "We'll discuss that later. But first I'm going to give you some advice. You can see that I am an old woman, but one who still remembers the old ways. There are very few of us left now. Science and religion have smothered the old traditions and have changed the way people think in every corner of the world. It is only in people like us, who have been forgotten or overlooked, where the old beliefs still reside. We are much closer to mother earth than those who have been touched by modern science or religion. We feel our mother's pain for it is our pain too. We cry when she cries, for her tears are for us. And we will die when she dies for it is she who is our mother. You must remember this Roberto. Science and religion are fine for those among us who need crutches in their life. But to really understand the truth of who you are, you must walk without such aids. Listen to our mother, because I know her voice echoes within you. It is certain my boy that with her guidance you will leave this life far richer than when you arrived."

Hinetitama groaned as she stretched her old body out changing her position on the mattress. For a moment Roberto closed his eyes and took a deep breath. The very air in this sacred space seemed to vibrate with an essence that soothed even a Spaniard, unfamiliar as he was to this place and from half a world away.

"We need to sleep now," Hinetitama said breaking the silence. "We must get up early tomorrow morning, before the sun comes up. There is something important we must do."

"Can I ask what it is?" Roberto inquired.

"You can," replied the old woman. "But I'm not telling you. Life is full of surprises. Learn to enjoy them when they happen. Now get some sleep, and don't snore. As you can see, I need my beauty sleep." She wriggled her old frame beneath the pile of blankets, which she had now managed to pull up over herself.

"You're younger than me boy, you can blow those candles out before you shut your eyes. We don't want to cook ourselves in this old *whare* to-night."

16

TOLAGA BAY, THE EARLY MORNING RITUAL

The old woman shook Roberto.

He woke with a start, "Wha…what the…"

"Come on, young fella, get up. We've got work to do."

He had forgotten where he was, and it took him a moment to recognize Hinetitama as she stood over him.

"Well—come on. The sun will beat us up if we don't get a move on."

The old woman led Roberto outside into the damp predawn air. A cold salty breeze swept in off the sea, and he could hear the waves rolling along the length of the beach in the distance. The pair carefully picked their way down the trail into the darkness toward the sound of the waves. Soon they had crested a small rise from which they could look down into the dark toward the beach. A cold wind blew into their faces and a light mist from the breaking waves moistened their cheeks. From here Roberto could see the horizon across the ocean far off in the distance. Its long thin horizontal thread seemed to divide the dawn. The murky darkness of the ocean lay below the line and a rising red trace in the early morning sky floated above it.

"This will do," croaked Hinetitama in the biting wind. "We'll wait here." From her shoulder hung the woven flax bag she had taken into the wharenui the evening before. She bent over and placed it onto the ground beside her.

As she did, Roberto noticed that she took something from it, but he could not see what it was; she had concealed the item in her hand.

"It's beautiful out here in the early morning," she murmured. "This is the time when I feel closest to my ancestors. They knew this place as Uawa. The land and the sea here sustained them for generations. But that's all gone now. We're different people now—everything has changed."

Suddenly the horizon was pierced by the first sliver of golden light. It sprayed upward like shards of gold exploding out from the sun disk as it glinted just above the horizon.

Hinetitama raised her hands, and to Roberto she smiled, "We have work to do young man."

She moved forward a few steps, held both her hands high in adoration of the rising sun and began chanting in her own language. It was now that Roberto noticed that in her right hand, she held an egg. It was this that she had removed from the bag that now sat beside her. Her voice was strong, and it boomed into the cold morning air. Its purity seemed to stir even the nearby trees, whose leaves appeared to shudder in awe.

Roberto did not understand a single word. But he could tell from her voice, resonating from deep within her old frame that her words echoed out into the universe of her Gods. As he watched, the old woman trembled in the cold morning air and tears, reflecting like drops of pure gold, began to trickle upon her cheeks. Sunlight streamed forth more strongly now forcing the surrounding darkness even further into retreat. And as Roberto listened to the old woman he was deeply moved. For he sensed with each word that left Hinetitama's lips, so went a precious fragment of the old woman's soul. And so it was that her Gods were honored at the break of dawn on a cold seaside morning with a prayer of rebirth.

Oh Great Father Pi-Ra! Oh Great Mother Isis!
Hear the prayer of an old woman.
It is I, the Dawn, who calls to you.
Oh Father—he who is born at first light to die at dusk,
Give warmth to this old body.
Great Mother it is Hinetitama, who calls your name.
Hear me now, you ancestors of eternity.
Look to the one, who stands before you, for he is yours.
Hear this prayer from she who knows, Oh eternal ones,
For none other would pass this way but me.

It is I who brought him here, for his days have all but gone,
Grant me a prayer Oh Father who sits newborn upon the horizon,
And in return a gift I make—of my years for his.
His energy will be your energy.
His light will be your light.
His spirit will be your spirit.
Let this be so that I may join my ancestors and live among them into eternity.

Roberto could feel the warmth of the sun upon his face as it revealed more of itself above the line of the ocean horizon. Hinetitama had now finished her prayer. She bent her old frame toward the ground, and with her left hand, scooped up a handful of soil. She straightened up, turned to Roberto, and began carefully rubbing the soil onto his cheeks. It was still damp with the early morning dew and the scent of mother earth filled his nostrils. Then, just as the golden disc of the sun sat full upon the line of the horizon, she offered Roberto the egg.

"Take this," she said. "I want you to carefully break the shell and swallow the raw egg inside."

Roberto looked at her in astonishment.

"Hurry up boy. We haven't got all day."

Before he knew it, the raw egg was in his mouth. It was cold and slimy, and a little of it dribbled from between his tightly pursed lips as he tried desperately to hold it in. He clenched his teeth and grimaced as the thick salty slime swirled about in his mouth. He knew he needed to swallow it quickly before he gave way to the singular urge to vomit it out. He closed his eyes and forced it down his throat. He shivered and immediately began to gag. But in that moment he could feel the old woman's eyes hard upon him and he knew that he must not disappoint her.

"Now you must remove all of your clothing," she said to him.

"What…"

"Take off your clothing Roberto—all of it, even your shoes." She was insistent.

"But why…" he asked.

"Because your new life begins at this moment, and it is here that you must leave the old one." She bent and took a white linen cloth from her bag and held it out to him. "Remove everything and wrap yourself in this. And please hurry, for our time here is fast running out."

He did as she asked, and within minutes he stood naked before the rising sun. His body was shaking as he unfurled the linen that Hinetitama had given him. He wrapped it around his shoulders and pulled it tightly around his waist to cover his nakedness.

Tears began to fill the old woman's eyes: by the golden light of the newborn sun, wrapped in nothing but pure white linen, Roberto had now become transformed—a holy and most beautiful transformation, wrapped in the pure, white spiritual armor of light.

"You have done well, my boy," she said as she wiped the tears from her eyes. She took a small bottle from her coat pocket and poured a little of the liquid it contained into her cupped left hand. She dabbed the fingers of her right hand into the tiny pool and raised them toward Roberto. She leaned forward and traced a circle upon his forehead. "With this sacred water I draw the sign of the sun disk upon you," she said solemnly. "It is the sign of Pi-Ra, and from now on, it will be your sign too."

By now the temperature of the early morning air had dropped, and Hinetitama could see that Roberto was shivering.

"Go back to the wharenui, you will find a change of clothes there. Put them on and wait for me."

He stared at her for a moment, and then looked down at his clothes in a pile on the ground.

"What about my shoes? Can I at least wear them back to the house?" he asked.

"No," she said. "What you see in front of you is now dead. I will weep for it and bury it when you are gone."

"But…"

She held her hand up to silence him.

"Please, you must go," she continued. "What I have to do now is between me and Him," she said, pointing to the sun that sat in the sky just above the horizon.

As she spoke, Roberto could see a beautiful soft glow within her eyes, and he knew that it emanated from somewhere deep within her. To him she looked just like an angel, and there was no choice now but to obey her. He smiled and turned to walk back to the house where he and the old lady had spent the night. The cold breeze blowing in off the sea had an edge to it and cut through the linen that wrapped him. His body shivered in the chilly air as he walked back up the gentle incline. As he made his way along the path an eerie feeling began to rise within him. In the distance he could hear the old woman speaking in her own language. And as he neared the entrance to the wharenui he heard an owl call from a tree near to where Hinetitama was standing.

He turned to look just in time to see her begin chanting to the bird. It called to her again, and she began to wail as though she mourned for a loved one. Roberto did not know whether the goose bumps on his arms were a reaction due to the cold, or to what he could see unfolding before his eyes.

He was still shivering as he made it back into the Meeting House—it was cold in there too. Neatly folded upon the mattress on which he had spent the night, he found a complete change of clothing. Beside the mattress on the floor was a new pair of shoes. By now he was too cold and confused to question anything. He got dressed and climbed back into bed to warm up. Pulling the blankets tightly around him and closing his eyes, he hoped that Hinetitama would return soon.

A strange silence began to settle into the large room. Suddenly, a tall man dressed entirely in black came through the door. His long shadow reached into the room silhouetted against the golden carpet of light laid down by the dawn glow now streaming through the door. The light behind him was bright but Roberto could still make out his form as he walked slowly toward him. In no time at all the stranger was standing over him. Roberto could see that he was an albino. His face was pale, his eyes were red, and several noticeable old scars ran across the right side of his face. Despite his appearance, the man was calm and seemed nonthreatening. He slid his right hand inside his coat and drew out an exquisitely decorated golden dagger. Roberto was dazzled by the beautiful weapon. The scabbard and hilt of the dagger were richly ornamented with rubies, diamonds, and emeralds, all sparkling in the glow of the morning light. The mysterious man then knelt and offered the beautiful weapon to Roberto. For an instant their eyes met, Roberto felt uneasy at accepting the gift and shook his head. The man again offered it, this time motioning with his eyes for Roberto to take it. He was nervous and a cold chill ran through him, but this time he reached out for the weapon. The man leaned forward and with a smile he placed the dagger into Roberto's hand. His task now done the mysterious man stood up.

He walked toward the door and disappeared into the golden glow of the early morning light. The next thing Roberto remembered was a rough hand shaking him.

"Wake up boy! It's time for breakfast."

Looking up he saw Hinetitama grinning down at him. He realized that he must have dozed off.

"Come on young fella, I'm starving—let's have something to eat," she said. "I promise this time, the eggs will be cooked." She chuckled at her own attempt at humor, but Roberto was still thinking of the strange man dressed in black. The early morning dream had left him shaken. He could tell that something wasn't right.

It was only a short walk from the Meeting House to another building where breakfast was being prepared. The only guests this morning were to be him and Hinetitama. The dining room was warm and smelt of bacon and toast as they came in through the door. A table for two had been set in one corner of the dining room and two young women were busy in the kitchen.

"Thank you girls," called Hinetitama as she and Roberto made their way to the table. "Two cups of tea, and make them hot. You do drink tea, don't you boy?"

"Do you have coffee?" he asked.

"Yes," a voice from the kitchen echoed.

"Make one a coffee," yelled Hinetitama.

The old woman pulled a chair from the table and sat down. Roberto did the same.

"Now young man, I expect you're full of questions this morning." She shot him a wily old smile.

"I have a few," he said.

"Good," she answered. "I always say, never trust anyone who doesn't ask questions. Remember that, it's a good piece of advice. But you know something, I don't have all the answers."

Roberto eyed her carefully, unsure of whether the old woman was joking with him. There was only one way to find out, and that was to ask.

"What was all that about this morning?"

"I can explain it to you—but only a part of it. The rest will be revealed to you in the fullness of time."

"I guess that's better than nothing," he shrugged.

"The thread of life for every soul upon this earth has been laid out by the hand of the Creator. No matter who you think your creator to be, all has been preordained. We call this the fate of the living. This morning, I asked that your fate be changed—and it was. Your old spiritual self with all of its problems has now been cast aside, and a new spiritual self was born to you. Whatever ailed you in the past has now gone. The illness that you carried here with you has gone. Now you will not die a young man, as you would have had you not come to me. Do you believe that?"

Without even thinking he answered, "Yes…I believe it."

Hinetitama could see the light in his eyes, and she was pleased with herself for saving him. "Good," she smiled. "Like I said before, you were right to come to me, for I am the only one who could have helped you in this way."

"Why are you the only one?"

"I am the only one who is prepared to sacrifice that which must be given. Don't doubt that you have been done a great honor today, and equally a great price will need to be paid for it."

"What price?" asked Roberto.

"Since it was I who asked for the honor to be granted and not you, the price that is due is mine to pay and not yours. Do not concern yourself with it."

"I'm not sure I follow what you're saying," he said.

"I can't tell you anymore, except this: Something will also be expected of you. I will tell you what that is a little later."

"Okay—now I'm confused," he said looking at her nervously.

"Don't worry," she smiled. "As the old song goes—what will be, will be. But remember this—I'll be with you."

Just then, one of the young women in the kitchen brought out the hot drinks. She placed one in front of the old woman.

"Thank you, dear," Hinetitama smiled. She took a sip of her tea. "Today, Roberto," she announced as she placed the cup back onto the table, "there is something very special we must do. To the north of here is a place called Te Araroa. We will travel there. In that place, there is an ancient tree. We will pay her a visit."

"What's so special about this tree?" Roberto asked.

"It's old…" she grinned, "…just like me and that's all you're going to get out of me for the time being."

"I can't wait," said Roberto as he stifled back a yawn with his hand across his mouth.

"You'd better be tired boy if you're gonna yawn like that around me. I'd hate to think that I was boring you…" Hinetitama leveled her eyes at him.

The two young women in the kitchen heard the tone in her voice and immediately stopped what they were doing. Their serious faces peered through the servery hatch at the wide-eyed Spaniard.

"I didn't sleep very well last night," he stammered, "and having to get up early this morning…"

"Okay, I've got the picture," Hinetitama said. A smile cracked across her face. "It's settled then, we'll head up to Te Araroa this morning." She giggled like a young girl as she picked up her cup of tea. "As for me," she announced, "I slept like a baby."

Roberto laughed out loud, partly out of relief, but mostly due to Hinetitama's mercurial personality. At times it was like dealing with fire and ice in the same moment. You never knew whether you would be burnt or frozen in any encounter. And that's obviously what had kept her family and the people in this village on their toes whenever they were around her.

"Come on girls, where's that breakfast?" called Hinetitama looking to the kitchen. "This young fella needs fattening up. And don't think I can't see you making eyes at him. You should know he's already taken, and she's waiting at my house. She'll sort you two buggers out. Don't you worry about that!"

It was a large breakfast, something Roberto wasn't used to. But it had been a chilly and early morning start for him so the hot food was welcome. After they had eaten, Hinetitama and Roberto made their way back to the old woman's house. There they found Hinetitama's daughter, Riria, along with Maya awaiting their return. Not long after, Hōne and Daniel joined them.

"Hōne, you can take Roberto and me up to Te Araroa today," ordered Hinetitama.

"But Ma, I'm going fishing with the boys today," he said.

"Forget those bludgers. You're helping your mother today. Now get going, fill the car up. I want to get on the road as soon as possible."

"Ma, what about him?" Hōne said, pointing to Daniel. "Why can't he take you?"

"Because I want you to take us—now get going. I'm not so old that I still can't clip you round the ears boy. Now hurry up."

"God sake!" grumbled Hōne as he turned and stomped out.

"And don't blaspheme," Hinetitama yelled after him. "You need all the help you can get in this life boy."

"I'd be happy to take you up to Te Araroa," interrupted Daniel.

"Hōne might look stupid," replied the old woman, "but he's the only one I'll trust my life to on the road. You could be blind in one eye and short sighted in the other for all I know. Hōne will take us. Don't worry; he's got one of those big four-wheel drive things. We'll all fit."

Forty minutes later, they were on the road out of Tolaga Bay heading north to Te Araroa. For centuries, Maori had lived in this remote and beautiful land. In ancient times, villages nestled into the fertile valleys and spread out across the rich, alluvial plains that rolled out toward the Pacific Ocean. This was a place of abundance, and the people felt safe living in the shadow of the towering fortress they called *Whetu-matarau*. This formidable stronghold kept vigil over the entire area.

The ancient name for this region was *Kawakawa-maitawhiti*, which in English meant Kawakawa brought from a far off place. But with the passage of time came a change of name—the modern seaside settlement is now known as Te Araroa. Only the cove with its beautiful sparkling waters hearkens to the ancient past, for it is still known as Kawakawa Bay.

This was a remote place, beautiful to the eye, peaceful to the mind yet resounding with the echoes of the past. Great personages in Maori history had left their mark here, both on the land and in the people. It was said of the great chief *Pawa* that his voice can still be heard resonating from the nearby cliffs. The people in this area would tell you the most famous warrior in their history, *Tuwhakairiora*, had imparted his genes into the genealogies of the people along this entire coast. And it was also in Te Araroa, where the ancient Pohutukawa tree known as *Te Waha-o-Rerekohu*—the mouth of Rerekohu—was to be found. It had stood in that place for hundreds of years. Its name derived from the food storehouse built by the great chief *Te Rerekohu*, which had stood nearby in olden times. The tree had always been considered sacred by the locals, and as such, dominated the surroundings—both physically and spiritually.

And so it was that on this day, after having traveled half way round the world, Roberto was to stand at the base of this sacred giant. Hinetitama hadn't yet shared her reason for bringing him here—but she would, and it would change his life.

Finally with a stony skid, the vehicle rolled to a halt. Hōne had stopped the car partway up onto the grass verge. Out in front of them, about fifty meters away, stood the giant Pohutukawa tree. As the small party clambered from the vehicle, the sight of the sacred colossus towering ahead silenced them.

For centuries Pohutukawa such as Te Waha-o-Rerekohu had formed an important link in Maori cosmology and helped the people to interpret the world they inhabited. To them, the awesome trees became spiritual bridges, linking one world with another. Reaching out as they did from the cliffs to the ocean, they were seen to span the gap between the land and the sea. Stretching their thick sinewy limbs across the divide between the living world and the spiritual world, reaching out like a parting lover to the one who has departed. Within these great sinewy limbs and powerful trunks, references to the energy and vibrancy of the people of the land were evident.

Hinetitama watched Roberto carefully as his eyes silently took in the great arboreal mass towering above them.

"Her name is Te Waha-o-Rerekohu," she smiled. "What do you think of her?"

"She is spectacular," he said.

"This old tree has been here for twenty generations, and with our love she will be here for twenty more." The old woman could not hide the adoration in her eyes. "She has become a symbol to us of the meaning of time, but perhaps not in the way you might think. You see in our world, we do not measure the actual passing of time; only that it has past."

Roberto was puzzled. "How does that work?" he asked.

"Can you touch or taste time? No—in fact there is no natural sensation of time anywhere. And so, for a people such as us, the truth has always been simple and real. We know our past, but never our future. Therefore our destiny is to be always trapped between the two. We are a people who walk backward into the future; we know where we came from, but not where we journey to."

"I see," he said as his eyes met the old woman's.

"The past," continued Hinetitama "is something that I share with all those who have gone before me right back to the beginning of time. But the future Roberto—the future is mine alone."

"I've never thought of it like that before…"

"Well you should," she answered. "Get that brain of yours out of its box, start using it. You'll be amazed at what you discover."

Roberto looked at her unsure of how to respond, but she saved him the effort.

"I've got something else you can think about. Do you know what the word *antipodes* means?"

"It means the exact spot on the other side of the earth to something that is on this side."

"Good," she smiled slyly. "Now if my knowledge of history serves me well, it was an ancient countryman of yours—Isidore of Sevilla, who, around 600 AD, was the first to mention the antipodeans. He was talking about us, the people who live on the other side of the world."

"I'm not sure…" said Roberto.

"I am," replied Hinetitama. "The books in my house are not there just to catch dust. That old man, Isidore, must have known something back then, because as it turns out where we stand now, I bet someone is also standing on the exact antipodean spot in Spain. You see, this country is the antipodes of yours. It's amazing, really, when you realize that more than seventy percent of the earth's surface is water, and less than four percent of the land surface is actually antipodal."

"I didn't know that," replied Roberto.

"Of course you didn't." There was a playful tone in the old woman's voice. "Who else but a crazy old woman like me with nothing else to do would know such meaningless things?"

Roberto looked at her for a moment.

"Alright my young friend," she smiled, "I think it's time you introduced yourself to Te Waha-o-Rerekohu."

"What do you mean?" Roberto asked.

"Go up to her and put your palms against her trunk."

"But…"

"Just do as I say boy, she'll know you're there and why you've come to see her. Let her warmth fill you. And when you've finished, take a handful of soil from the ground at her base."

"Why *have* I come to see her?"

"Listen, we'll get to that later. Now go to her…"

"And the soil, what will I do with that?"

"Bring it back to me of course. Now go…go to her…she is waiting for you…"

At first Roberto was reticent, but the old woman nodded again toward the tree, and then watched as he walked to the Pohutukawa and did what she had told him to do.

When he returned, she was smiling, and held something in her hand.

"Put some of that soil into this," she said, handing him an envelope. "Now, in your country, do you know where the town of A Coruña is?"

"It's a city in the north of Spain."

"Good, I want you to promise me something."

"What is it?"

"Promise me that you will take the soil in this envelope to A Coruña. There you will find another ancient Pohutukawa tree. She is as old as Te Waha-o-Rerekohu. I want you to sprinkle the soil at her base."

"How is it possible that an old Pohutukawa grows in A Coruña?" he asked.

"I will tell you, but first you must promise to do this for me."

"But…I don't even know why," he said.

"Just promise me, and you will find out."

"I promise…" he said, finally giving in to her insistent stare.

"Good—it's settled then. Now as far as the Pohutukawa tree in A Coruña is concerned, it was taken from here a very long time ago. It is not important to us how that happened, only that it did. What is important is that you sprinkle that soil at her feet. From that small act, she will know that a memory—a spiritual echo of her—still lives within the bosom of her homeland. As it was for you with echoes of your line having survived for centuries in ours and through the words of ancient mariners, echoes of our lines lingered in yours. That probably sounds romantic to you, but I can assure you it's not good to have all those unresolved memories just lying about. The circle of life that they are a part of must be closed. If it isn't, those unresolved memories are destined to languish forever, caught between worlds, and haunted by the souls trapped within them. By coming to this country and to me, Roberto, you have carried out an important act—that of completing the circle of life of which your past is a part. By doing that, you have freed all those poor souls trapped within it. Just you being here among us was enough to close that circle forever. But in doing so, another circle has been uncovered, and therefore, an obligation has now arisen."

"What obligation? I don't understand."

"Life is full of incomplete circles, my young friend, and it is people like me who are obliged, when they are discovered, to close them. It doesn't matter how much time has elapsed or how far we have to travel—we must close them, and free those poor souls trapped within them. The soil you take to that old tree in A Coruña will close that circle and bring peace to those poor ghosts who cry out to be free. On this particular occasion, you will be my messenger, and in that envelope of soil that you carry, is my message. You will do this, Roberto, because it is an act of spiritual thanks for what I have done for you. Do you understand now?"

"I understand that, but the bit about the circles…"

"You don't need to understand that part—just know that they exist," replied Hinetitama. "It takes great courage to think outside the confines of what we have been taught. Remember the story I told you about Isaac Newton. He is remembered by us today as being a great scientist, so great in fact, that we know him as Sir Isaac Newton. What has been forgotten is that he was also a renowned occultist and an alchemist who spent many years searching for the fabled Philosopher's Stone. You might think that it was silly on his part to even think that such a stone ever existed, but the British government didn't. They were so afraid that he would find it, they actually banned his research. They believed that the discovery of such a stone would completely undermine the value of gold. But what really made Isaac Newton the great man that we know him to be wasn't his science or his discoveries. It was the simple fact that he always kept an open mind, for without it, I feel sure that he would have remained in obscurity. There have been many others like him, both before his time and after. The single contributing factor to their greatness was that they always kept their minds open to all possibilities. Even to possibilities that directly challenged the very core of their own personal beliefs, or worse, even when they challenged the established belief system. Like Galileo for example, another great man. He was shut down by the Inquisition, which even went so far as to threaten his life. So you see, it takes real courage to keep an open mind. And from what I see, there's not a lot of that about in the world these days."

Roberto smiled as he nodded in agreement. His eyes were once more drawn to the spectacular tree in front of him. As he gazed upon it he could feel its ancient energy drawing him to it like a magnet.

"Well I think we're done here," said Hinetitama finally. "Let's get back to Tolaga Bay. I'm finished with you now. You can spend the rest of your time relaxing on the beach with that beautiful girlfriend of yours. Then you can go back to where you came from."

Roberto was silent. He was surprised at how dismissive of him Hinetitama had now become, especially after all that they had shared. Suddenly he remembered something. "Before we return to the others, there is something I want to talk to you about."

"What is it?" she asked.

"This morning just before you woke me, I had an unusual dream. A man dressed entirely in black came to me carrying a beautiful jewel-encrusted dagger. He knelt down beside me and offered the weapon to me."

"Did you accept it?" asked Hinetitama, her eyes narrowed as she fixed them on him.

"I took it" he said.

Hinetitama's expression changed to one of concern. "Why?"

"I don't know. I guess I felt I had to take it," Roberto saw the disappointment in Hinetitama's eyes.

"Did you get a look at his face?"

"I've never seen him before. He looked like an albino with scars on his face—here…" he said, brushing his right cheek.

"We have been undone. Everything has now changed," she muttered, her expression crumpled into a scowl.

"What do you mean?"

"The dagger you so eagerly took up represents that part of you—however small it may be—which stubbornly refuses to believe."

"Believe in what?" asked Roberto.

"In anything," Hinetitama said. "We humans are a fickle lot; we are easily persuaded and taken advantage of; that is why our fates never rest with us. By accepting the dagger, you have accepted control over your fate. It is now within your power to sever the sacred bond that exists between you and what was done for you this morning. By giving you the dagger, that spirit has ensured that your fate has been placed firmly into your hands. And that, Roberto, is a very dangerous position for you to be in."

"Why?" he asked.

"As long as your fate rests with you, your life is in great danger, because you will not be able to prevent it from being taken from you. And if you don't get rid of the spirit who gave you the dagger, he will do just that—take control. From that moment on, Roberto, your soul will belong to him, and believe me, you would not want that."

"I don't understand."

"The man you described in your dream placed that dagger in your hands in the hope that you will use it. Mark my words…he will work on you. If you use it, I cannot save you. Your safety is in the power of your belief. As long as you believe in what has been done, you will be safe. You must not give him an opportunity to come between us."

"But who is he?" Roberto asked.

"He is a spirit from the other side, who took an opportunity when he saw it to become your nemesis. He wants your soul. You must heed my warning—he is very dangerous to you."

"But he was a dream…"

"Like that dog that follows you around he is now a very real part of your life. But all is not lost, because unlike the dog, you can deal with him—and you must, and quickly, or he will have you."

"But how?"

At that moment, a small gust of wind blew in from the sea and picked up a white seabird's feather. It fluttered in the wind for a moment then fell and tumbled lightly across the ground a few meters from the pair. It immediately caught Hinetitama's eye.

"Fetch me that feather," she said pointing to it as it came to rest on the grass.

Roberto walked over and picked it up, then returned to the old woman and gave it to her.

She held it for a moment, cupping it in both her hands as if she was about to pray. She closed her eyes and whispered something that Roberto could not make out. She opened her eyes again and looked at him.

"Take this feather, find an ancient Egyptian temple, and place it in the shrine room saying aloud these words—'I call upon the Goddess Isis for whom I have brought this symbol of Ma-at. It is for the sake of my soul that I offer it and that order once again may return to my life.' This is very important, Roberto. You must make this offering as soon as you can, for while things remain as they are, your life is in danger. Promise me that you will do this."

"Where I am going to find an Egyptian temple?"

"Promise me…" demanded Hinetitama.

"Alright…I promise—I'll do it. But where I am going to find an Egyptian temple?"

"Seek and you shall find Roberto…you know that." Hinetitama smiled. "You found me, didn't you? And surely, if you can do that, you can find anything."

"But…" Roberto was struggling to come to terms with the promise he had just made.

"Listen, I don't make the rules, and neither for that matter do you. We are simply the players in this game," said Hinetitama.

"But why an ancient Egyptian temple?" asked Roberto.

"On the great spiritual journey, they were the first to see the light, and they will be the last. All that we know and do even today, we find root with them." Hinetitama now turned from Roberto and faced the east. "They are the Alpha and the Omega, and their Gods are my Gods. That is why."

"And if I do as you ask, what then?" asked Roberto.

"Your nemesis will be returned to his cage," smiled Hinetitama. "And you will then be free to follow the new path that has been laid before you."

"Why do I feel as though this is some sort of wild dream, and any moment now, I will wake up, and everything will be back to normal?"

"I'm afraid, Roberto, this is not a dream. Do as I say, young man, and you will be fine." She smiled, then reached out and wrapped him up in a hug. "Boy, if I didn't already have a son, I would snap you up in a flash. You're a good young man, and one day, you will make us all proud. Come on, let's get out of here. I can see the curtains in the houses around here twitching. These lonely buggers have got nothing better to do than to spy on us. Come on, this old woman wants to go home."

Early the following day Roberto, Maya, and Daniel said their goodbyes and prepared to leave Tolaga Bay. Hinetitama, in her own inimitable way, said goodbye to Roberto. Standing at her gate, she leaned forward and embraced him; she whispered into his ear, "While you are in this life, I shall see you just once more. Prepare yourself, because it will not be an easy time for you."

When Roberto asked her to explain further what she had meant, she simply smiled and kissed him on the cheek.

"Goodbye Roberto. You are my messenger. Remember the promises you made to me."

He knew as they parted that the memory of this old woman would be with him forever.

The occupants of the car were silent and completely lost in thought as the vehicle wound along the narrow road heading away from the remote bay. Daniel was driving, and Roberto sat in the front passenger's seat, his expression blank and his eyes closed. Maya was in the back seat staring out the window, trying to catch a last glimpse of Tolaga Bay as it retreated from view.

A moment later, Roberto's expression changed. He smiled as the vision of Hinetitama, washed by the golden light of the rising sun, entered his thoughts. He would never forget that dramatic morning as they both looked out over the sea and faced the pure light of a new dawning day. The glow of the sun from the east upon Hinetitama's face seemed to honor her with a sacredness that only she, with the blessing of her Gods, could have borne. She had healed him that morning—there was no doubt in his mind. At last he felt happy. He had done the right thing by coming to this place. He turned back and looked at Maya sitting silently in the back seat.

"I owe you my life," he said to her in Spanish.

She smiled at him and held out her left hand, "Don't be silly. You owe me nothing," she said.

Roberto took her hand and kissed it. "How did you know that I needed to come to this place?"

"I told you that this trip would be good for us," she said. "But if it wasn't for your amulet, we would not have come here. We probably would have gone somewhere else. I'm so glad that we came here though."

"So am I," said Roberto. "So am I…"

Daniel looked up. He could see Maya in the rearview mirror. *How devoted she is to him*, he thought—it was in her smiling eyes as she spoke. He could not understand what they were saying, but whatever it was; he could see love for Roberto written all over her face. A twinge of sadness touched him. One day he hoped that someone would feel that way about him. But lately, work seemed to be the only thing in his life, and as long as that situation remained, there would be no room for anyone like Maya.

For the next few days after they arrived back in Auckland, Daniel had arranged sightseeing tours for the pair. They were fascinated by the thermal wonderland of Rotorua and fell in love with the beautiful islands of the Hauraki Gulf. In the end, it had been an amazing holiday for both of them. They took with them many wonderful memories. But for Roberto, he would never forget Tolaga Bay or the old woman they called Hinetitama. She had led Roberto to the light.

Two short weeks after they had arrived in New Zealand, Daniel said goodbye to the pair at Auckland International Airport. It had been a whirlwind tour, but they had enjoyed every moment of it. As the wheels of the Boeing 747-400 lifted off the tarmac beginning their long flight back to Barcelona, Roberto nestled into his seat and closed his eyes. Suddenly, he sat up with a start. It seemed almost unbelievable, but above the roar of the jet engines, he had heard a whisper in his ear. The voice was old and familiar, and the words he had heard before: *"Remember, Roberto, you are in danger as long your promises remain unfulfilled."*

17

RETURN TO BARCELONA

As the sun rose over the horizon a blaze of light burst forth into a new day. Roberto felt its warmth upon his face. There in front of him facing the dawn, an old woman wept. She made no sound; but he watched as tears fell from her cheeks like drops of liquid gold falling from the sun itself. Suddenly a voice called his name—a deep voice that reverberated into the still morning air like a stag roar through a silent forest. Roberto turned; there, on a rise behind him, was the sunlit form of a man, almost angelic in the light of the newborn day. A cold shiver ran through him for he recognized that man, and in an instant the dream had dissolved and he was awake.

For a moment Roberto lay numbly staring at the ceiling. *Another one…* he grumbled to himself, tired now of the strange dreams that had plagued him since he and Maya had returned from New Zealand. All of them contained images of Hinetitama and the early morning ceremony on the beach at Tolaga Bay. Others were haunted by visions of the mysterious devil who had given him the precious and troublesome dagger.

"Foolish young man," the demon mouthed. "Beware of that old witch, for she has blinded you with her lies."

Sometimes Roberto woke shivering and drenched in sweat only to find, sitting in the corner of the room, his friend, the white dog. The little creature kept a vigil over his dream-plagued companion.

"Help free me from the nightmares," he whispered in desperation. But those bright red eyes simply watched; then the little ghostly canine melted away.

Soon Roberto had convinced himself that the dreams bedeviling him were due to jet lag. The trip to New Zealand and back had been the longest journey he had ever undertaken. Perhaps his mind had become disoriented—maybe that would explain the unusual dreams? Surely now all he needed was time to get over the experience.

Several days after returning home to Barcelona, Roberto finally received the phone call that he knew would come, and he was dreading it.

"How was your trip?" asked Alejandro Rivera, who had been Roberto's doctor for many years. It was he who had originally broken the bad news about the terminal illness.

"It was fantastic," Roberto said. "It was everything that Maya and I had hoped for."

"Good," said Rivera. "It's about time we had a catch up, don't you think? I just happen to have a gap in my appointments this afternoon. I can fit you in—if you're not too busy, that is."

The phone suddenly felt cold against his ear, Roberto knew now that the moment of truth had finally arrived. He had travelled halfway around the world and succumbed to the stories of a strange old woman who said that she had cured him—and he'd believed her. But now it was time to stand beneath the microscope of medical science—and what would it have to say? He suddenly felt faint. "I'll be there," he said. "Just tell me when."

At three-thirty that afternoon, a nervous Roberto appeared at the door of Rivera's surgery. The doctor was pleased to see him and wasted no time in getting down to business—after all, he was concerned that the trip had affected his patient's health. From the beginning, Roberto could see that the examination was going to be thorough. But he understood—it was something that just had to be done.

Two hours later, all had gone according to plan, and eventually, Roberto was free to go.

Early the following morning Rivera called Roberto. He sounded concerned, but would not discuss any details over the phone, saying only that it was urgent that he see Roberto as soon as possible.

Later that morning, a now very anxious Roberto returned to Rivera's surgery.

"Come in," he said as the nurse showed Roberto into his office. He could see immediately the apprehension on Roberto's face, and stood up from his desk to welcome him into the office.

Alejandro Rivera was a kindly man, tall and lean and in his late thirties. His deep-olive complexion and long black hair gave him the look of a flamenco dancer rather than that of a doctor.

"How are you this morning?" he asked Roberto as he offered him a chair.

"I don't feel at all like someone who's about to die, if that's what you mean," replied Roberto as he sat.

"Now that's the strangest thing," said Rivera. "I just can't figure it out." He scratched his head as returned to the chair at his desk.

"What can't you figure out?" asked Roberto.

"The results from your tests are puzzling me," said Rivera. "They seem to indicate that the cancer is gone."

Roberto eyed him carefully before answering. "I see."

"You don't seem surprised…" Rivera was a little taken aback by Roberto's calmness.

"I'm not," said Roberto.

"Why not?" Rivera was puzzled.

"Like I told you, I don't feel like a man who is about to die anytime soon."

To Rivera, Roberto was now beginning to sound as though he actually believed the results.

"Look, let's not get our hopes up," he said. "I think we need to run these tests again."

"Why? How do you know these results aren't telling you the truth?" Roberto sounded firm.

"That's the problem, we *don't* know. That's why we need to run them again," said Rivera. "It would be a miracle if this disease has disappeared from your body. Only God can grant such things, and as you can see, I am not God. So please, Roberto, let's just take this for what it is, something we need to explore further."

Roberto thought for a moment. "What if I don't want any more tests? Maybe I already know as much as I ever want to know about this thing."

"Of course, it's your choice, Roberto. But I want you to think very carefully about this," urged Rivera. "Look—I understand how you feel. Medicine is not an exact science. We make mistakes; test kits are sometimes faulty. But whatever the reason, this is serious. It's something we need to take another look at. What do you say?"

Over the years he had known him, Roberto had come to respect Rivera. He knew he was a good man—and Roberto trusted him. But this time, he felt that the doctor was wrong. And although he had no scientific evidence to back himself up, Roberto was convinced that the disease that had once afflicted him had now completely disappeared.

"I'm sorry Alejandro," he finally replied. "I don't want any more tests. I just want to get on with my life."

Rivera could now see that Roberto was not going to change his mind. There was no use in pressing him further. "Like I said, it's your decision Roberto. But remember, I'll always be here, should you need me."

"Thank you." There was relief in Roberto's voice. "You're a good doctor, but my mind is made up. I just want to get on with my life. If your concerns are correct, and the illness hasn't gone, then so be it. But if it has gone, and I do feel that it has, then I don't want to waste a single minute of what's been given back to me."

Roberto didn't remember leaving Rivera's office that morning. All he could think about was that he'd been cured, and the realization of how this happened had completely overwhelmed him. For a while, he simply wandered the streets aimlessly and became lost in the thoughts that tumbled about in his head like lottery balls in a spinning cage. Hinetitama had been right all along. The ceremony on the beach had cured him. And D'Anjou—Roberto was sure now that he had foreseen it all. And even Maya, who had been so persistent in getting him on a plane to New Zealand—what did she know?

It wasn't long before that whole morning had simply become a blur. He wandered about in a daze, not going anywhere; and for a while, he was lost—even to himself. *Life had played a trick on fate—that cruel decider of us all. And fate, it seemed, had lost.*

As he wandered, he thought about how his life had suddenly changed from one of confinement and certain death, and now to one of light and living; and of uncertainty; and even, perhaps, of happiness.

But he was struggling, too. The thoughts churning in his head were now beginning to wear him down. He needed to find somewhere quiet to think things through—somewhere where he could be alone. It only took him a moment's thought, and he knew where he must go.

Like his grandfather before him, he loved books. They were the true window on life itself. Through books, Fernando had once told him, it was possible for one to look out upon the world—and know that the world looked back. And it was true—a book might indeed possess an echo. But not everyone, it seemed, was lucky enough to hear it, or even understand its meaning.

He needed to find a place that was full of books. Only then would he find the tranquility and the space where he could untangle the knot of thoughts in his mind.

Suddenly, as if guided by some invisible, yet knowing hand, he came to a halt in front of the monumental fountain at the center of Plaça Espanya. It was as though he had been struck by a thunder bolt—standing here was nothing less than an omen, and at that moment, it was one that he could not ignore. He knew that the immense fountain's grand proportions and architectural promise hid a dark and almost forgotten truth. The city gallows had once stood on that very spot. Men's lives had been cut short by the voracious hand of vengeance and death.

Darkness once lived here, he thought.

But now, this celebrated architectural tribute to water rose up and dominated the space where death had reigned. Water—the very essence of life itself—had now banished the shadows and darkness of the past. *Now*, thought Roberto, *it is a place of life*. The parallel with his own small life on this morning of discovery was almost spiritual.

He had seen enough. He was now desperate for the book-filled refuge that he knew would ease his mind, and beneath that spectacular fountain was where his journey would begin.

He headed underground to the metro station below the plaza, and caught the next train to Liceu. From there, the biblioteca on carrer de l'Hospital was but a short walk.

Surrounded by books, and in the comfortable anonymity of the library, he spent the next few hours. There he attempted to untangle the thoughts and emotions that had earlier threatened to overwhelm him.

As time ticked by, it became clear that the biblioteca had worked its therapy, as Roberto had known it would. He was a lot calmer now, and soon it was time to go. But when he left, he was disappointed too. He still did not understand anything of what had happened to him. The more he considered the questions that stirred in his head, still others sprang to mind. Soon he began to realize that perhaps there were no real answers to be had.

Maybe this is what life was all about—a journey without answers.

It was just after four, when he returned to their apartment. Maya was out, and the place seemed cold and empty without her. A late lecture at the university would keep her there this evening, until at least seven.

Roberto made himself a drink, and clutching it in one hand and a library book in the other, he headed for the sofa. A modern copy of *The Book of the Master of the Hidden Places* by W. Marsham Adams had caught his eye. Perhaps in it, he would find the answers he sought, for he was sure that he had seen this title among those upon Hinetitama's cluttered bookshelves. But before he reached the sofa, the phone rang.

It was his mother. He detected at once the serious tone in her voice.

"What is it?" he asked.

"Can you and Maya meet me this evening?"

"Yes, of course—but why?"

"Around eight o'clock would suit. Is that alright?"

"Yes, but you haven't told me why."

"Roberto, we'll talk about it this evening. Don't worry—it's not bad news, I just want to discuss something with you—that's all. Do you know Mudanzas, near Santa Maria del Mar?"

"Yes..."

"Good. I'll see you there about eight." She hung up.

It was obvious to Roberto that his mother didn't want to say anymore than necessary over the phone. *But why?*

He was intrigued—and at the same time, annoyed. After all, he was her son. What could she possibly want to discuss with him that they couldn't discuss on the phone? He reached for the receiver again and went to dial her number. As his finger hovered above the keypad, he thought again, and decided that whatever it was, it could wait.

After all, she had already told him that it wasn't bad news.

That evening, when Maya got in, the pair set out for Café Mudanzas on carrer Vidrieria, near to where Amalia worked. When they arrived, they could see the downstairs bar was packed. Amalia was already there. She looked anxious, seated alone at a table near the bar. In front of her sat an empty glass and a plate that contained what was left of her tapas.

She waved to them through the crowded, smoke-filled room, and smiled as the pair approached her. Roberto kissed her on both cheeks before sitting down; Maya did the same.

"Would you like something to drink?" asked Amalia.

"I'll get it, Mama," replied Roberto and signaled to the waiter. They made their orders, tapas, and two glasses of Cruzcampo. Amalia ordered another orange juice. She never drank alcohol. Roberto could see that she was nervous in their company. It was totally out of character for her, and it puzzled him.

"What's all this about?" he finally asked.

"I have been talking to your grandmother," she said, almost with a sigh. "Since Fernando's death, she has been desperately lonely, rattling around in that big old house of hers."

As soon as he had heard these words, Roberto knew at once where this discussion was heading. It all made sense to him now—why his mother had been so uneasy. Ever since his grandfather had died, he'd known that this was a conversation just waiting to be had. But right now, he wasn't ready to have it. He already had too much to deal with.

"I'm happy where I am, mother," he said, forcing her to cut to the chase. "I like living in the city. For me it's close to everything I need."

Amalia studied him for a moment. She wasn't expecting such a direct response so soon. Like Roberto, Maya could also now see why they had been summoned here tonight.

"Be reasonable, Roberto," Amalia pleaded. "You know that the place will be yours. Why not move up there now? Your grandmother needs help."

"But Mama…"

"Talk to him, Maya. You're a woman—please make him see reason." Amalia appealed to Maya with her eyes.

"Oh I don't know. We're very happy here—"

When she realized that Maya wasn't going to support her plea, Amalia cut her off.

"He's a writer Maya—and a good one. The clean air in the Collserola Hills and the quiet…it will be good for him—for you both. Think of it! All that room, and quiet too. It will be such a creative space for you, Roberto."

"Mama, why are you doing this?" he asked.

"Your grandmother will be eighty-eight years old this year, and she is in desperate need of your help, Roberto."

"She has a live-in maid and a nurse. What more could I do for her?" he said.

"They're not family. She needs family around her now that Fernando has gone. She loves you, Roberto—you mean the world to her. To have you around would make the last years of her life the happiest."

"I'm not sure…" he answered, struggling to find the right words.

"Well *she* is," Amalia said. "That's why we're here. She has asked me to talk to you about moving in with her—as soon as possible."

Roberto was stunned. He could not go against his grandmother's request. He remained silent, barely able to conceal the bitterness he felt at being pushed into something he wasn't ready to do.

Amalia could see that he was unhappy.

"Please say something, Maya. He needs you to show him that this is the right decision."

"Roberto is capable of making his own decisions," Maya said. A forced smile could not hide the tension on her face.

Roberto and Maya left Café Mudanzas soon afterward. It was cold when they got outside. Maya could see that Roberto was still upset with his mother. She suggested that they catch the metro up to Plaça De La Universitat and walk home from there along the Gran Via. She hoped that the walk in the night air would give Roberto time to calm down.

The streets were busy when they came out of the metro station near the university. As they walked through the plaza toward the Gran Via, they could see the Edificio Histórico, the heart of the university complex ahead of them. By night, lit by the golden wash of spotlights, it seemed almost enchanted. To Maya, the exterior of this grand edifice resembled an ancient fairytale castle. She loved the place and perhaps even more so because of its long history, for its university foundations went back as far as the year 1398. And best of all, she now worked there—in one of the oldest universities in Europe.

She pulled her coat collar up to keep out the chilly night air. It swirled around them as the constant flow of traffic and pedestrians streamed noisily through the streets and avenues adjoining the plaza.

Soon they had made their way on to the busy arterial known as the Gran Via. As they neared the intersection with carrer de Casanova, a short way ahead, Roberto noticed a tall man wearing a long black coat. He stood casually puffing on a cigarette outside the farmacia on the corner of the street. His dark, wide-brimmed hat was pulled low across his brow, and the brim hung down and partially obscured his face. Wisps of cigarette smoke eddied up from beneath it into the cold night air. The luminous cross set above the door of the farmacia cast its green light across the man as he loitered beneath it. The glow added a sinister tone to the scene. As the pair neared him, Roberto could see the man's eyes glinting from beneath the brim of the hat, staring out, keenly watching as they approached.

Alongside him now, the pair could see that his face was mostly hidden. His collar was pulled high and obscured much of what the brim of the hat did not. As they passed, the stranger raised his head slightly to better view the passing couple. As he did, Roberto turned to face him. In the green light, he glimpsed the stranger's expression. There was a crooked smile, but the right side of his pale face looked badly scarred. A shiver shook Roberto as their eyes met, and he nodded as they passed.

A moment later, behind them, they heard a gasp. Turning quickly, they noticed a couple walking a dog, a young Labrador. The man in the black coat had recoiled in fear at the proximity of the dog. He gasped loudly and stepped backward so quickly that he dropped his cigarette, and within an instant, he had backed himself flat against the front glass window of the farmacia. He seemed terrified of the dog. The woman, who held the lead, reacted quickly and pulled the animal close to her side. She apologized profusely for startling the man. He did not answer, and as soon as the way was clear, he fled, heading quickly down carrer Casanova toward Ronda Sant Antoni. Roberto was surprised by the stranger's reaction.

"What do you make of that?" he asked Maya.

"He gave me the creeps," she whispered.

"He doesn't like dogs—that's for sure," replied Roberto. He couldn't explain it, but at that moment, deep down, something troubled him about the stranger.

As they made their way home, the image of the man in black played on Roberto's mind. There was a strong resemblance between him and the man who had held the dagger in his dream while they were in New Zealand. But was it really possible that a living person could actually resemble anyone in such a bizarre dream? To Roberto, the coincidence was disturbing.

That evening when they had arrived back to their apartment, Roberto and Maya talked again of the move to Vallvidrera. Both agreed, almost from the outset, that they would keep the apartment. It was well placed for them both, and for a time, they could see themselves living between there and the villa in Vallvidrera. It was obvious, after the discussion with Amalia, that the move should occur as soon as possible. After all, Nuria wasn't getting any younger. And so that night the pair decided to begin their shift within the next few days.

Later, when they went to bed, Roberto again found it difficult to settle. When he finally did, he was once more assailed by the weird and confusing dreams that had plagued him since they had returned from New Zealand. Between the images of Pohutukawa trees and brilliant sunrises, and those of Hinetitama, the man in the black coat seemed to shadow them all. Roberto woke several times during the night, but as soon as he had returned to sleep, so returned the dreams.

When morning finally arrived, he'd had enough, and in desperation, he decided to talk to Maya.

"Do you remember that man last night—the one you called creepy?" he asked.

"Yes"

"I dreamt of him," Roberto continued.

"He must have left quite an impression for you to do that," she answered.

"I dreamt of him while we were in New Zealand."

Maya looked astonished.

"I can't explain it," he continued. "But that guy in the street last night reminded me so much of the man I dreamt of while we were with Hinetitama."

"What happened to you there?" Maya asked. "What did that old woman do to you?"

"There is so much I have to tell you, Maya," he said. "But right now, all I can say is that she saved my life."

"How?"

"It's a long story, and I promise I'll tell you everything," he replied. "But there is something I must do first…"

"You and your secrets…you'll drive me crazy," she shrieked, as she threw her hands up in exasperation.

"I'm sorry," he replied. "But the sight of that man last night was a warning to me—I know it was."

"A warning about what," she asked.

"I must go to A Coruña; there is something important I must do there. After that, I have to find an ancient Egyptian temple."

Maya was flabbergasted. "A *what?*" she squealed.

"I know it sounds crazy…and maybe it is, but I made some promises to Hinetitama. I have to keep them, Maya—they're important."

"What on earth has she got you doing?"

All he could do was shrug his shoulders.

She stared at him for a moment. "You *are* crazy," she finally said. Then her astonishment gave way to a grin. "Of course, now you'll have to go to Egypt. For someone who just a few short weeks ago didn't want to go anywhere, you're sure pushing the boundaries now."

"Have you heard of the Temple of Debod?" asked Roberto.

"No," she said.

"Well it's right here in Spain, in the Parque Del Oeste, near the Royal Palace in Madrid."

"Sometimes you amaze me, Roberto," she said. "How can it be an authentic temple? The Romans were here in Spain, not the Egyptians."

"I know," he said. "I've done the research, and I know what I'm talking about. The temple is not a replica. It's an authentic building from the second century BC, given to Spain by the Egyptian people. The Spanish government helped save the Abu Simbel temple complex in Egypt from being lost into the rising waters when the Aswan Dam was built. In 1968, the temple of Debod was brought to Madrid stone by stone, and carefully erected on its own dedicated site in the gardens near the Royal Palace. In re-erecting the temple, everything was kept just the same as it was in Egypt. Even the original east/west orientation of the building was retained. Besides the temple in Madrid, there are only three other places in the world outside of Egypt where temples like this can be found: New York in the USA, Turin in Italy, and Leiden in the Netherlands. But the one in Madrid is the only one to have kept faithfully to the original setting and to have retained the proper alignment. The rest are all housed in museums as relicts of the past. So you see, the Temple of Debod is about as authentic an experience as you can get outside of Egypt."

"You really have done your homework," she smiled. "But why do you need to visit it?"

"Hinetitama believes in the ancient Gods of Egypt. I know—that also sounds strange, but I promised her that I would take an offering and leave it in the temple. She believes that this offering will also help me."

"Help you?" said Maya. "Why do you need help?"

"I'll tell you everything," he said. "But only after I've fulfilled the two promises I made to Hinetitama."

"I can't wait," Maya jeered. "This is one story I definitely want to hear."

That morning, after Maya had left for the university, Roberto called Nuria to tell her of their decision. When the old woman heard that her grandson and his girlfriend had decided to move in with her, she was overwhelmed and began crying on the phone. She told him that she had been very lonely since Fernando's death. Through her sobs, she said that these last months had got so bad, that she had even begun to wish for death to come for her. Roberto choked up when he heard this. After he hung up from his grandmother, he called Amalia.

"I'm sorry, Mama, for being angry at you last night," he said. "Maya and I have decided to start the move to Vallvidrera in a few days."

"Your grandfather wanted you to have that house, Roberto, and Nuria has wanted you there since he died. But she has been too afraid to ask— she didn't want to pressure you. She knows what young people's lives are like today. She didn't want to be the lead weight around your neck, slowing you down from getting on with your life."

Roberto's guilt began to bite. He was embarrassed that he had been so reluctant during the conversation with his mother, and for not noticing sooner his grandmother's loneliness.

"I'm sorry, Mama. Will you ever forgive me for last night?"

"You were forgiven even before you left the table. I'm your mother, Roberto. You grew from the love between your father and I, just as I grew from the love between my parents. Those powerful linkages make us a family who cares about one another. Your grandmother loves you, and she wants to spend what's left of her life with you. All she wants is for you to take care of her—as I know you will."

Roberto was close to tears when he hung up, and he was glad that Maya wasn't there to see him. It had been an emotional time for him since arriving back in Barcelona, but he knew that there was more to come—and he didn't mind admitting that the thought of it frightened him.

18

A CORUÑA – EL ÁRBOL DE POHUTUKAWA

On the day that he and Maya had finally moved in with Nuria, Roberto roamed about the old villa almost as if he were a stranger. The ghosts from his past were suddenly all around him. He felt anxious, and in his head, he could hear the echo of his grandfather's voice, *"Old families harbor old secrets."* And now that he was to take control of it, this house of Hernandez seemed to be full of them—whispered from ear to ear and from heart to heart. He had no doubt that behind those stone walls was a treasure trove of echoes from the past, lost memories, and even ghosts. He shuddered when he remembered Hinetitama's words, "It's not good to have unresolved memories lying about. The circle of life that they are a part of must be closed."

At least, he thought, there was always the little apartment in the city where he and Maya had been so happy. Perhaps he could hide there when it all got too much for him in Vallvidrera.

In almost every room of the old villa, he could close his eyes and remember the sounds of his youth. But it was his grandfather who he remembered most of all. Roberto longed again for those balmy afternoons on the balcony, where he had learned so much about life; and the cold winter evenings by the fire in the living room, where he would lie on the chaise, mesmerized by his grandfather's stories.

For the first few days, the shift to Vallvidrera brought nothing but disorientation to the pair. The daily commute for Maya to and from the university had changed. Her day had become longer, and the drive into the city would take some getting used to. Roberto, on the other hand, did not have to leave the house to work. For him, the place and its surrounds had become a mine of inspiration. He relished being able to slip back into his boyhood memories, recalling the days of his youth spent wrapped in the security of the villa Hernandez.

All the while, Nuria sat quietly observing. Her old eyes never missed a beat. She enjoyed every moment of the young couple being around her. It made her feel young again.

Lolita, the family's faithful maid, eagerly welcomed the change in the household. Things had not been the same since the señor's unexpected death—and the señora, she had changed. Although she loved Nuria dearly, for Lolita, being left to cope all those months on her own with the old lady had turned out to be *very* hard work. But now Roberto, whom she'd once had a hand in raising, was home to stay. And with him came his beautiful señorita. It had been a long time, she thought, since the sounds of real passion stirred the languid air of the old villa. A beautiful place such as this was meant to be full of love and passion and laughter too—not the decaying air that had filled it for far too long.

The first week seemed to pass quickly. Roberto had managed to cope with the cascade of memories that the move had brought with it. Maya, always the innovator, had adapted quickly to the new surroundings, and soon had Lolita laughing aloud again. Even Nuria, who had not taken to Maya when they first met, was now utterly captivated by her.

"Roberto," she whispered. "Maya is such a sweet girl. Be careful that another man doesn't slip a ring on her finger before *you* have a chance to."

"Thank you for pointing that out," he whispered back. "I'll keep that in mind."

"I'll be eighty-eight this year…" a sly smile lit her old face. "I may need a celebration to cheer me up before God calls me to him."

"Of course, mi abuela," he said. "We won't forget your birthday."

Together they burst into laughter.

"It's so good to have you home again, mi corazon." Nuria reached for him. He leaned forward, and she kissed his cheek.

As the weeks passed, the household settled happily into its new routine. Maya's day started early, and by seven, she had usually already left for the university. Roberto also started early, having taken over the library as his writing room. He would spend most of the day in this "temple to writers"—as his grandfather once called it—a magnificent room, completely crammed with books both old and new. Nuria would often join him there in the early afternoon. After an hour, Lolita would return and take the old lady away for her nap.

All of the fears that Roberto had harbored about the move to the villa were now gone. He felt embarrassed when he thought back to the night at Café Mudanzas when his mother had angered him by her suggestion that he and Maya move in with Nuria. But happily, all that was in the past, because right now, there was nowhere else he would rather be.

One evening, just over a month after the move, Roberto again raised with Maya the subject of his promises to Hinetitama. He had waited until he and Maya were alone; he did not want anyone else in the house to know—Nuria in particular, who he knew would be furious with him.

Maya listened carefully as he told her that in three days' time, he had decided to fly to A Coruña. Once he had finished there, he would fly on to Madrid and the Temple of Debod. He would spend the night in Madrid and fly back to Barcelona the following day. His conscience would then be at rest, having carried out both of the promises he had made.

"You have it all worked out, don't you?" Maya sounded unhappy.

"I need to do this," he answered. "It's important to me, Maya."

"I know," she said. "But now, I want you to promise *me* something. When you get back, I want you to tell me what this is all about. I think I've been very patient with you, Roberto."

"You have, Maya, and I'm grateful for that. I'll tell you everything when I get back."

The night before his flight to A Coruña, Roberto opened the envelope that contained the soil that he had brought back from New Zealand. He felt goose bumps as he poured it from the envelope into the palm of his left hand. What he held was a memento of a journey that had changed his life. He brushed the dried soil gently with his right forefinger, and as he did, he remembered the day that he had scooped it up from beneath that old Pohutukawa tree in Te Araroa. He poured it back into the envelope, and as the last of it fell from his hand, he could not explain the sense of loss he suddenly felt. He still couldn't shake the feeling as he closed the envelope and placed it into the inside breast pocket of the jacket he would wear the next day.

Into the same pocket, he also put the white feather that Hinetitama had asked to be placed on the altar of an Egyptian temple. He had earlier wrapped it in a small piece of white linen cloth.

Both of these items, which had now journeyed with him for almost twenty thousand kilometers, were offerings to a religion that was foreign to him—a religion that he did not understand, nor ever thought he would.

The next morning, as he boarded the Iberia flight from Terminal B, he struggled to ignore the voice within him that kept asking a question to which he had no answer: *Do you really understand the journey that you're about to embark on?* He tried hard to put this to one side and focus on the promise he had made in New Zealand to the old woman who had saved his life.

But he could also hear the voice of another old woman—his grandmother. She would not understand the reasons for this trip. He knew that if she ever found out, she'd be outraged that he could somehow be trapped into an adventure such as this. Roberto had made up his mind that she would never know the real reason for his trip. When he kissed her that morning before leaving for the airport, he told her that he was going on a research trip—one that he needed to take for a book that he was working on. She believed him and wished him a speedy and safe return.

The flight to A Coruña would take an hour and fifty minutes. As the plane climbed into the air, Roberto's thoughts drifted to the Pohutukawa tree that grew in that city. The more he thought about the tree, the more he wondered about Hinetitama's beliefs. The spiritual message that he carried had waited centuries to be delivered—a message that only she and the tree understood. On this journey, he was simply the messenger. But now that his journey had begun, and he was in the air high above Barcelona heading north, he began to realize just how bizarre it all was. He was delivering an ethereal communication in an envelope filled with dirt to a five-hundred-year-old tree. If his mother knew what he was doing, he felt sure that she would have him put in an asylum.

Hinetitama's words seemed so distant now. He could not even remember the sound of her voice. But one thing was sure, back when she had told him to do this, it had sounded much more sensible than it did right now.

The plane finally touched down at A Coruña airport at 1:00 p.m., and the seven-kilometer ride into town took the taxi just twenty minutes to complete. The city of A Coruña had ancient roots. It sat on the northern coast of Spain in the autonomous region of Galicia. It was cold and wet in the winter, and folklore had it that fairies played in the valley mists that lay in the country vales. The people there had strong Celtic traditions and held ancient kinships with the people of Scotland and Ireland. For thousands of years, those hardy souls had won a living from the land and from the often-treacherous seas that surrounded it.

The Tower of Hercules, close by the city, was the oldest lighthouse still in use anywhere in the world. Through its golden eye atop the great stone tower, it had been a witness to two thousand years of history, from the Roman Empire to the Catholic monarchs in the Middle Ages who had finally united the disparate kingdoms of Hispania. The golden eye looked out and saw the coming of Napoleon Bonaparte and the invading French hordes, and it witnessed the birth of Francisco Franco and wept for the dead of the civil war. But all those were now embers glowing faintly in the great hearth of time, and the golden eye watched still.

The phone call that Roberto made before leaving Barcelona was to confirm his arrival. He was expected at the police station on calle Tui at one-thirty. In the station courtyard, he would find what he had come all this way to see—the ancient Pohutukawa tree. The locals knew the tree's story. Originally from the South Seas, it had been brought to Spain by a returning caravel around five centuries ago. The old Pohutukawa had been living in the city so long now it had been afforded special protection by the city authorities.

As the taxi came to a halt, Roberto caught his first glimpse of the tree. The thick, sinewy limbs reached out, towering above the walls and surrounding buildings. Any doubts that he might have harbored on the plane about this trip had now gone. He was full of excitement as he emerged from the vehicle. The entrance to the police courtyard was open. He entered the covered access, and the reception window set into the right-hand wall slid open.

"What can I do for you, señor?" said the stocky policeman seated at a desk behind the glass window.

"My name is Roberto Torres. I called earlier…I'm here to look at the old tree in your courtyard."

"Ah yes, señor. Velasco will take you in," he said, nodding to a younger policeman seated beside him.

Velasco eyed Roberto for a moment, and then stood up. The door near the window swung open, and out stepped the younger man. He was tall and well built.

"Follow me señor," he said, as he placed the police cap he held in his hands onto his head.

As the pair made their way into the courtyard, Roberto could see that the Pohutukawa tree held almost the entire space in its shadow. Its huge limbs stretched skyward in all directions and the foliage appeared almost to blot out the sun. The courtyard seemed completely overwhelmed by the large and ancient tree. Roberto thought back to his visit to Te Waha-o-Re-rekohu in Te Araroa, and how she had also dominated her surroundings. Compared to her, though, this poor tree seemed almost imprisoned. But it was obvious to him that, like the old tree in New Zealand, this grand old Pohutukawa was also greatly respected. Even though the Pohutukawa spe-cies was alien to Spain, this one had been here in A Coruña so long that the townsfolk had adopted it as an official emblem of the city. It had become special to the people of this place, just as Te Waha-o-Rerekohu was special to the folk of Te Araroa—an entire world away.

"Are you an arborist?" asked Velasco.

"No," Roberto said. He walked up to the tree and placed the palm of his left hand against the enormous trunk. Velasco's keen eyes narrowed slightly as he watched the visitor.

Then Roberto stepped back, removed a small envelope from his pock-et, and sprinkled something at the base of the tree.

Suddenly, the raised voice of the young policeman echoed into the courtyard: "What are you doing señor?"

"I have placed some soil at the base of this tree."

"Why?" Velasco asked sharply.

"It is the soil from the base of a tree just like this one—but the other tree lives almost twenty thousand kilometers away, on the other side of the world."

"I don't understand señor," Velasco appeared concerned.

"In a strange way, these two trees have given me the opportunity to think about some important things in my life. The soil is simply an offering of thanks."

Velasco's policeman's eyes examined Roberto for a moment. Then he shook his head. "We get all sorts in here to look at this old tree, but no one quite like you. Have you finished? I've got work to do."

"Yes," said Roberto, "I've finished." He raised his eyes upward, taking one last look into the vast crown of the tree. He could see the sunlight flickering through the leaves silhouetted against the deep blue sky beyond. He smiled to himself as his thoughts drifted back to New Zealand. He turned to the policemen to thank him for allowing the visit. As he did, out of the corner of his eye, he caught a fleeting glimpse of something that surprised him. A tall figure dressed in black had been standing across the courtyard, watching him. Startled, Roberto quickly turned back to take a better look, but the shadowy figure had vanished. The hair on the back of his neck was already bristling in the gentle breeze blowing across the yard. The vision had unsettled him—something about it now made him feel very uneasy.

"What's the matter?" Velasco asked. "You look like you've seen a ghost."

"It's…nothing…" Roberto stammered. "Listen—thanks for your time. I really appreciate you letting me see the tree."

"De nada," replied Velasco. "Now, if you don't mind…"

As he walked out of the police station, Roberto could see the taxi waiting on the other side of the street. From here, it would take him back to the airport for the flight to Madrid and the ancient Egyptian Temple of Debod.

As it pulled out onto calle Tui, Roberto looked back through the rear window of the vehicle. He gazed one last time upon the old giant that dominated the courtyard and dwarfed the surrounding buildings. And as he did, he suddenly realized something—something that he felt sure

Hinetitama had already known and wanted him to discover, also. Like the ancient Pohutukawa here in A Coruña, brought from a far-off land centuries ago, he was also the seed of an ancient journey. Both had started and ended in A Coruña. For Roberto, eighteen generations had passed since his ancestor, Francisco de Villanova, had set sail on his voyage of discovery. Years later, he had returned from the South Seas with a son spawned in the very land of this giant tree.

For the Pohutukawa, it was also a sailor returning to A Coruña from the South Seas, this time with a seed, which grew into the giant now casting its aura across the police courtyard and even the city. For a brief moment, beneath the crown of that old tree, two spirits were united—one of nature and one of man.

For the man, this moment had indeed been an awakening. He could feel his heart quake within his chest as he thought back: Hinetitama had been right all along. He would never doubt her again. Now he needed to keep one last promise to her. But this one was also for him, because once it was done, he would be free of the nemesis who haunted him. He slipped his left hand into the inside breast pocket of his jacket. His heart calmed as his fingers touched the cloth that wrapped the white feather. Soon, he thought, it will all be over, and he would return home, just as Hinetitama had told him, with his spirit free.

As Roberto had hoped, the traffic on the road was light. The trip from the city to the airport had been a quick one. He'd known when he'd originally booked this particular flight that catching it in the time he had allowed was always going to be tough. But someone was obviously watching out for him, because to his relief, all went according to plan, and within twenty minutes of arriving at the airport, his flight was airborne.

As the plane climbed above the city, Roberto could see the harbor waters glistening in the bright sunlight. For hundreds of years, ships had sailed from here to all parts of the known world. From the comfort of his seat, Roberto imagined what it would have been like in the days of his ancestor Francisco de Villanova. He imagined the small fleets of caravels as they sailed their way up the harbor, heading for open water. In his mind, he could hear the lieutenants aboard the ships barking orders to the sailors scurrying over the decks and dangling in the rigging. He could almost taste the salty breezes as they spilled into the canvas sails, billowing and flapping, flicking sea spray into the faces of the toiling men.

As the ascending jet banked, setting its course to the southeast, Roberto caught sight of the city below. The older precincts huddled closely around the ancient, sheltered port. The surrounding modern city sprawled outward in every direction and ran northward, clinging to the coastline. For hundreds of years, A Coruña had been a port city—and it was still a port city. Huge luxury liners and ferries packed with commuters now carved their way through the rippling waters, pushing inexorably onward to the waiting quays. A myriad of small boats and watercraft bobbed and swayed at moorings, or splashed their way through the white tops, weaving to points up and down the harbor shore.

Soon the waterfront and the city had gone from view, replaced by the rolling geometric patchwork of hued regularity that industry and agriculture ultimately impressed upon the land. As the jet reached its maximum altitude, clumps of cotton wool cloud drifted slowly by. At times, they obscured from view the natural carpet of land rolled out below. Roberto settled back in his seat and closed his eyes. He would remember this day—the day that he touched his past and closed an unfinished circle of life, Friday, April 16, 2010. He promised himself that one day he would return to A Coruña, and with him, he would bring Maya.

19

Amalia Hernandez trembled as she stood by the telephone, her features tensed in shock and disbelief. The dreadful news had shaken her almost beyond her limit. Roberto's flight from A Coruña to Madrid was now overdue. The man who called from the airline sounded worried, but he assured Amalia that the airline was doing everything in its power to locate the plane. He would call back the moment he had more news.

As they waited for what seemed to be an eternity, a grim silence began to settle over the three women. Everything they did that afternoon became a struggle; even breathing was a task. The *not knowing* made it all excruciatingly painful. Somewhere a son, a grandson, and a lover was lost and in danger—but where?

When the clock which stood in the hallway of villa Hernandez chimed six, their hearts sank. It had now been more than two hours since Roberto's flight should have landed in Madrid—and there was still no word. None of them could ignore the terrible feelings that welled up within them. Amalia sensed that her son was in danger; Maya too began to feel the fear within her heart. And Nuria, who sat with Maya on the sofa, silently began to grieve for her grandson, whom she now felt was in mortal peril. The pair held one another close, bracing for the worst. Tears had already been shed that afternoon, but a dreadful feeling in the room told them that this would just the beginning.

When the phone rang, the sound of it almost stopped their hearts. Amalia's quivering hand reached for the receiver. She froze for an instant—what if the unthinkable had happened? Maya held Nuria's hands as the old woman began to moan. The stress of that afternoon had already taken its toll on her. Her tear-soaked eyes looked up at Amalia, who was also struggling to control her own emotions.

She raised the receiver and placed it to her ear. The voice on the other end told her that the airliner on which Roberto had been a passenger had crashed at three-thirty that afternoon. The site of the crash had been located, and a search team was on its way. The remains of the airliner lay in a remote area on the side of a mountain. The man's voice choked up as he added that it was unlikely that anyone had survived. Amalia never uttered a word.

Maya and Nuria could see the blood drain from her cheeks. Slowly the pale and chiseled expression upon her face began to melt into a landslide of raw and quivering emotion. She did not replace the receiver—it slipped from her hand and landed on the floor. The agonizing cry of a mother for a lost child is a sound that once heard, will never be forgotten.

Amalia collapsed down onto her knees, doubling over in anguish and losing herself into grief. No words were needed for Maya and Nuria. The room was filled with the appalling sound of a mother's agony. Nuria simply fell into Maya's arms. Tears streamed down Maya's cheeks as she shrieked out Roberto's name. Its shrill echo carried through the halls of the villa Hernandez, only to be swallowed by the wailing of heartbroken women.

A cloak of darkness concealed the dreadful scene. Freezing winds howled through the shattered pieces of fuselage strewn along the mountain slopes. The atmosphere was foul with the stench of death. This night, the Reaper rode the icy air as it hastened and roiled over desolation and carnage. Pieces of fuselage flapped and debris clattered, caught in the freezing currents as they hurtled up the narrow gully and swept through the gutted remains. Hot metal crackled as it cooled in the sharp, swirling gusts—no other sound could be heard. And of hope, there was almost none—no beginning or end…only blackness, freezing cold, and death.

Then suddenly, out of nowhere, a shimmering apparition appeared in the darkness. A tall, thin man knelt close to a crumpled human form, tossed like an unwanted doll into the broken and twisted wreckage. The ghost reached out for something that lay next to the twisted male body. But a white dog, an ethereal image itself, which had been lying close by, reared up and bared its teeth at the ghostly man. He had not seen the dog until this moment. He was shocked, and reeled in fear, hissing back at the growling creature.

He eyed the dog cautiously and tried again to move in and grasp the folded white cloth lying next to the body in the wreckage. But the dog attacked, this time running at the ghostly man who lurched backward, greatly alarmed. His eyes glared ferociously as he lashed out, but the dog held him at bay.

Just then, the gossamer outline of an old woman appeared. She came to the male form lying in the wreckage. The dog, recognizing her at once, let her pass as the tall aggressor now melted into the night.

The old woman knelt down beside the unconscious man and whispered to him, "You must wake up." Her shimmering form was almost invisible in the dense blackness. Now that the ghostly man had gone, the dog returned to the crumpled form caught in the debris. He lay down beside him and rested his head upon the man's chest as if guarding his heart.

The old woman leaned closer. Her lips almost touched his ear. "Wake up Roberto—it's not your time," she whispered. He did not move, hovering on the very edge, trapped in that delicate spark of light between fragile life and certain death.

Then he recognized the old woman's voice. It was Hinetitama. His eyelids flickered faintly. His lips quivered. "Help me."

"Hold on Roberto, they will be here soon." The old woman knelt beside him. His frail grip on life seemed to be fading. His weak flame spluttered in the wind—threatening at any moment to go out. The old woman tenderly stroked his forehead. "I will stay with you, Roberto. Hold on… they will be here soon."

He lay perfectly still. Icy fingers of wind ruffled through his hair, pulling it across his bloodstained brow. Freezing and in shock, he had lost a lot of blood. His life had almost fully drained away. If help did not come quickly, he would die here. The expression on his face was one of calmness. His lips lay slightly open, no longer trying to speak. His eyes were closed—he had lost the will to open them. Beside him on the ground lay the folded white linen cloth. It had fallen from him in the turmoil. Hinetitama took it up and opened it. Inside, she found the feather that she had given him as an offering to Isis. She refolded the cloth, still containing the feather, and put it back into Roberto's pocket.

"Take good care of this, my young friend," she whispered to him. "For you will need it."

Suddenly, something stirred within him. His eyelids flickered, but without opening them, he spoke softly, "Father."

His voice was little more than a frail murmur.

"Where are you father?"

"Your father cannot come. It is me, Hinetitama—I have come to you, Roberto."

"Father, I cannot see you. Where are you?" he pleaded weakly.

"You must not reach out for him, Roberto—he will take you. It is not your time. You must stay with me." It was then that the old woman sensed his presence. She turned slowly, and behind her stood a man, his hand outstretched toward his dying son.

"I have always been by your side Roberto, watching you as you grew." His voice was gentle in the freezing wind.

Hinetitama smiled at him. The white dog had also spotted the man and rose up. Cautiously it walked to Hinetitama's side. Its eyes were fixed on Roberto's father.

Hinetitama held out her hand to Sebastian, he bowed and kissed it. "I can see you love your son dearly," she said.

He nodded to her. "I did not say goodbye to him, and I regret that."

"I will see that he knows what is in your heart," she said. "You must go now. Don't worry; he will be well-cared for—I will see to that."

Sebastian eyed them both for a moment, then he smiled, "Save your energy, my son—they are coming for you. You will be safe now." A moment later, his eerie form faded into the cold and windy night.

The woman knelt again. "Hold on, young one. They have arrived."

In the distance, the low rumble of helicopter engines could be heard. Spotlight beams stretched like golden rods from the aircraft and painted the ground with an eerie white glow, and as the noise intensified, the glowing lights found their target. Within moments, the terrible wreckage was illuminated, and that first awful image of the carnage would be etched into the rescuers' minds forever. It was hard to believe that what lay spread out before them had once been an aircraft.

Soon rescuers began scouring the debris, searching desperately for any survivors. But of the 173 passengers and crew, only one person was found clinging precariously to life.

"It's a miracle," said the leader of the search party later in a television interview. "To have survived this crash would have required the intervention of a guardian angel or even of God himself. The sole survivor removed from the wreckage tonight must have had assistance from both."

It was now after midnight, and a heartbroken Maya sat alone in the dark. She had, not long ago helped Amalia to bed. Roberto's mother was so numbed by her loss that she could hardly stand or walk unaided; even speech had abandoned her. Nuria had long since cried herself to the point of utter exhaustion. And between them, Maya and Lolita had carried her to her room. And now Maya could not sleep. In fact, at that moment, she did not think that she would ever sleep again. Her loss was enormous, and like the others in the house, at present, she could see no further than that which was in front of her own eyes. There seemed no future for her now. What would be the point to even continue on? How would she do that without Roberto?

Then the phone rang. Maya's first instinct was to leave it; everyone was asleep. She didn't feel like talking. If it was important, they would call back tomorrow. But something whispered inside of her: *At a time like this, any phone call—even at this late hour—should be taken.*

The man on the phone asked for Amalia Hernandez. Maya explained that she was asleep, and under the circumstances, should not be disturbed.

"When she wakes, please tell her that her son, Roberto Torres, has been found alive. He has been taken to Madrid and is in hospital there in a critical care facility."

Maya did not hear the rest. The tears streamed down her cheeks as she reached out to steady herself against the table upon which the telephone sat. Overcome with emotion, she crossed herself whispering thanks to God for the miracle that He had granted.

As she turned, Maya was startled to see Amalia's silhouette in the doorway. In the twilight of the room, their eyes met.

"He's alive…" Maya said softly. She made her way across the room and embraced Amalia who crumpled into her open arms.

"I need to see him," she sobbed.

"So do I."

The airline put the families of the victims on a special plane. Amalia and Maya were aboard when it flew out of Barcelona bound for Madrid.

Nuria had decided not to go with them. Instead she would wait for news from Amalia after she had seen her son.

Early the next morning, the pair arrived at the hospital. They had no idea what to expect—all they knew is that Roberto was alive. The two anxious women were taken to his room and left alone with him. The son that Amalia had raised to manhood and the lover to whom Maya had given herself, now lay in front of them. He was unrecognizable, a tangle of tubes and wires protruded from him. His bed was surrounded by bleeping monitors and medical equipment. His face was so badly injured that the sight of him nearly stopped their hearts, but despite all of this, their man had survived.

The doctor, around Roberto's age, was worried. Amalia could see immediately the same concern etched on his face that she held in her heart. Was her son going to survive this ordeal?

"We cannot say yet," said the doctor. "But we have been able to stabilize his condition, and at present that's all we can hope for."

As each day passed, the two women were Roberto's constant companions. And even though he was in a coma, they refused to leave his side. During those long days and nights, they heard the fluid that rattled in his chest and watched as tremors shook his body. They flinched as new tubes were inserted into him and were reduced to tears when the bandages were replaced. Some of the wounds were so bad; they could not bear to look at them. It had been an ordeal for them both. But they knew that in this situation, love and prayers were all they had to offer. And they prayed to God and the Virgin Mary and all the Saints that their man would once again be restored to them. In this quest, they were steadfast. As long as he drew breath, they would not give up.

Then, one day, Roberto opened his eyes. It had been almost two weeks since he had last looked upon the world. At first, he did not know where he was, or who the two women were who sat beside his hospital bed. Though they were familiar to him, their names eluded him. Amalia wept when he finally called her "mother." Then Maya kissed his hand and whispered into his ear "I love you" when he called her to him. The nurse on duty that afternoon left the room to dry her eyes. When she returned, she held a box of tissues in her hand.

Many more days passed before Roberto began to remember what had happened to him. It would be another eight weeks before his injuries had healed enough for him to go home. On the day that he left the hospital, one of the nurses who had cared for him came to his room with a small package in her hands.

"You are the luckiest man alive to have survived such a devastating air crash," she said to him as she handed him the package. "This bag contains the belongings that were in what was left of your clothing when you were admitted to the hospital."

When Roberto opened it, he saw that it contained three items: his wallet, a set of keys, and a folded piece of white linen. He removed the items and placed them among the belongings that he would take with him. A short while later Maya arrived to take him home. That day, as he walked from the hospital, a crowd of medical staff and well-wishers had gathered to see him off. They clapped and cheered as he, with Maya supporting one arm, courageously limped his way to the waiting taxi. She carried his bag, for to walk he needed the assistance of a cane. The hospital had arranged the transport to the airport, and the airline had supplied special tickets for their flight to Barcelona.

In the first few days at home, it became evident that the accident had taken a heavy toll—not only physically, but also psychologically. His memory loss, particularly of simple things and even words, frustrated him enormously. His moods had changed, and at times, anger flared. His concentration had been badly affected and he could no longer write—not even a simple correspondence. But the women who cared for him were told that they would need to be patient. And so they placed their trust in Time, the great healer and their faith in God the Father—and eventually, their faith and trust were rewarded.

As time moved on, Roberto's memories began to return—at first as simple flashbacks, disturbing, confusing and disjointed. But with professional help, and dedication from those who loved him, each day they became clearer. Even his mood swings had mellowed now, and with every passing day, he seemed to return more and more to the old Roberto. His concentration had also improved, and he was now able to spend time writing again. The recurring nightmares that plagued him, even while he was in hospital, had now let up. Physically, he had been left with lasting injuries. His left leg had been badly damaged, and although the doctors did their best, it would never be the same again. For a long time afterwards, he would need the aid of a cane to walk. Other permanent reminders of the day he almost lost his life were the scars that littered his body, and in particular, the one he carried on his right cheek. Every time he looked into a mirror he would be reminded of that fateful journey to Madrid.

It had been a very long recovery for Roberto, but life now had returned to a normality that he could handle. And with it also came the return of the memories and the reasons for him being on the plane that crashed. Soon a recollection of the fleeting and shadowy figure who had been watching him in the police courtyard at A Coruña had also returned. It was the same shadowy figure that had haunted the nightmares that plagued him after the crash. And the same figure who had given him the dagger all those months earlier in New Zealand.

Then he remembered Hinetitama's words: "You must make this offering as soon as you can, for while things remain as they are, your life is in danger." And with this, he remembered what still needed to be done.

Among this flood of returning memories, there was one more that he knew was important. It was his promise to Maya, that when he returned from Madrid, he would tell her everything. She had waited long enough, he thought. That evening, when he and Maya were alone, he sat next to her on the sofa and told her his story.

He described to her the illness that had dogged him and how it had threatened his life. He told her that he believed the trip they both took to New Zealand was somehow preordained, for he now believed that he had always been destined to meet Hinetitama. That evening, Maya learned from Roberto how Hinetitama had cured him of his illness. He described to her the ceremony that took place on the beach at sunrise. He explained that he believed a dark spirit now pursued him, and that he had seen this same spirit in the courtyard at A Coruña only hours before the plane crash. With tears in his eyes, he told Maya that he remembered Hinetitama by his side while he lay in the wreckage of the plane on that cold and desolate mountainside.

"I don't know how any of this is possible," he finally said. "But I firmly believe that, had she not come to me that night, I would have died along with all the rest."

Maya sat patiently; her heart had been moved by Roberto's story. She saw that he desperately wanted her to understand what he had been through.

"I remember Hinetitama's voice," he continued. "She kept urging me to hold on; 'It's not your time,' she said, 'They are coming to rescue you.'"

Maya reached out and rested a hand on his.

"I know now that I must complete this journey," he said. "I have to go to the Temple of Debod as soon as I am able. There, as Hinetitama instructed me, I must make an offering that will free me from the spirit that pursues me."

Maya smiled at him. "I can tell you right now that you won't be going anywhere without me," she said. "This time, I'm coming with you. But I want to talk to Hinetitama first."

"Why?" he asked. "I've told you everything."

"Look at you Roberto! This thing has almost claimed your life. I need to know what else can be done to protect you, and she will be able to tell me."

That evening, Roberto called Daniel Potae in New Zealand. He was hoping that Daniel would give him Hinetitama's phone number. But he was shocked to learn that the old lady had died some months earlier. The circumstances of her death had been so unusual that Daniel not only remembered the date—Saturday, April 17, 2010—but also the exact time. Hinetitama's daughter, who had been staying with her, was woken that morning by what sounded like an explosion. It seemed to shake the entire house. Her first instinct was to call the police, and she reached for the telephone that sat on the bedside table. Near the phone was the alarm clock, and as she placed her hand on the receiver, she noticed the time—3:30 a.m.

Suddenly, she thought of her mother, and hurried to check on her before making the call. To her horror, she found Hinetitama dead. The old woman lay face down on the floor, her body still warm. She had somehow been thrown from her bed. Despite a thorough investigation, no evidence of an explosion was ever found, and the circumstances that resulted in Hinetitama being cast from her bed had never been properly explained. Even now her death remained a mystery. The case was still open, but the police feared that with no real evidence, it would never be solved. Hinetitama was buried three days later, and when the ceremony had finished, it began to rain. It poured relentlessly for seven whole days.

When Roberto hung up, Maya could tell from his face that he was in shock. It took a few moments before he could tell her what Daniel had just conveyed to him.

"April seventeenth was the day after the plane crash…" she observed. "What was the time of her death?"

"Three-thirty in the morning," he said.

She looked at him in shock, "You know something, with the time difference between us and New Zealand, Hinetitama's death would have been Friday, April 16, at three-thirty in the afternoon—the exact time of the plane crash."

Stunned, both knew that the trip to Madrid was now urgent. And Maya, who had become quite anxious after hearing the news from Daniel, would begin the preparations immediately.

The following afternoon, Roberto received an unexpected visitor. He was at work in his study when Lolita appeared at the door.

"Someone is here to see you, señor. She is waiting downstairs. Her name is Juanita Suárez, and she wishes to speak with you personally."

"What does she want?"

"She would not tell me, señor. She only said that it was important that she speak with you in person."

"Have her wait. I'll be down shortly."

Ten minutes later, he made his way downstairs. His visitor greeted him with a smile and a firm handshake.

"I am Juanita Suárez. Thank you for taking the time to meet with me." She was confident, polite, and in her late twenties.

"What do you want of me, señorita?" asked Roberto.

"My father has asked me to visit and pay to you his respects. He is unable to do so himself."

"Who is your father?" asked Roberto.

"His name is Henri D'Anjou."

"Yes, I remember señor D'Anjou," said Roberto.

"He was saddened to hear of your tragic accident," she said. "And he hopes that your recovery has been speedy and full."

"Thank you, señorita," replied Roberto. "And how is your father?"

"He is very ill, señor," she said. "But he wanted me to give you this." She held out an envelope.

"What is it?" asked Roberto.

"It contains his phone number," she smiled. "He asked that I bring it to you personally, and that when you are able, please call him. But señor, do not leave it too long."

"Your father's illness—it is serious?" asked Roberto.

"He will not survive it."

"I see," he took the envelope from her. "I will call him. And now, if there is nothing else señorita…"

"Thank you for seeing me, señor Torres."

They shook hands, and Roberto summoned Lolita, who showed señorita Suárez out. After she had gone, Roberto returned to his study and called D'Anjou.

"Your daughter has come to see me, as you asked her to," said Roberto. "I am sorry to hear that you are ill, señor."

"Juanita is a wonderful daughter to me," replied D'Anjou. His voice was frail.

"And as you also requested," said Roberto, "I make this call to you. How can I help you, señor?"

"Please Roberto…call me Henri," replied D'Anjou. "I knew your father and your grandfather as well. We are not strangers, you and I. And besides, it is not your help that I require. It is I, who offers help to you."

"What do you mean?" asked Roberto.

"I read about the plane crash," said D'Anjou. "Please forgive me for bringing this up. I'm sure you're thoroughly tired of hearing it. But it is rather astonishing that there were one hundred and seventy-three people on board that plane, and you were the only one who survived the crash. Someone, it seems, is looking out for you, Roberto."

"Perhaps," he answered, not wishing to reveal anything to D'Anjou.

"The question is," D'Anjou responded, "Why you?"

"Why not me?" Roberto asked.

"You must understand that I have spent many years as an occultist," replied D'Anjou. "More, I would estimate, than all the years of your life. I can sense when something's not right. And in this situation, my friend, I see the signs—something is definitely not right."

Roberto remained silent.

"Are you still there?" asked D'Anjou.

"Yes…I'm here…"

"Well then…am I correct?"

"You are," Roberto added reluctantly.

"Tell me," said D'Anjou. "Are you in trouble?"

"And if I am?" answered Roberto.

"Then I can help you…" D'Anjou replied; his words were dry and almost whispered.

"Your daughter tells me that you are…very ill," said Roberto. "If this is the case, how will you help me?"

"You know already the answer to that question Roberto," D'Anjou said. "Do I really need to waste my time with an answer for you?"

Roberto thought for a moment, "No," he replied.

"Good," said D'Anjou. "Your time now will be better spent explaining to me what is going on. Because once I know, I can help you."

"Why would you do that?" asked Roberto.

"Why not?" D'Anjou said. "You need help—and I have it to offer. It is the perfect match. And besides, what else would I do? As it is now, I simply sit here in my room, waiting to die. This way, I can help us both."

"Then I will tell you, but on one condition…"

"No," D'Anjou interrupted. "I don't want your conditions; I don't have time for them. I have a few weeks left to my life—those are *your* conditions…take it or leave it."

There was a moment of silence.

"Alright," agreed Roberto. "Have it your way."

He told D'Anjou everything, of the trip to New Zealand, of Hinetitama, of A Coruña, of the demon that pursued him, and of the impending trip to the Temple of Debod. By now D'Anjou had gone silent on the other end of the phone. Roberto could still hear him breathing and waited for him to say something. After a moment D'Anjou spoke.

"I will come with you when you go to the Egyptian temple."

Roberto was surprised. "Why?" he asked.

"Because you will not survive this time if you don't have me with you," said D'Anjou.

"Why do you say that?" asked Roberto.

"Because it is the truth," D'Anjou replied. "The dark spirit that wants your soul will have you this time if you are not prepared. I can help you prepare."

After he and D'Anjou had said their goodbyes, fear settled over Roberto as he hung up the phone. At that moment, he thought of Hinetitama. So much had happened to him since he had met her, and now she was dead. A feeling of loneliness filled him that afternoon as he sat in his study. How he wished that she was still alive. She had saved him from peril before, and he felt sure that she would have again. But he knew that, like his father and his grandfather, she had gone, and he would never see her again. It was just him now; him and the old man that Nuria and Amalia blamed for his father's death. How ironic that in this battle, it had come down to this. His only ally would be the seriously ill man whose name he dare not speak in the company of his family—Henri D'Anjou.

20

BARCELONA NOVEMBER 2010

The clock in the departure hall read 8:45 a.m. when Roberto and Maya arrived at Sants station in Barcelona. The train they were to catch, the AVE high-speed service to Madrid, was due to leave from platform two at nine o'clock. The 621-kilometer trip would take just two hours and thirty minutes to complete.

Since she and Roberto had discussed the trip to Madrid, Maya had been busy. Through her contacts at the Universidad de Barcelona, she was able to organize some private time for them at the Temple of Debod. The university, on her behalf, had asked the relevant authorities in Madrid for the temple to be closed to the public for a short period. They were told that Maya had planned to carry out some research while she was there, and the closure of the temple would greatly assist in this matter. The authorities agreed, and a time was set. Once this was known to Roberto, he contacted D'Anjou, who told him that he and his daughter Juanita would meet them at the temple site.

"If you arrive before me," he cautioned Roberto. "Do not, under any circumstances, enter the temple. You must stay well clear of it."

The trip to Madrid that morning allowed Roberto time to reflect. So much had happened to him already—and now this; a journey to seek the intercession of ancient Egyptian Gods. *There are more things in Heaven and Earth, Horatio, than are dreamt of in your philosophy.* Shakespeare had got it right thought Roberto. He had studied the English playwright when he was at school. Hamlet was his favorite play, and this particular phrase had always fascinated him. And now in truth, all these years later, it seemed to sum up perfectly his life.

And of course there was D'Anjou—how things had changed. If Amalia and Nuria knew what he and this man were up to, they would be lying in front of the train right now to stop him from going to Madrid. Roberto was the first to admit that D'Anjou was not the man they thought he was. And he also knew that the question may well be asked—*who was he really?* But to him, it no longer mattered. *It is strange*, he thought, *how circumstances conspire to unite even the most disparate of people.* Perhaps when this was all over, only then would he know the real Henri D'Anjou.

And Maya, sweet Maya, he thought; *she has been with me through it all.*

She looked up from the magazine she was reading; he was looking at her. "Did you say something?" she asked.

"No," he smiled.

"What are you thinking about?"

"Once I was a normal happy kid with two loving parents. I should have grown up to become just another normal man going about his business. But look at me. My life so far has run like a Stephen King novel. And today I'm off to an Egyptian temple to make an offering to an ancient Goddess. How open must an intellect be to actually comprehend all of this?"

"I don't know," replied Maya. "Perhaps, for starters, your definition of *normal* needs changing. Maybe that's the bit preventing you from finding the real answers."

He thought for a moment, and then smiled. "You're right. What is *normal* anyway, and who really gives a damn about it. There are more things in Heaven and Earth, *Roberto*, than are dreamt of in your philosophy." He grinned as he finished the quote.

"What?" Maya asked.

"I was just reminding myself of something that I read a long time ago. I think the man who wrote that phrase agrees with you. Being *normal* is only a state of mind; the reality is something quite different."

"That's my boy," she smiled.

"So now, all I have is you," he said with a big smile. "And that must make me the luckiest man alive."

"We have each other," replied Maya. "And that makes us both lucky."

The journey was now almost over, and the train had begun to slow. The tenement suburbs of Madrid were in sight and Atocha station was only minutes away. Roberto reached for his walking cane. Some days the pain in his left leg was bad enough for him to need it; and today was one of those days. He and Maya readied themselves to disembark, and moments later in electric silence, the train glided softly to a halt. Their aim now was to get through the large station as quickly as they could, then to a taxi, and on to Parque Del Oeste.

It was a beautiful autumn day in Madrid, and when they drove into the grounds of the large park they could see that it was full of people. The Temple of Debod stood on a natural rise in the center of the sprawling parkland. As the taxi made its way up the narrow road toward the crest and the temple, Roberto caught sunlit glimpses, like photo flashes, of the ancient structure through the trees. The sight of it filled him with dread.

As the taxi came to a halt at the top of the rise, Roberto spotted Juanita. D'Anjou's daughter was standing near the entrance to the temple grounds. Beside her was an old man in a wheelchair—presumably this was D'Anjou himself. But Roberto was unsure, for the man looked too old and frail to be the D'Anjou he remembered at their last meeting in Café Nudivel.

Maya paid the taxi driver, and as the vehicle drove away, the pair headed toward the entrance to the temple grounds. Illness had utterly ravaged Henri D'Anjou; he looked frail and thin. His pale and wrinkled features were expressionless, and his almost-lifeless eyes stared blankly into space.

Roberto was shocked by D'Anjou's appearance. As he and Maya approached, Juanita greeted them.

"Buenos dias," she said as she held her hand out to Maya. "I am Juanita Suárez. May I present to you my father Henri D'Anjou."

Maya smiled and shook Juanita's hand. D'Anjou did not present his, though he managed a smile, which Maya politely returned.

"You should not have come here today señor," Roberto said to D'Anjou. "You are far too ill for this."

D'Anjou ignored his concern and greeted him with a frail smile. His voice was weak, "These men won't let us in." He nodded toward the guards gathered at the entrance to the temple grounds. "Otherwise, we would be waiting up there in the shade."

Maya pulled some documents from her bag and approached one of the guards. He examined them, and a few moments later Maya called to the little group to follow her. Roberto was the first to go, leaning heavily on his cane as he walked. Behind him, Juanita pushed D'Anjou in his wheelchair.

"You have changed since our last meeting," said D'Anjou softly as he and Juanita followed Roberto. "You have grown an extra leg, my friend."

Unfazed, Roberto called back to him, "and you have grown wheels, señor." D'Anjou smiled at the quip. If nothing else, he still had his sense of humor.

One of the guards led the small group to the temple entrance and unlocked the doors. "As the university requested," he said. "The temple is now closed to the public. You have the afternoon in which to do your research, señores. You will not be disturbed."

"Thank you," said Maya. "We really appreciate this."

The guard nodded and left.

"Research," said D'Anjou, a smirk twisted his lips. "If only they knew…"

"Can we get on with this?" Roberto interrupted. "We have all come a long way."

"And have so much further to go," added D'Anjou, dryly. "Let us make our way into the entrance hall—but go no further."

The little group made their way up the access ramp and into the two-thousand-year-old building. As Roberto entered the small vestibule, he felt the eerie ambience within the ancient temple. He could feel the ghosts of history in this place. The very thought of them made him lean even more heavily onto his cane. The pain in his left leg had now increased. Outside it was unusually warm for an autumn day, but within the temple, the temperature was cool. Still, Roberto was perspiring, and had begun to feel light-headed. Ever since the plane crash he hated the feeling of being confined, and in this small room, being confined was all he could think about. It wasn't long before claustrophobia had him by the throat.

D'Anjou could see now that he was struggling. "Do you have the offering?" he asked Roberto.

"I have it here," he replied, and he slid his hand into his jacket pocket and pulled out a folded white cloth. He opened it and held the feather out to D'Anjou.

"No," said D'Anjou shaking his head, "It is yours—I must not touch it."

Roberto drew back when he heard this.

"The words you will use are very important," said D'Anjou. "Have you memorized them?"

"I have," replied Roberto.

"Good—we are almost ready," D'Anjou said. His voice now sounded stronger. "Do you know why we are here?"

Roberto seemed dazed and had begun to sway as though he were about to faint. Maya saw that he was in trouble. She reached for him and caught him just as he began to fall. She pulled him to her and took his weight as she held him close.

"Are you alright?" she asked as she quickly scanned the room for a chair.

"I don't feel so good…" he stammered.

By now Juanita, who had also noticed Roberto's struggle, had located a wooden chair and had positioned it behind him. Maya helped him seat himself.

"You must fight it, Roberto," called D'Anjou. His voice now filled the vestibule. "Your nemesis has arrived."

A cold wind blew through the entrance hall, and D'Anjou began to laugh out loud. Then his voice grew stern. "Come in, demon," he called. "We have been expecting you."

A chill shot through Maya; there was now no doubt in her mind that evil had just entered the hall.

D'Anjou raised his arms in the air. There was no sign of the weakness in him. "Dark demon," he called, "I know your name, and I will write it in ash, and you will be no more."

The wind blew even colder now; it whistled around the ancient pillars. Suddenly, out from under him, Roberto's chair flew backward, pulled and tossed violently by some invisible force. It splintered into pieces as it struck the wall.

Maya screamed out to Roberto, but it was too late. He hit the floor hard, headfirst. Blood began to ooze from his right temple. His eyelids twitched as though he were about to slip into unconsciousness. Maya ran to his side.

"Leave him," yelled D'Anjou. "The dog will protect him now."

Maya ignored D'Anjou. She took Roberto by the arm and tried to lift him to his feet.

"Do as I say, girl," yelled D'Anjou angrily. "You must come to me now, or the demon will take you—*quickly!*"

D'Anjou's fiery eyes shocked her; the anger in his voice boomed with almost superhuman strength. Roberto seemed barely conscious, and Maya's heart sank as she saw the pool of blood spreading out from beneath his head. Reluctantly she left Roberto and walked slowly toward D'Anjou.

Juanita reached into her pocket and pulled out an amulet that had been threaded onto a leather thong.

"Here," she said to Maya. "Put this around your neck. It will protect you."

Maya did as she was told. She looked back to Roberto lying on the floor; his eyes were now closed, and his face was pale and blank.

"I'm going to him," she yelled to D'Anjou. She was determined to go now, no matter what happened.

"Stay where you are!" he screamed.

But to her astonishment, before she could make a move, Roberto stood up—shakily at first, but then he miraculously seemed to gain strength.

"Can you see the dog?" D'Anjou cried out to him.

Roberto nodded. He had also spotted his cane that lay near to where the chair had smashed against the wall. He turned to retrieve it.

"Leave it!" yelled D'Anjou. "Follow the dog."

Roberto looked confused.

"Do it!" D'Anjou ordered. "He will lead you into the holy sanctuary. Place the feather into the altar chamber and speak your prayer to the Gods. Once that is done, the dog will lead you out. The demon is afraid of the dog and will not harm you as long as the animal leads the way. Do not walk in front of him, or the demon will take you."

Fresh blood ran down the side of Roberto's head as he hobbled toward the door of the sacred chamber situated immediately to the rear of the entrance hall.

The freezing wind howled even more loudly now as D'Anjou watched Roberto disappear through the door to the inner sanctum. Then he cried aloud, "Dark demon," and held up a paper bag in his right hand. "Your name is written here." D'Anjou flung the contents of the bag into the air.

A cloud of ash erupted into the wildly swirling air currents. Suddenly, the freezing wind stopped. There was now complete silence.

From where Maya stood, she could see through the open door into the sacred chamber. Roberto was standing next to the altar stone. He pulled the feather from his pocket and placed it into the chamber that was cut into the stone and began his prayer: "I call upon the Goddess Isis for whom I have brought this symbol of Ma-at. It is for the sake of my soul that I offer it, and that order once again may return to my life."

D'Anjou could hear the prayer from where he sat, and he smiled to himself as Roberto pronounced its final words.

"Amun-Ra is pleased," announced D'Anjou. His voice sounded weaker. "I see his face—and the demon is no more…" His voice now trailed away.

Juanita bent and kissed her father's forehead.

A moment later, Roberto emerged shakily from the sanctuary.

Maya ran to steady him, "Are you alright?" she asked.

"I think so…" he said. "Where's my cane?"

Juanita retrieved it for him and Roberto thanked her.

"We're done here," she whispered to Maya. "You go with Roberto, and I will bring my father out in a moment."

Roberto noticed that D'Anjou was slumped over in his wheelchair.

"Your father needs you," he said to Juanita.

"He needs his God," she said softly. "He is dead."

Maya now realized that Juanita had been crying. She reached out and took her by the hand.

"I'm okay," said Juanita. "My father is happy now."

Roberto went to D'Anjou and knelt down beside him. He leaned over and kissed the old man's cheek. "I was wrong to have ever doubted you," he whispered. "Without you, I would have failed here today."

Sirens echoed across the crowded park as emergency vehicles made their way up the hill to the temple. As the paramedics attended to Roberto, Maya explained to the concerned guards that in the temple, Roberto had accidently dropped his cane. As he attempted to retrieve it, he slipped and fell, hitting his head against the stone floor. It was a simple accident and one that he felt greatly embarrassed about.

D'Anjou's fate however needed a very different approach. But as it happened, an explanation wasn't necessary. He had been pronounced dead by medics' only moments after they had arrived. Preliminary cause of death, they ascertained, was heart failure.

"He was in the final stages of a terminal illness," said the paramedic in charge. "It was only a matter of time—today or tomorrow or even next week. But rest assured, it would have happened—there is no doubt of it."

Maya and Juanita looked on forlornly as D'Anjou's body was placed into a body bag and then strapped onto a stretcher. As they watched the stretcher being loaded into the back of the ambulance, tears rolled down Juanita's cheeks.

Maya reached out and put her hand on Juanita's shoulder.

The pair watched in silence as the ambulance slowly drove away. Juanita wiped the tears from her eyes, she turned to Maya and nodded that she was okay.

"What will happen now?" Maya asked.

"We discussed this—he and I," Juanita said, looking to the ambulance as it disappeared from view. "He wanted to be taken back to his village in France. He will be buried there."

"We can help," offered Maya.

"Thank you," Juanita said. "But we don't need help."

"You know, what your father did today…" said Maya.

Juanita interrupted her, "What my father did today was what he always did for people who needed him." Her voice was full of a daughter's love. "He knew that he had a special gift, and his mission was to help where he could. It sometimes got him into trouble, but he never gave up. Even today, he could have simply stayed in his bed and let you both come here alone. But he knew the dangers, and he knew that without him you would have been in trouble."

By now, the paramedics had cleaned and dressed Roberto's head wound, and he had made his way over to where Maya and Juanita stood talking.

"I don't know how I could ever have thanked your father for what he did today," said Roberto.

Juanita looked surprised. "You would have wasted your time if you thought he wanted you to thank him. He never did this for thanks. His mission was to eliminate evil wherever he found it. And today, he found it here.”

“What will happen to you now?” asked Roberto.

“Me? I guess I’ll pick up my life where I left it. The day Henri called, asking me to help him live out his last few months usefully; I dropped everything and went to him. Now that he’s gone, I’ll go back to Barcelona and get on with my life as it was before.”

“Barcelona…” Maya said, a little surprised.

“That’s right. It was a shock to Henri’s family in France when they discovered that he had a love child in Spain. They didn’t exactly open their arms to me. But who did he turn to when he needed help? Me. Those bastards would have let him die alone in some sterile room—and he knew that.”

“Since you will be coming back to Barcelona, perhaps we can keep in touch,” suggested Maya.

For a moment, Juanita eyed them both. “I’d like that,” she said.

On the train trip home, Roberto slept, he was utterly exhausted. Maya though, sat thinking about the dramatic events at the Temple of Debod. At one point she smiled to herself, she remembered that she had to submit a research report to the university on the “project” at the temple. Of course, she would have to spend a few days in the library to prepare something that was scientifically acceptable to them. For she knew that the truth would destroy her career and get her kicked off campus—probably for good.

Roberto awoke just as the train was pulling into Sants.

Maya was smiling as he opened his eyes.

He reached out and took her by the hand. “What would I do without you?” he whispered.

“I was just thinking the same thing about you,” she said.

That night, when he was finally in bed, ghostly images filled Roberto’s sleeping mind. He was once again in the temple and could see himself being led by the white dog into the holy sanctuary. Set upon the stone altar was an ancient bronze bowl. Hinetitama was in the sanctuary, and D’Anjou was with her. The old woman held something in her hand. But from where he stood, Roberto could not make out what it was. She walked to the altar and carefully placed the item into the bronze bowl. Flames immediately rose from the altar bowl, and from the flames a trail of smoke snaked its way into the air. As he watched, Roberto could hear Hinetitama's voice intone, "You are free now, cleansed by the sacred fire and by the Gods themselves."

He saw her turn to D'Anjou. She placed an object to his mouth. Then she raised her hand, and the pair seemed to melt into the air. The flames in the bowl had died now, and the smoke that eddied into the air of the temple had cleared. Even the white dog had disappeared. Roberto was alone. He walked over to the ancient bronze vessel that sat on the altar and looked into it. To his amazement, lying in the bottom of the bowl was a scroll. He reached in and picked it up. It was sealed with a small clay seal, which he broke. He opened the scroll and discovered that it was a letter. His heart almost stopped when he realized that it was from his father.

My son,

Understand that what I did was to save you. I sought, with D'Anjou's help, to take the curse that was upon me to the grave before it infected you. However I failed, for it did not follow as I had planned, and you were left, a mere boy to its evil fate. Now you have been saved, and my heart is full of joy. But great sadness fills me too, for that which has so long bound me to you is no longer. And now it is time for me to say goodbye, my son.

Roberto woke up and lay for a few moments, staring into the darkness. In his freshly woken state the dream had unsettled him. Finally though, after a short time, he managed to return once more to sleep.

When he woke in the morning, the memory of the dream still had not left him. He remembered vividly its content.

He tried hard during the day to forget the dream by burying himself in his work. But by the afternoon, it had once again begun to occupy his thoughts. Finally, he got up from his desk and went to his bedroom. When he returned to the study, he carried with him a wooden box, which he had kept hidden away for decades. One day, he'd hoped that he would have the courage to burn its contents. But that day had never arrived, and the box and what it contained, were destined to become ghosts trapped in his past—unresolved echoes wandering in time.

That autumn afternoon, Roberto cut a forlorn figure sitting alone at his desk. The box he had brought from his bedroom was full of letters, and it now sat open in front of him. He held one of the letters in his hands. Torment was upon his face when he finished reading it. His hands trembled as he folded it and carefully placed it back into the box with the others. He closed the lid, and as he did, tears filled his eyes. Now he understood.

His father had come back to say goodbye. He had found a way to return to him.

Roberto wiped his tears and placed his hand upon the box. "Goodbye Papa," he whispered. "Until we meet again."

That night, for the first time in many nights, Roberto slept soundly. Finally, the circle that had been opened by the boy had been closed by the man. He was at peace now—with the world, and finally, with himself.

POSTSCRIPT

THE LETTER FROM SALAMANCA, 1579

To Señor Bartolomé Diego Lopez, the Lord Archbishop and Inquisitor General

Sir,

I write to inform you of the judgment upon the sorcerer Francisco de Villanova of A Coruña. The punishment of burning was carried out on the 17th April 1579. He was brought before the Holy Tribunal in January of this year on a charge of sorcery, it having been substantiated by the many who gave witness against him. Each of them told how he commanded a demonic presence in the form of a savage white dog. His trial was a lengthy one, he being of a mind to prove his innocence before God. But in the end, when put to the knot, he gave up the truth and condemned himself by his own words.

The punishment was carried out in the Plaza Mayor, and he and two other heretics were put to the fire for their sins. And like the sinners they were, none of them chose the cross when it was offered, so all were burnt while alive. On the appointed day, large crowds gathered to witness the Holy Tribunal carry out its verdict. The people, mostly of a celebratory disposition, fully condemned the sinners for their fall from the grace of our Mother Church. Some souls among the throng called for their repentance, but it was too late, for judgment was at hand.

My Lord Archbishop, in this matter, I must also inform you of some disturbing events that took place during the execution of this same sorcerer. While the firelighters were putting flame to his pyre, we noticed the demon dog of Francisco de Villanova standing beside him. As the inferno grew around the sorcerer, neither he nor his demon beast cried out as the other sinners did. The beast remained by his side until the blaze had completely consumed the sorcerer. Then, like a devil bounding from hell, the beast leapt from the inferno and rushed toward us, growling as it came. We ran as fast as we could to make it to the church, where God protected us. The demon did not follow us inside, and some have since said that it disappeared into the air at the very doors to God's sanctuary. Many people have afterwards come to the church to receive blessings. They are now fearful that, having seen the demon, they may become possessed. We have done our best to protect them and allay their fears.

It is troubling, my Lord, to know that the Devil has now sent sorcerers and demons into this town of ours. We must be more vigilant than ever. But the most troubling of all is the evidence, seen with my own eyes, that these demons are not affected by the flames. The trials put to Francisco de Villanova the sorcerer, subdued him greatly. He had to be carried to the stake, but even in this condition, one would have expected him to cry out in the inferno. But never once did he make utterance.

Further, our investigations have revealed that Francisco de Villanova's father, Juanes, was a close friend of the Jew Josef Jimenez. It is said that the Jew practiced regularly the forbidden arts of witchcraft. Jimenez, it is alleged, passed something secret to Juanes before the flames of judgment took him. We know not what it was, but know only that which is begat of evil shall remain evil forevermore. Surely this must be the curse that now sits upon the entire de Villanova family, even upon those yet unborn. We now know that de Villanova has a son called José.

I believe, my Lord, that it is the Church's responsibility to put an end to this line of evil while we are able, and we must put all our efforts into finding this man, José. For it is certain that the father now resides with the Devil, and so too should his only begotten son.

I am your servant my Lord,
Silvestre Gonzales of the Holy Tribunal
Salamanca
20th of April 1579.

Fin

9 780473 218737